MW01125537

Gravity Breaker

Jonathan R. Miller
Copyright © 2016

www.JonathanRMiller.com

contents

chapter one

chapter two

chapter three

chapter four

chapter five

chapter six

chapter seven

chapter eight

chapter nine

chapter ten

about the author

All the heroes of tomorrow are the heretics of today.

- E.Y. Harburg

chapter one

On the day everything started falling apart, Isaac was running around the Rockridge neighborhood of North Oakland collecting loads of dirty laundry from the doorsteps of rich folks who were too busy to handle the task themselves. His job back then was simple: to drive, pedal, jog, or walk his way through the trendiest, most upscale neighborhoods of San Francisco, Oakland, and San Jose, knocking on clients' doors and picking up bags full of their clothing for the wash. Button-down dress shirts, floor-length gowns, silk bedding, luxury bath towels, hundred-dollar hoodies, delicates—all of it. Twenty-pound minimum was the only requirement.

The company was called Quixit, for some reason. Premium laundry services right at your front door.

By the time he'd finished his collections that day it was late afternoon, and he was pushing a blue grocery cart overflowing with fat plastic laundry bags along the road shoulder of Claremont Avenue in Oakland, weaving in and out of traffic to avoid the cars parked along the curb. It was summertime—the heat was so fierce that you could actually see it in the air, radiating in thick waves off the blacktop—and he was hauling something like fifteen bags in total. At twenty or more pounds per bag, that meant he was moving three hundred pounds of clothing in the cart at a minimum. The goal was to transport everything back to his truck (a 2001 Ford F-150) which he'd parked in a metered space nearby, as was his normal routine when he had a group of pickups in an apartment building with no visitor parking.

With his shoulder lowered against the cart handle, he muscled that heavy load up Claremont, doing his best to ignore the soaring temperatures, the waves of diesel exhaust, the rumbling of engines to his left, and the coldly curious stares of folks walking on the pavement to his right. It was a lot to juggle at once, to be honest. But he was getting the job done as best he could, and everything was fine—until he came upon a white SUV double-parked next to a sandwich shop, blocking the right-hand lane (and blocking his path). There was no way around that beast, other than to swerve out into the road. It wasn't his first choice, but it was also the only way forward. So that's exactly what he did: he waited for a lull in traffic, raised his hand high to signal any oncoming drivers, and when everything looked clear, he swung the cart around the rear bumper of the SUV, quickly passed the vehicle on its driver's side, and immediately went back to hugging the curb. Safely out of traffic, he continued pushing the cart up the road, rolling by a seemingly endless line of storefronts on the way back to his truck. And everything seemed fine again, at least for a while. But then he heard a sound that made his stomach drop: the short, staccato blast of a police siren behind him.

On instinct, Isaac brought the cart to a stop, let go of the handle, and turned around slowly, raising both hands with palms facing outward. He saw what looked like the same white SUV he'd passed moments earlier—only now there was a red beacon rotating on the dashboard, sending a dizzying red glare through the vehicle's interior. The driver, a tall white man with dark slicked-back hair, stared at him over the steering wheel with a blank expression. The SUV was idling slowly in his direction.

When the vehicle was about ten yards out, the driver put on the brakes, raised a black CB transmitter to his mouth, and clicked the side-lever with a meaty-looking thumb. Isaac heard the crackle and squeal of a loudspeaker coming to life.

"Show those hands," the man said. "Hands, please."

Even amplified, his voice sounded calm and professional, which came as an absolute surprise. There was no trace of the threatening approach—the preemptive strike of straight-up hostility—that he'd come to associate with law enforcement over the years.

"They're shown," Isaac called out. He brought his arms up a bit higher and flattened his palms a bit further to drive the point home. "No problems here, officer. They're shown."

The man lowered the transmitter from his mouth; the static

from the loudspeaker went silent. Moments later, the driver's side window whirred down and the man leaned his head out.

"Up higher, sir," the man said. "As far up as they'll go."

Isaac did what the man told him to: he reached for the sky.

"All right, then," the man said. "That's good right there. Hold steady."

The man rolled up the window, looped a gold badge around his neck, and exited the SUV, never once taking his eyes off of Isaac's face. Meantime, Isaac stood beside the cart with his head held low and his hands held high, painfully aware of every car that slowed down to watch the spectacle. Getting gawked at while he was rolling a shopping cart up the street was one thing—Isaac could handle that much negative attention—but getting caught up with the police while doing it? That was more outside scrutiny than he'd signed up for.

As the man approached, Isaac saw a service pistol holstered in his belt next to a handheld radio and what looked like an industrial-sized can of pepper spray or mace. He was dressed in everyday street clothes—a black t-shirt and loose-fitting jeans—and his movements were less like those of an overzealous soldier on his first patrol (in other words, less like a typical police officer), and more like those of an ordinary man walking on familiar ground, showing a certain level of caution, but not fear or animosity, toward a stranger he's encountered. Other than the contents of the man's belt and the badge he wore on a chain around his neck, there was nothing about his appearance that screamed out *authority*, but Isaac didn't feel as though he had a choice but to take the man's identity on faith. Uniform or not, the man was a cop.

The officer stopped about ten feet away from Isaac and stood on the road shoulder, staring off in the direction of the storefronts, then the traffic, then the men and women on the sidewalks, a few of whom had stopped to document the drama unfolding in front of them, their phones held high in outstretched hands.

Finally the officer stared straight at Isaac; he seemed to be wearing the faintest smile.

"It's a scorcher today, yeah?" the officer said, shaking his head. "I mean, what the hell. I thought the climate around here was supposed to be all mild and Mediterranean and shit."

Isaac wasn't sure how to respond.

He wants to talk to me about the weather we're having today?

"No question," Isaac said, nodding. "The heat is no joke."

He couldn't think of anything else to add.

The officer kept on shaking his head in apparent disbelief as he stared off at his surroundings again.

"Do I have to keep doing this?" Isaac asked.

The officer continued to look around as though he was alone. "Doing what?"

"My hands," Isaac said, glancing upward. "Is it necessary, officer? I'm not a danger to anybody out here."

The officer didn't respond right away. "Let me ask you something," he said. "Are you carrying anything on your person that you shouldn't be carrying?"

"No, sir."

"And what about over there?" the officer asked, nodding toward the cart. "Are you hauling anything in the basket you shouldn't be hauling?"

"No, sir," he answered. "Some clothes is all."

The man's eyes widened. "Seriously? Some clothes? That's your answer?"

"Just clothes. That's all there is."

The officer didn't respond; he continued scanning the cart for what felt like a long time. "That's a hell of a lot of clothes you got there," he said. "I don't suppose all those bags came out of the Goodwill donation center over on 56th and Park, did they?"

Isaac wasn't sure what the man was talking about.

"Pardon?"

"The bags," the officer said, gesturing toward the cart. "Did you take them from the collection box on 56th—yes or no."

"No, sir," Isaac answered. "I'm just working. That's all."

The officer snorted.

"Working on what?" he asked. "What could you possibly be working on out here with a bunch of bags?"

Isaac nodded toward the cart. "See the logos on those bags? Just look at the bags for a second," he said. "*Quixit*. I'm on the clock for Quixit."

The officer paused.

Even before Isaac saw the expression on the man's face, he knew that he'd crossed a line, that he'd committed a cardinal sin as far as the authorities were concerned. He'd taken a tone. He'd shown a hint of attitude. A fine edge.

"You need to be careful right now," the officer said. "You keep that mouth real civil. I'm just asking a few questions here is all."

"I'm sorry," Isaac said, nodding. "All right? I apologize. Please look at the bags. Please. You see how they're all the same? Same color, same tags, same name on the sides. Quixit. I'm just trying to tell you, sir. I'm on a job out here—that's all."

"Quixit?" When the officer said the word, his face looked like he'd just swallowed something rancid.

"It's a wash service. Pickup and delivery. Quixit. All I'm trying to do right now is finish my pickups so I can head home like everybody else."

"Okay. So you're telling me that you're an employee of Quixit."

"A contractor, actually. But yes. I do jobs for them."

"A contractor," the officer repeated, almost to himself. He was smiling faintly again.

"I'm independent. It basically saves the company from having to pay out benefits. But I'm telling you, sir, I work for them."

The officer didn't respond right away. He kept staring at Isaac with the same half-smile on his face.

"All right, then," the man said. "If you are who you claim, then shouldn't you have some kind of uniform on? A name tag, at least? Something that tells me who you work for?"

Isaac was at a loss. As much as he hated to admit it, the officer was absolutely right. He should have been wearing his company button-down with the logo on the pocket, but he'd skipped it on account of the heat. And as for his badge? He'd forgotten that back in the apartment on the hall table, something he'd done far more often than he would've liked to admit.

"Yes. You're right about that," Isaac said. "I absolutely do have all of those things, but they're just not *on me* at the moment. Okay? And I'm sorry for that. But can't you see that I'm just out here trying to get on with it? I'm not hurting anybody. I have a daughter back home. I'm just out here trying to do the right thing and get my deliveries made."

"With a shopping cart?" the officer said, shaking his head. He wasn't smiling anymore. "One that says *Costco* on it, I might add. I mean, what the hell am I supposed to think, sir. What do you expect me to do?"

"All right. Yes. It's my fault on the cart. It was wrong of me to borrow Costco property. But I just needed a way to get the load from Point A to B, sir, that's all. My truck is just up the road a ways."

"Your truck?"

"Yeah. It's close. I'm telling you."

"Okay. Assuming I believe that—and everything else you're saying—why not just drive the truck door to door and make your pickups? Wouldn't that make a lot more sense?"

"Yes," Isaac answered. "It would. And I do that, usually. But at the building I was just at—the Eastmont, back there on the 800 block—there's no guest parking, no metered spots, nothing on site for visitors."

"So you have no other option but to obstruct the lawful flow of traffic with a stolen shopping cart," the officer said, nodding.

"Look. I know this seems bad from where you're standing," Isaac said. "But please hear me out, sir. I know I did wrong on the whole cart thing. Yes. I'll return it to the store as soon as possible, okay? And I should've worn my company attire, but like you were saying before—in this heat? I mean, come on, now. You know how those work shirts can be. With the collar and the starch and the thick-ass fabric that doesn't breathe right. The long sleeves. You know? Can't you put yourself in my shoes for one minute?"

"So you're just a simple contractor pushing these bags up the road to your truck," the officer said. "And then it's off to the washing machines you go. That's what you want me to believe?"

"It's the truth, sir. Absolutely."

"And if you took me to this truck of yours, would I see the company name on the side, at least?" the officer asked. "Or would that be hoping for too much."

"Sir. Please. I just want to do my job and get home to see my kid."

"Answer the question," the officer snapped. "Is it a company vehicle or isn't it?"

"No," Isaac answered. "It isn't."

"Exactly. So how the hell am I supposed to believe you, sir? Yeah? From where I'm standing, it seems a lot more likely that you snatched these bags and made off with them in a shopping cart that you've already acknowledged is stolen. There's no compelling reason for me to believe otherwise."

"How about this," Isaac said. "You could call up my supervisor. Okay? He'll tell you exactly who I am. Or better yet, check this out. I have this company app on my phone that I use to check in orders—to scan the forms and the tags and whatnot. Only contractors have access to it. I can show you."

"Hey," the officer snapped, his hand dropping to the pistol in his belt. "Get those hands back up, sir. What the hell is wrong with you?"

Isaac quickly raised his hands above his head. Without thinking, he'd started reaching into a pocket for his cell phone.

"Listen to me carefully," the officer said, his hand still resting on the weapon. "You stay exactly where you are. Do not fucking move, and do not say another fucking word."

Isaac did exactly as he was told. Hands held high, he stayed rooted to the spot and watched helplessly as the officer pulled a butterfly knife from his pocket and flipped it open, approached the cart, and punched the blade into one of the laundry bags. He sawed a foot-long gash in the plastic, reached inside, and pulled out a fistful of fabric. After studying the material for a few moments, kneading it carefully between his fingers, he shoved everything aside and moved on, repeating the same process with eight or nine more bags. By the time he'd finished, the cart had been all but ransacked; Isaac had no idea whether he'd be able to put the customer orders back together again, assuming that he could even make it out of this situation without being taken into custody himself.

"All right, then," the officer said, folding the knife closed. "Go on and relax, now. At ease."

Isaac lowered his hands, being careful to keep them visible, glued to his sides.

"Look here," the man continued. "I saw some pretty expensive-looking shit in a few of those bags, yeah? So I want you to tell me, sir. And try being straight about it this time. Where did you get the clothes from?"

"I already told you. I'm working."

"Yeah. *Working*, I know. Working a fucking angle. That's the only thing you're working."

"You don't even know me," Isaac said. "You don't know what I do or don't do."

"Please. I see people like you every single day. Always trying to run some kind of hustle game, trying to treat everybody like they're a simple fucking mark, but that's not going to happen between you and me right now. So let's move past it. If you don't want to talk real with me, fine, I won't take you in, but you can be damned sure, I'm about two seconds away from calling Impound to come down here and take this goddamn cart and everything in it, lock it down tight until we can get this thing sorted out properly. How's that sound?"

Isaac didn't answer. He couldn't. It was becoming clear that there was nothing he could say or do to make this situation right.

Out of the corner of his eye, Isaac noticed that a few of the bystanders who'd been taking video of the incident—either to protect him, to protect the officer, or in hopes of capturing something truly horrific, something horrific enough to eventually go viral—began to lower their phones and move on, and Isaac couldn't help but wonder how many of them did so with a feeling of disappointment rather than relief.

"Hey," the officer said. "Hello? I'm talking to you."

Isaac shrugged. "I've got nothing else to say. Go on and do whatever you're going to do."

The officer paused for a moment, staring at him with an expression that could only be described as one of disgust, before reaching for the radio on his belt, unclipping it, and raising it to his mouth. He clicked the side-button and barked out something into the microphone, but Isaac couldn't make out what the man was saying; his words were drowned out by a sharp creaking sound, followed by a low groan, as though something made of metal was giving way, buckling under. Isaac looked around and immediately found the source.

It was the officer's white SUV.

The front end of the vehicle was rapidly, inexplicably, caving in. By all appearances, it was being crushed under the force of an invisible weight, as though the hand of the Almighty were pressing down from heaven above.

Isaac watched in disbelief as the windshield and both headlights shattered, the front tires burst—first the left then the right—the hood folded in on itself, driving the engine block downward until the front axle snapped cleanly in two, dropping the vehicle's undercarriage onto the street with a resounding *crack*, fracturing the surface of the street underneath, spraying black fragments of asphalt in every direction.

Isaac spent a long time seated on the curb with his face in his hands, staring through his fingers as the officer tried to piece together the events he'd just witnessed. His radio still in hand, the man slowly circled what remained of the SUV, alternating between barking out a series of urgent-sounding requests into the handset, and barking out a string of futile commands to the gathering crowd of onlookers, pointing this way and that: *stay back, move the fuck on before I make you move on, turn off those goddamn cameras right now.* Nobody was paying a bit of attention to him. How could they, honestly? After everything they'd just seen with their own eyes?

As for Isaac, the primary emotion he was feeling wasn't curiosity or awe, but fear. Not only was he still reeling from the interaction with the officer, but the sight of a full-sized vehicle caving in like a paper model directly in front of him, with no obvious cause, had shaken him to the core. Every logical explanation he could think of (a structural weakness in the metal frame?) was woefully inadequate— laughable even—given what he'd just seen, leaving him with no other choice than to simply sit with the terror of witnessing an absolutely breathtaking display of destructive power without a clear perpetrator, without any perceivable warning signs or justification. The destruction had been completely indiscriminate, which made it all that much more frightening to consider.

But there was more to Isaac's emotions than just fear: a side of him was also euphoric. He couldn't have been happier to see that son-of-a-bitch cop get a taste of his own medicine, to see him stripped of the power he'd wielded so effortlessly moments earlier, to watch him grapple with a situation that he couldn't readily control, even with all the power and authority he had at his disposal. Did a part of Isaac enjoy watching the officer stare at his broken ride like a helpless child on the street? Absolutely. He wasn't proud to feel that way, but he took pleasure in it without a doubt.

Eventually the officer let Isaac go—*dismissed* him would be more accurate—without confiscating the cart or anything in it, thankfully. The man obviously had more pressing matters on his mind, what with the crowd of rubberneckers assembling on the sidewalks, the standstill traffic on the roadway, and the fact that he was going to need a little assistance from a taxi, a bus, a train, *something* if he was going to get himself back to the station. In any case, Isaac was free to leave. And he didn't waste any time, either; while the officer was busy taking pictures of the remains of the SUV's front end, Isaac hurried to the cart, steered it past a group of young boys standing on the road shoulder with skateboards under their arms, and continued pushing the load up Claremont in the direction of his truck.

Not long after Isaac left the scene, he reached the mouth of a wide alleyway between a Starbucks and a realtor's office, where he pulled off the road and stopped the cart, letting it settle in a shallow valley in the asphalt. Even though he was only a couple of blocks from the truck, he needed to take a moment to check the laundry bags, to figure out the extent of the damage done by the officer, and see if he could fix it before the situation got any worse as he bumped his way up the road.

Using the order inventory information saved in his phone app, he spent some time sorting the loose clothing back into its proper bags and tying knots in the plastic to close up the holes as best he could, but even after checking and double-checking, he couldn't be absolutely certain that he'd made things right again. But he'd done as much as he could; there wasn't any other option but to move on and hope for the best.

He pulled a yellow bandanna from his pants pocket, wiped the sweat off his forehead, and stuffed the bandanna back in its place. He sipped from a bottle of water he kept inside the cart and watched the rush-hour traffic go by, allowing himself to take a quick breather before getting back to the labor of pushing the load.

He was just about to continue on his way when he heard a familiar sound cutting through the buzz of traffic: a piercing *beep-beep-beep* coming from behind him. He knew the sound; it was a warning signal, the kind you hear whenever an industrial-sized truck is rolling in reverse.

He turned around to face the alleyway.

A green-and-white Waste Management recycling rig—absolutely monstrous—was backing directly toward him.

It wasn't too terribly close, maybe fifty yards away, but it showed no signs of stopping or slowing down, so Isaac decided it would be prudent to step aside and make way. He dropped the water bottle into the basket, lowered his shoulder against the cart handle, and started shoving. Not panicking, but not acting casual about it, either.

The load shifted forward by an inch, then promptly rolled back to where it started. He tried again right away, but this time he was serious about it; he laid into the basket with every ounce of strength he could muster, doing everything he could to overcome the inertia of all that dead weight, but again, nothing happened other than a subtle rocking back and forth. It felt like he was trying to move a tree stump rooted to the ground.

The truck was steadily approaching—*beep-beep-beep*—bearing down on him as though he weren't even there. Isaac stopped pushing long enough to try and flag down the fool behind the wheel: he whistled sharply through his front teeth, hollered out a string of desperate salutations, and waved his arms like a castaway on a remote island seeking rescue, wildly leaping up and down, but none of it had any noticeable effect. At this rate, in about ten or fifteen more seconds, the truck was going to be right on top of him.

Isaac decided to give up on the driver and go back to pushing; he couldn't let himself abandon the cart, not just yet. If all that precious laundry ended up scattered on the road in a jumbled-up mess, run down by thirty tons of steel, he might lose his job, which would mean losing what little stability he'd established for his daughter since they'd moved up to the Bay Area. So he dug in even deeper. Soon he felt a shift in the right direction—the cart began to creep forward, inching toward the curb cutout on the opposite side of the alleyway. It was progress, *hallelujah*, but it wasn't going to be enough to save the load. The ground ahead of him was sloped upward by a few degrees, so he wasn't able to generate any real momentum. It was an uphill battle in every possible sense.

The truck was only around fifteen yards away.

This was it. If Isaac was going to make it out of the situation with his own skin intact, he needed to clear the load, right then and there. His shoes scrabbling against the concrete, teeth grinding, he leaned low and hard into the back of the basket, bulldozing it with his shoulder again and again, until finally he felt something change. Dramatically. The cart didn't just move; it *shot forward* as though the wheels were suddenly riding on greased rails. Isaac lost his grip on the handle, took a few floundering steps toward the curb, and fell face-first onto the asphalt, skidding to a hard stop just a few feet off the path of the oncoming truck. He looked up and stared, dumbfounded, as the cart careened down the sidewalk, veered into the outer wall of the realtor's office and overturned, spilling the load of laundry bags onto the concrete.

It took a lot longer than it should have, but eventually Isaac dragged himself back to the pickup. Once the bags were secure in the truck bed, he sat in the driver's seat with his eyes closed and his forehead resting against the wheel. Just breathing. He needed the recovery time—not only from the experience of nearly getting rolled over by a recycling truck, but from the experience of watching, of *feeling*, the cart leave his hand. The fluidity of its forward motion. The sheer power behind the mass. Isaac couldn't help but dwell on the way he felt at the moment he lost contact with the handle: it seemed effortless. It felt as though the wind had been at his back, for the first time he could remember since he was a child. The purest ease he'd ever felt.

* * *

When Isaac was around ten years old, he was running outside on the red dirt track with some kids during school recess when the sky above them suddenly split wide open. A true and proper cloudburst.

No warning whatsoever, at least none that he'd noticed. The squall didn't act up for very long, but he was soaked to the bone in seconds. All of them were. The other kids made a mad dash for the corrugated metal tool shed next to the wooden bleachers, but Isaac kept right on running around that red dirt track in the middle of the storm as the others watched him from underneath the eaves, a line of brown faces only partially visible in the shadows. *Running* may have been the wrong word for what Isaac was doing; he was practically swimming on his feet. Wheeling and kicking his way around and around in muddy circles while the heavens crashed down on every side.

And then, in a matter of moments—just like that—the downpour quit. It was as quick as a spigot turning off. Isaac stopped running and stood on the track with his hands on his hips, water streaming off his forearms and chin as he listened to the sudden, blessed quiet. Watching the steam rise up off the pinehill bluestems. The scent of sweetgum and tupelo drifting in from the thicket surrounding the glen. This was Mississippi, after all: beauty and drumfire in almost equal measure.

The other kids gradually emerged from the shed and wandered back onto the track, staring and blinking like they were seeing the world in the light of day for the very first time. As for Isaac, he started to run again almost immediately. *Always forward.* That was his unwritten mantra. Before he could make it even halfway around the track, the wind picked up again—no rain this time; just a stiff gale rolling in from the direction of town. But there was a difference: As Isaac made his way around that oval of wet earth, he could feel the wind blowing at his back for the first time in his recollection. Lifting him up, urging him forward instead of keeping him at bay.

Everything was suddenly easy. In fact, his movements felt too easy to be real.

Still running, Isaac glanced down at his feet and saw what could have only been described as a betrayal of basic physics. His sneakers weren't making a bit of contact with the ground any longer; they were skimming an inch or two above the muddy surface on what felt like a cushion of air. Startled by the sensation, Isaac immediately broke stride, lost his balance, tripped over his own two feet, and fell face-first onto the track, triggering a chorus of raucous laughter, cheers, and whistles from the other kids as he lay there in disbelief. Before long, a handful of boys approached and pulled him to his feet, slapping him on the shoulders and wiping off the worst of the mud, joyously recounting his spectacular face-plant down to its finest details, but none of them—not a single one—mentioned what had happened directly before the fall. No one seemed to have noticed that he'd been *hovering above the ground* only moments earlier. That, combined with the healthy sense of skepticism Isaac had already developed by that early age, helped convince him that he'd imagined what he'd seen, that it had been a trick of the light filtering in through the trees, and that the feelings he'd experienced had been a function of the slick surface underneath his feet, a natural effect of reduced friction between his well-worn shoe treads and the saturated earth.

* * *

Once Isaac felt calm enough to drive, he headed to the company's laundry facility in Fremont, a city that lay roughly in between Oakland and San Jose. Given how he felt at the time—exhausted, confused, unnerved by what he'd seen and felt—he wanted nothing more than to leave this job behind, slink back to the apartment in San Jose, put Tallah to bed early, and watch a mindless movie on the couch until he could fall asleep himself, but that wasn't an option for him. Always forward. That was the only way he really knew how to live.

From the outside, the Quixit facility wasn't much to look at. A series of long, faceless gray buildings behind a length of chain link—there wasn't even a sign with the company name. To the casual eye, the place could have easily passed for a simple storage warehouse or possibly even a minimum-security prison. And that was just fine. Quixit's actual company headquarters was miles away in the city of San

Francisco, and *that* building was everything one might imagine it would be—all black-smoked glass and gleaming chrome, hundreds of feet in the sky. But this place? It had no reason to be particularly beautiful. Only one basic task was performed on site—cleaning clothes. A whole lot of clothes, trucked in from all over the Bay. North, south, east, and west. That was its only reason for being.

The drop-off process at the facility worked like this:

First, Isaac was supposed to drive around to the docks at the rear of the main building, back the truck down a ramp into an underground loading bay, and park in the far back corner near the elevators.

Next, came the weigh-in. A Quixit employee (Leti Sanders, if he was lucky) would scan the bags with a handheld reader, place them one by one on a stainless-steel platform scale, and print the total weight on a receipt.

Last but not least was checkout. That was when you brought your receipt over to the payroll desk back in the main building, where somebody would make sure the weight on your receipt matched the number logged in the computer system. Payments were made on the first of every month.

A three-step process. That was all it took.

But Isaac always did things just a little bit differently. Not out of rebelliousness, but out of an abundance of care.

Instead of driving straight to the loading docks, Isaac parked the truck in the nearly abandoned lot in *front* of the main building. That was the site of his pre-game ritual: whenever Isaac so much as set foot on the Fremont facility grounds, he always weighed his own bags first, just to be certain, before letting the Quixit folks get their hands on them. No offense to the company, but in the end, that's exactly what it was—a company, and a publicly traded one at that—which meant that its only function was to squeeze every last dime out of the operation for its shareholders, giving it every incentive in the world to tip the scales in its own favor.

Some people will tell you to *trust but verify*. But they've only got it half right. Just verify. That's all you really need to do. The trust part comes later, if you're lucky.

Isaac pulled an old bathroom scale from underneath the passenger seat and got out of the truck, holding the scale under his arm. The sun was about ready to quit on the day, but the summer heat was still stifling. It would be another hour, at least, before the dark would come and bring some measure of relief. Already sweating, he walked around to the back of the truck and lowered the tailgate, stepping aside as a few laundry bags spilled out at his feet. He set the scale down on the blacktop and got started.

After about ten minutes of back and forth, he had his total:

Three hundred and thirty-one pounds of good, wholesome weight.

Isaac reloaded the truck and drove around to the rear of the main building, backing down a long ramp that led into a storage warehouse underneath the load docks. Wide-open, dark gray, and abandoned—not a single worker in sight. Just rows and rows of crates filled with laundry supplies, a collection of empty wooden pallets stacked along the north wall, five yellow forklifts sitting idle along the south. Isaac parked the truck near the freight elevator and got out, piled the laundry bags into a heap next to the platform scales, and slammed the tailgate closed, double-checking the latch. He punched the call button by the elevator and leaned up against the wall, took out his phone, and started killing time scanning box scores online, waiting for somebody to come down and conduct the official weigh-in.

Before too long, a bell sounded and the elevator doors slid open.

Out walked Leti Sanders, hallelujah. Praise Jesus' name.

She smiled at him.

Double hallelujah. The day was starting to look a whole lot better all of a sudden.

Leti Sanders had worked for Quixit for a couple of years—

twice as long as Isaac had—and he'd gotten to know her pretty well, considering their only time together had been spent standing around a set of industrial weigh scales inside of a dank warehouse. Isaac had never even seen Leti outside of a company setting, and it wasn't for lack of trying on his part; he'd asked her out on two different occasions and been shot down (kindly) both times. At first, he spent a fair amount of energy trying to figure out why (something he'd said? just not her type?), but before too long he grew to accept her decision and appreciate *this thing* he had with Leti for what it was: a welcome distraction from the monotony of a job in the service industry, yes, but also a true friendship, the truest friendship he'd ever had, matter of fact. They texted back and forth, they talked on the phone, and they chatted at work—about nearly everything going on in their lives. Almost every single day, they were in some form of contact, and their bond was undeniable, but friendship was where it ended and seemingly always would.

Did Isaac occasionally wish for more out of their time together? Without a doubt. Not only was Miss Leti Sanders a good-hearted soul, wickedly funny, smart as could be, and tougher than any woman he'd come across before, but she was also *fine* in a way that only ladies of a certain age (she was somewhere in her forties) could manage their fineness: full-bodied, laugh-lined, throaty-voiced, confident, and open, wielding wisdom like a samurai's blade. Powerful—that was the word that came to mind when you spent even a minute with Miss Leti Sanders. With her dark brown skin and crop-cut hair, a tiny diamond stud glinting in the crease just above her left nostril, she exuded a certain kind of sophistication and class, always, even though Isaac never saw her wearing anything fancier than the dull tan drabs of a full-time laundry worker.

Isaac wouldn't have gone so far as to say that he was *in love*—their relationship was too easy to fit into the category of romantic love—but he did love Miss Leti Sanders, and he knew for a fact that she loved him too, somehow. The truth was that she was the only real friend he had in the world, and she was the only human being he trusted completely other than his daughter, Tallah.

"How've you been, Ize?" Leti asked, giving him a hug. She always called him *Ize*—as in, "all *eyes* on me"—her own special take on his name, which he liked more than he cared to admit.

"Good, everything's good," Isaac said. "Can't complain. And yourself? It's been a while now, yeah?"

Actually, it hadn't been that long since he'd been to the warehouse—maybe a week or so ago—and they'd talked on the phone as recently as yesterday, but for some reason it felt like it had been a long time since he'd seen her face.

Leti stared at him for a few seconds with her head cocked, then took a step backward, looking him up and down. Her hands went down to rest on her hips.

"I don't believe you," she said flatly.

It wasn't at all what Isaac was expecting to hear. He was at a loss for words.

"What do you mean?" he asked.

"You're straight lying. Badly. That's what I mean. *'Good, everything's good.'* That's some hogwash and you know it. What's going on with you, boy?"

Isaac smiled.

"How could you tell?" he asked.

"Your face. You're not exactly designed for hiding things, are you. Face like a Times Square billboard, only slightly smaller."

"I don't know about all that. I think I'm pretty good at keeping things under wraps."

"Oh, really?"

"Yeah, really," Isaac said. "Check this out. You ready? What am I thinking at this moment, right now. Go on. Try and read me, Miss Magic."

Isaac put on his most serious expression.

"Subject changer," Leti sang. "Subject changer."

Isaac shrugged. "That's fine. No problem. If you're afraid to try, I understand completely. You don't want to embarrass yourself out here."

"Afraid?" She shook her head. "Please."

"I'm just calling it like I see it."

"Okay, fine. You want to play? I'll play your little guessing game."

Leti folded her arms and stared at him. She stared hard, *appraising*, until Isaac's face felt so warm that he thought he was going to pass out on his feet.

"I think I got it," she said. "Here's what you're thinking. You want to ask me out, for the third time, but you're pretty sure it would only mess up the good thing we got going, so it would probably be best to just keep it friendly and professional between us. Sometimes the imagining of a thing is so much better than the reality of it. It's so sad but it's also so true."

Isaac had no idea how to respond.

"You're also thinking that I sure am a wise one—wise beyond my years," she added.

"Wow. You're pretty good," he said.

"Don't I know it," she said.

After a few more minutes of banter, Isaac decided, against his better judgment, to tell Leti everything.

He started with the incident between him and the officer on Claremont Avenue in Oakland, continued with the part about the SUV getting pulverized, and ended with the shopping cart careening up the sidewalk as though it were somehow possessed by the Devil himself.

When Isaac was finished, Leti stared at him with what looked like a mixture of pity and admiration. She placed a hand gently on his arm for a second, which he liked. More than he wanted to admit.

"Lord, Ize," she said. "That's quite an afternoon you had."

"I know," Isaac said, shaking his head. "I know. I can't explain any of it. All I know is what I saw."

"What you saw."

Leti gave him one of her looks—lips pinched together, eyebrows raised—which meant that she was especially skeptical about something (her default orientation was, in fact, slightly skeptical).

"I mean, yeah, Let," he said. "It happened right in front of me, didn't it? I was there. I saw it."

"Okay. But that's what I'm wondering," she said. "Did you really?"

"What does that even mean?"

"It means are you sure you saw what you saw? Maybe it was something else."

Isaac looked at her. "Something else how?"

"I don't know. I'm just saying, is it possible that something hit the truck, fell on top of the truck, *something?*"

"It was an SUV."

"Whatever," Leti said. "The big cop buggy that got smooshed. Who cares?"

"All right, fine. Maybe that's what happened. But let me put it this way. If something did fall and land on it, that joint was *invisible.* That's all I know."

"Okay. I hear you, all right? Relax."

"Don't tell me to relax," Isaac snapped, immediately regretting it. "I'm perfectly capable of deciding when I need to relax."

Leti was absolutely right: Isaac needed to relax. He was getting more and more irritated by the fact that the first thing Leti felt the need to do after hearing his story—the very first thing—was to question what he saw, what he *felt,* like he was some kind of unreliable witness to the events of his own life.

"Let's just get the clothes weighed, yeah? Let's get it done," Isaac said, turning to the pile of bags near the scales.

"Ize—"

"I'm done talking about it. Just weigh the bags and I'll be up out of here."

Leti sighed. "Look. I'm not trying to cast doubt on you. Okay? I'm sorry if it seems that way."

Isaac picked up the closest bag and tossed it onto the scale platform.

"Well, it sure doesn't sound like you believe me, either," he said.

"All right. Just give me a second before you start foaming off at the mouth. Lord, Isaac. You have to admit, it all sounds a little improbable, what you're telling me."

"Granted. I've got no problem admitting that," he said. "I'm not trying to tell you that I've got everything figured out. I'm just reporting the facts of the matter. What I saw in front of me. What I felt. If you've got some theory to fill in the holes, by all means, Let. Do your thing. Hypothesize away."

"You want my theory?"

"Sure," Isaac said, shrugging. "Why not?"

Leti paused, thinking for a moment.

"For starters, how about hysterical strength," she said.

"Pardon?"

"All right. You know those stories you hear about some lady, some ordinary lady, who was somehow able to lift a Chevy Impala off of her brother-in-law when it slipped off the jacks during a tire change, even though the lady herself only weighed about a buck twenty-five, fully clothed?"

"Come on, Let."

"No, I'm serious. Hysterical strength. You said yourself that you were almost run down by a garbage truck, right? That had to have produced some wild levels of adrenaline—even Mr. Isaac Williams himself isn't that cool under pressure. Maybe that explains how the cart took off running the way it did."

"It was a recycle truck."

"Exactly," she said. "Aren't those even bigger than garbage trucks? A bigger truck equals more adrenaline, at least in my book."

Isaac shook his head. "Adrenaline. That's what you think this is about?"

"I'm just throwing out some conjecture. Maybe you just

Hulked-out is all."

Leti was trying to inject some humor into the mix, trying to be flip about the whole situation, a tactic she used whenever she knew Isaac was irked and needed a reminder to calm himself down. Usually it worked—even though he knew good and well what she was doing when she did it—but the emotion he was feeling at the moment had gone beyond mere irritation. Isaac needed her to believe him, and he was flat out upset that she very clearly didn't.

"I'm done talking about this," Isaac said. "Just weigh the bags, please."

Leti stared at him.

"You really want to try and order me like that?" she asked.

"I want you to do your job, that's all. Please."

"Look, Isaac. You know me. The way I'm built," she said. "I can do sympathy all day, regardless of the circumstances, whether you're right or wrong in a given situation. I can *feel* you either way, because I care. And I mean that. It's not a put on. But listen, Ize: I absolutely cannot do reassurance unless I think you're right. I'm sorry, but that's just the way I'm put together. You want me to tell you that I think a truck got flattened by itself? And a shopping cart what? Grew its own motor and drove away down the sidewalk? Just because that's what you think happened? Well, I can't do it."

"It was an SUV. But that's fine, Leti. I'm through talking. Can we just get on with this?"

"No, Isaac. We can't. I'm sorry about what happened with the cop giving you a hard time, I really am, and I'm beyond thankful that nothing worse happened to you on account of that asshole. And I'm willing to talk through the rest of it with you, too, the stuff about the cart and the SUV and whatnot, but you can't ask me to cosign your explanation without letting me use my own mind on it first. You know me better."

"Just weigh the bag, please, Leti. Or I'll find someone who will."

Leti shook her head.

"You're sure this is how you want it to be?" she asked.

Isaac wasn't. But at that point he was too upset with her to change his mind.

"Just do it, please," he said. "I'm done talking about it. Let's move on."

Leti stared at him for a few seconds before nodding, approaching the terminal for the scales, and logging in.

Over the next fifteen minutes or so, she worked in silence, recording the official weight of each bag, one after the other, while Isaac stood in the same spot next to the elevator and read the news online, glancing up at the scales every now and again. Normally, he would've helped her shuttle the bags back and forth, but not this time around. It wasn't part of his official job description, and he wasn't exactly in the mood to extend himself for the sake of Leti Sanders at the moment.

When she was finished, Leti printed out his receipt, ripped it from the feeder, and left it sitting on the workstation. She logged off the terminal and left the warehouse through the door to the stairwell without another word.

Isaac went to the workstation, picked up his receipt, and checked the number.

Five hundred and fifty-three pounds.

He spent a long time staring at the readout.

Five hundred and fifty-three pounds?

Isaac couldn't remember the exact total he'd rung up on the bathroom scale during the weigh-in outside in the parking lot, but he knew it was somewhere in the low-to-mid three-hundreds *at most*, a whole lot less than the figure sitting in front of him.

Five hundred and fifty-three pounds?

Obviously, the bathroom scale was the culprit—it had cost him $15.99 and it was as old as hell is deep, while the Quixit model had a label on the side that read, "Contains four IP68-rated, hermetically sealed, stainless-steel weigh bars"—but that didn't make the situation any clearer as far as Isaac was concerned. Even if he accepted that the bathroom scale was faulty, it was hard to imagine how it could possibly be wrong by such a significant amount. A few pounds per bag, maybe. But this?

And that wasn't the only problem.

If Isaac were willing to accept that the Quixit scale was the accurate one, it would mean that he'd just hauled in *five hundred and fifty pounds* of cargo, which presented its own set of issues as far as believability was concerned. First and foremost, it just didn't feel right. Isaac had brought in a lot of loads in his thirteen months working laundry delivery as a rag runner, and in that time he'd developed a pretty keen sense of where each load would fall in terms of final weight. For this particular load? Three hundred and change felt right. Mid fives? Mid fives felt plain ridiculous. Not only that, but in the entire history of his employment with Quixit, the largest load Isaac had ever brought in—and this was two truckloads of twenty-five bags, mind you, a far cry from one load of *fifteen* bags—was only in the mid four-hundreds on the scales. This? This was absolute fantasy. In fact, the only reason that Leti hadn't flagged the load and reweighed it *had* to have been that she was too annoyed with him to have noticed the absurdity of the total.

Isaac stared at the heap of laundry bags, mulling everything over. Eventually, he decided that he needed to weigh them all again.

Isaac went and fetched the bathroom scale from the truck, and over the next hour, he weighed and reweighed each bag using both scales—five times per bag, per scale—making notes in tiny script on the back of the receipt.

What he discovered didn't make the situation any clearer. In fact, it made things more complicated than he could've possibly imagined.

For each bag, the weight was the exact same on both scales. There was no discrepancy between them whatsoever. But that wasn't the real problem.

The real problem was that the weight for each bag was *different each time he weighed it*. Higher one time. Lower another. But always consistent on both scales, which meant that the scales themselves weren't even the issue at all.

The weight of the bags was actually *changing* as he went.

And—although this officially made him doubt his grasp of reality—Isaac felt as though he was exerting some form of influence over the change.

chapter two

Isaac spent the next few weeks quietly experimenting.

Whenever he would haul a load of bags to the Quixit facility in Fremont, he'd stop in the front parking lot for the pre-weigh routine as usual, but this time, instead of worrying about the total weight of the entire load put together, he'd record the weight of each individual bag in the stack. Then, once it was time for the official check-in by a Quixit employee (never Leti Sanders; she was definitely avoiding him intentionally), he would stand next to the scales in the underground warehouse and watch as each bag was placed on the stainless-steel platform, and at the moment that the plastic touched the surface, he would try his best to focus—on *what*, exactly, he couldn't always decide, but on *something*. On the shape of the bag. On the fabric of the clothes inside. On the metal of the scale. On the air that surrounded it all. On himself. Isaac tried a hundred different strategies to trigger what he was increasingly beginning to think of as his influence. His *sway*.

Things started to happen.

During one particular weigh-in, Isaac caused a ten-pound bag to tip the scales at nearly one hundred pounds, which would've been a nice boost to his check on the first of the month if it hadn't caused an immediate do-over by the (completely baffled) attendant manning the console. The second time around, the weight of that same bag skyrocketed to just north of *five hundred pounds*, prompting the attendant to send Isaac home until a technician could come and recalibrate the scales. After that incident, Isaac made it his singular goal to modulate, to tone down the effect he was having on the target in question, but then he accidentally swung too far in the opposite direction: at the very next weigh-in, he caused a twenty-pound bag to register as nothing more than a pound and a half. At the end of the day, after dozens of visits to the scales, Isaac wasn't able to master the technique, but he was able to confirm what he'd suspected to be true—that he somehow had the ability to affect the weight of objects, for the love of God—but he also determined that *an effect* was all he could have at the moment. Control was another matter altogether.

* * *

During the weeks that followed, Isaac worked on refining the craft of breaking gravity. Changing the amount of attraction between two masses—reducing or increasing the natural force of their interactions. Even reversing those forces entirely. Creating a kind of gravitational microclimate around a given set of objects. This was how he'd come to understand the task in front of him.

From that point onward, Isaac started focusing on his perception of the *fields* surrounding different objects, rather than focusing on the objects themselves. He thought about context. The milieu. The medium.

In fact, *focus* might have been the wrong word for what Isaac was doing. He was able to hold an image of the fields inside his mind—he imagined them as a kind of bluish aura around every object—but he *felt* them more than he focused on them. The process required less concentration, less single-mindedness, and more letting go, more oblivion.

As soon as Isaac started using his abilities in this way, by surrendering to a feeling of release, everything started to change for him. The scales started to read precisely what he wanted them to read. There were fewer re-weighs, fewer recalibrations, fewer surprised expressions on the faces of the attendants. After two months' worth of practice, Isaac had made enough progress that he could comfortably and reliably pad the weight of each laundry bag by between five and seven pounds, which (although it seemed like a trivial amount) had done wonders for his overall financial health. Isaac wasn't remotely proud of his actions in the least—not only was he using his ability to bilk money from his employer, but he realized that it had been his natural instinct to do so, the very first act he'd thought to commit with this newfound power of his. It was shady, pure and simple, and it probably spoke volumes about his true character, as did the fact that any remorse that he was feeling didn't stop him from continuing. The truth was, Isaac could live with the shame of it. *Always forward.* He honestly couldn't imagine giving up the control he was wielding after spending so much of his life feeling as though he'd had none. And who was he really hurting, in the end? Some faceless corporation? Himself?

* * *

Those first few months brought a torrent of different emotions—Isaac ran through the full gamut. He experienced denial, shock, awe, confusion, guilt, joy, and relief, repeatedly, and not always in that order. It was becoming too much for him to bear; he found himself falling apart. The intensity of his ever-changing feelings, the lack of solid sleep, the mental energy required to manipulate *one of the four fundamental forces in the physical universe*—the combination of everything was slowly breaking him down. Even his attempt at embracing his abilities didn't reduce the emotional toll. Isaac still felt the exact same range of feelings, and on top of that, he couldn't shake the idea that he hadn't done anything in particular to earn this power, this privilege, this gift—and that's exactly what this was, wasn't it?—so the abilities themselves often felt tainted by the fact that they were so clearly undeserved.

It didn't help that Isaac was going through everything alone.

He wasn't able to tell a single soul about his struggles—namely, that he was somehow able to affect the behavior of matter itself—for the most obvious reason that it sounded preposterous, which would inevitably mean that he'd be required to show immediate proof of his abilities in the form of a demonstration, which would be either terrifying or awe-inspiring, depending on the viewer. But either way, that person would never be able to see him in the same way again.

* * *

Eventually Isaac decided to stop. Not to stop using his abilities altogether (that would have been an absolute tragedy). But to stop using them to do the wrong thing on an almost daily basis. He couldn't let himself continue to defraud Quixit on every job he took—he'd thought that he could live with it, but he felt too guilty, and while the extra money was nice, it wasn't the kind of money that was going to elevate his family to the next level or somehow *change their station in life* for the better. In the end, it just wasn't worth the amount of pain it brought on. So Isaac decided to return to doing his job the way he always had before: as a normal, unenhanced, dedicated rag runner. But a relatively honest one, at least.

Instead of exercising his skills at work, Isaac started practicing at home. Freeing himself from the confines of the workplace had an unexpected effect: it broadened his understanding of what was possible. He quickly realized that he'd only been using his abilities for the most pedestrian of tasks—to affect the weight of a plastic bag on an industrial scale—meaning that he'd only been working along one geometric plane, one single axis, and in one direction almost exclusively. He had already established that he was proficient at *pulling objects downward*. But what about lifting them upward? What about moving them horizontally from one place to another?

Sitting cross-legged on the carpet of their one-bedroom apartment, Isaac laid out a line of Tallah's old toys in front of him—a blue die-cast metal tractor, a plastic Pegasus, a stuffed lion, a small foam ball—and set out to accomplish the seemingly simple goal of raising them off of the floor by even a miniscule amount. He started with the foam ball, the lightest of the group, and got to work.

The process felt like trying to create both an updraft and a downdraft simultaneously while holding the ball in between, where the two drafts came together and met.

Like before, Isaac had no problem *influencing* the target: within the span of an hour, he was able to bring the ball off of the carpet on each attempt.

The problem, like before, was control.

On some attempts, in spite of all his best efforts, he could only raise the ball by an almost imperceptible degree. Millimeters, at most. Other times, without even thinking about it twice, he would rocket the ball into the air, sending it ricocheting pell-mell throughout the apartment, or—during one particularly misguided attempt—sending it upward with enough force to punch a hole into the plasterboard above his head. A ball made of foam. And to make matters worse, his goal at the time had been to raise the ball into the air by no further than a couple of feet, at the absolute most.

Isaac spent nearly every minute of his free time practicing, as long as he was certain that Tallah was out of the apartment or asleep in the other room. His days off, his evenings, his weekends—Isaac used every possible opportunity to broaden his skill set and hone his technique, to improve himself for some higher purpose, still unknown. He told himself that he was doing it all for his family, but he knew that was only partially true: this was about more than just his daughter. Crossing barriers that no one had imagined could be crossed, upending one of the most fundamental scientific disciplines known to humanity, rewriting the very rules of how the universe behaves: it was just plain addictive. Isaac's initial feelings of ambivalence and guilt, the concerns that he hadn't actually earned this power of his, had all but disappeared, replaced by a feeling of calm self-assurance, a sense of independence, and a level of control that may have been better described as dominion. As mastery. He wanted to believe that he was working this hard for his daughter—for the family—but he knew better than that. Everything he did was for himself much more than it was for anything or anybody else.

With so much of his time spent practicing, Isaac advanced at a breakneck pace, and the speed of his development further fed his desire to improve, which in turn made him practice even more. It was a spiraling cyclone of self-fulfillment.

Before long, he was able to raise the foam ball to any given height and hold it there, steadily, for a full minute or more before setting it down in a location of his choosing. After that, he moved on to the stuffed lion and practiced until he could do the same. Next came the toy Pegasus. Then it was the metal tractor, the heaviest object he'd tackled to date.

Once he was comfortable with that (which happened over the span of a few hours), he left Tallah's toys behind and graduated to household objects and appliances—the garbage bin, the blender, the stereo system, the toaster, the microwave oven. From there, Isaac moved on to the furniture in the apartment. A folding chair, the wooden TV stand, an old card table, the brown leather La-Z-Boy recliner. By the time he'd mastered those, he felt ready to try his hand at the most unwieldy items that the household had to offer: the stainless-steel refrigerator, the sleeper-sofa, the queen-sized bed in Tallah's room, the chest of drawers where all their clothes and other valuables were kept.

He worked for weeks, painstakingly teaching himself to raise each object to any given height and hold it in place, motionless, for a minute or longer before setting it down again. Once that goal had been achieved, he set yet another goal for himself.

To do it again. But this time, to move all of the objects at once.

* * *

Isaac started going out at night.

He would leave the apartment while Tallah was asleep in her bedroom and he'd walk the streets of the Alum Rock neighborhood of East San Jose, soaking up the brisk air and searching for opportunities to exercise his abilities in a real-world setting without attracting any unwanted attention. He knew that it was unforgiveable to leave his girl alone—the parental neglect he demonstrated was staggering (even to him), as were the rationalizations he used to justify it—but he honestly believed that the potential gains were worth the risks. Worth the *price*.

He was being driven by an almost physical need to push his limits, to reach the next objective on the horizon, to become more powerful than he was at any given moment, a need that felt akin to a hunger or thirst that could never be quenched.

Just off Laumer Avenue, Isaac discovered a vacant lot—no streetlights, no vehicles passing by, no real foot traffic to speak of—a place where he could practice what he'd learned in relative seclusion. *Vacant* may have been the wrong word to describe the place. It was abandoned and lifeless enough, but there were a number of objects scattered across the property among the debris—large objects, much larger than anything he could have found in the apartment—including the burnt-out chassis of an old school bus, a wall of crumbling cinderblocks about fifteen feet high and thirty feet long, and the remains of an abandoned two-story office building, all of its windows broken out and its roof entirely caved in on one end. All of these objects—the bus, the wall, the broken-down building—represented nothing more than targets to Isaac. Means to a greater end.

He started with the school bus. From a position concealed between the cinderblock wall and a mound of still-damp earth from an old dig site, Isaac worked on raising the rusted hulk of the vehicle into the air. Some fifteen thousand pounds of weight, by his estimate. Night after night he tried to move the bus in any direction, including sinking it straight into the ground, but he couldn't make it budge a single inch. By the eighth night of trying, he had no choice but to consider the possibility that he was being overly ambitious, that he was simply too far out of his depth. It was a disappointing conclusion, but perhaps he'd discovered the limits of his newfound abilities.

* * *

Isaac woke one morning unable to drag himself out of bed. He had a spasmodic pain in his lower back, radiating downward all the way into his groin area. It was excruciating.

After calling in sick (going into work wasn't even an option), he lay on the mattress for at least a couple of hours, alternating between breathing deeply with his eyes closed and browsing through a series of mindless celebrity entertainment news sites in a futile attempt to distract himself from the agony. Nothing helped. The only reason he was eventually able to work up the nerve to get out of bed was his overwhelming need to use the bathroom—his bladder felt like it was about to burst, which made the suffering even more difficult to bear. He moved to the edge of the mattress, climbed gingerly to his feet, and—hunched over, with both hands pressing hard against his stomach—staggered from the sofa bed across the living room to the master suite.

Tallah had already left for school, which was a good and bad thing. On one hand, he wouldn't have wanted her to see him like this, debilitated and on the verge of tears, but on the other hand, he really could've used some help in getting from Point A to Point B, even if the distance between them was only twenty feet or so. He stepped over an array of dirty clothes strewn across the floor and made his way into the bathroom, pulling his sweatpants down around his thighs along the way. When he reached the toilet, he couldn't stay on his feet any longer so he sat down hard on the seat and immediately tried to take a leak.

He wasn't able to.

Isaac drove to the Urgent Care department of Valley Medical Center, a few miles west of downtown San Jose in the Fruitdale district. He was feeling a little bit better by that point—the worst of the pain seemed to come and go in waves—but he wasn't going to sit around and wait until the next round of misery hit. He needed to get help right away, while he was still able to get from one place to another in an upright position. He hurried through the automatic doors at the front entrance, approached the receptionist at the desk and, after waiting in line for around fifteen minutes, checked himself in.

Isaac listed "stomach pains" as his primary (and only) symptom. His foolish pride wouldn't allow him to mention the ache in his groin or the part about lacking the ability to perform a basic bodily function on command. The way he figured it, his problems were almost definitely all related to each other, so if he could get the stomach issue squared away, the other problems would likely resolve themselves, falling *one-two-three* like dominoes in a line.

Isaac didn't bring enough money for the co-pay, but they took him in anyway. After sitting in the waiting area for about half an hour, a young Filipina nurse escorted him to a corner cubicle with a greenish-blue, retractable privacy screen, which she promptly yanked closed with a practiced hand. He sat down on a swivel stool with caster wheels and watched as the nurse stood near an empty instrument tray and swiped the screen of a tablet computer over and over again with her middle finger—it looked like she was aggressively flipping herself the bird. It was an interesting technique.

After a few minutes of silence, the nurse tucked the tablet underneath her arm, opened the privacy screen, and left the cubicle without a single word. Isaac sat on the stool and waited.

The cubicle was larger than what you might find in a typical office space, but otherwise it wasn't much different: six-foot-high walls covered in a beige print fabric, no ceiling, a couple of desktop writing surfaces, a gray metal filing cabinet. The most obvious differences were the sliding privacy screen, the paper-covered exam table, and the fact that the aforementioned writing surfaces were covered with medical supplies—glass jars with long cotton-tipped swabs, packages of bandages, a box of two hundred nitrile gloves—instead of office supplies.

After a few minutes of looking around, Isaac spent some time paging through a two-month-old issue of *Sports Illustrated* before putting it aside, folding his arms, and closing his eyes.

"Mr. Williams?"

Isaac nearly jumped out of his chair. A tall Black woman in a white lab coat was standing in the entryway.

What struck him immediately (other than the shock of realizing that he wasn't alone) was how painfully thin the woman was—the type of thinness that spoke of near-starvation and a lack of decent sleep, a constant stream of coffee and not much else. Her long hair was loosely pinned back, falling into her face in certain places, and the wire frames of her glasses were slightly crooked, which only furthered his impression of her as exhausted and overworked.

"Isaac," he said. "Just Isaac is fine."

The woman smiled warmly and stepped forward, her heels clicking on the tile. She extended her hand.

"Dr. Thompson," she said.

Isaac struggled to get onto his feet.

"Sit. Please," she said. "It's all right."

He didn't argue; he settled back onto the stool and shook her hand—calloused, wiry, and cool to the touch.

"So, Mr. Isaac," Dr. Thompson continued. "What brings you in today?"

Over the next ten minutes, Isaac talked about his pain in more detail than he'd ever thought possible. Was it stabbing or burning? Throbbing or pounding? Constant or intermittent? Localized or radiating? How would he rank its intensity on a scale of one to ten?

When he was done telling Dr. Thompson everything he could think of (other than the part about his groin and his problems making water), she asked him to lie down with his back on the exam table and lift his shirt hem up to the level of his ribcage, which made him feel a little uncomfortable—overly exposed—even though he knew that it was just part of the normal process.

Dr. Thompson plucked a pair of blue gloves from the box, pulled them on as she approached the table and, without a word of warning, started pressing against Isaac's stomach with her fingers. Gently but firmly. She didn't stay in one area for long before moving to another spot and continuing the same routine.

Eventually Isaac closed his eyes and tried to think of something else.

"About how often do you urinate each day?" Dr. Thompson asked quietly, palpating just below his navel.

Isaac opened his eyes. "How often?"

"Yes. How often?" she asked. "On the average. I don't need a statistical analysis."

Isaac really didn't want to talk about something as personal as his bathroom habits with a perfect stranger—it felt like crossing a line. And the fact that she currently had her fingers awfully close to his sensitive areas wasn't helping matters any.

"On average, everything's fine," he replied. "There's just the right amount of activity going on down there. All good."

Dr. Thompson paused and stared down at him.

"Look, I don't know," he continued. "I don't count the frequency, okay? I just know everything down there is working how it should be. I'm good."

"Are you having trouble urinating today?" she asked, pressing slightly harder.

Isaac winced, gritting his teeth.

"It's just some stomach pain," he said. "Stomach, not private parts. Isn't there some kind of medicine you can give me for the stomach area?" He waved his hand in a circular motion near the region in question.

Dr. Thompson ignored him. She continued to dig her fingers into different areas of his belly. At this point, her fingers felt like a pair of sewing needles.

"When did you have your last period?" Dr. Thompson asked, moving to another spot.

He thought he must have heard her question wrong.

"Pardon?"

"Your last period," she said. "Your flow. Are you having regular cycles, or do you think you could be premenopausal?"

Isaac stared up at her, dumbfounded.

"Relax. I'm just messing with you," Dr. Thompson said, smiling. "I'm trying to get your attention, Mr. Isaac. Do I have your attention?"

Isaac couldn't believe it—this strait-laced lady had a sense of humor, and a pretty brutal one at that.

"To the utmost," he replied. "You have my fullest attention." He couldn't help but chuckle a little bit—even though it hurt to make a sound.

"Look. I'd like to be the one to help you," Dr. Thompson said, taking a step back and pulling off the gloves. "Unfortunately, that will mean asking some tough questions. Personal ones. There's no two ways around that. So, if you'd feel more comfortable talking with another doctor, maybe one of my male colleagues—"

"No," Isaac said. "I apologize for acting like a baby. It's all right—I'll be fine with the questions. Go ahead and ask whatever you need to."

Dr. Thompson spent at least an hour trying to help Isaac. Asking personal questions (as promised), running tests, drawing blood, requesting lab work, gliding a gel-covered ultrasound wand across his stomach like he was pregnant (at first he thought she was messing with him again, but she was completely serious), and writing out a couple of prescriptions for codeine and something called *tamsulosin*. She even tossed in a tasteless joke every once in a while, which made it all easier for him somehow. Her smile helped too; when Dr. Thompson smiled, she seemed to transform into an entirely different person—warm and full of life, as though she'd suddenly been nourished after a long period of deprivation. Isaac ended up telling her everything that he'd been feeling since he woke up that morning. Even the most difficult parts of the story.

The verdict, in the end, was kidney stones.

"Kidney stones?" Isaac said.

Dr. Thompson shrugged. "I'm sorry. But don't worry too much about it—they'll pass through you, given enough time."

"How much time?"

"Two, maybe three weeks, tops," she replied. "After that, follow up with your primary if you're still experiencing pain."

"I don't have a primary to follow up with," he said.

"You don't?"

"Not unless you're it."

"I can't be your primary, Mr. Isaac," she said, shaking her head.

"Why not?"

Dr. Thompson gestured toward her surroundings. "Because this is Urgent Care. Emphasis on the word *Urgent*. This isn't about day-to-day health, Mr. Isaac. I'm nobody's primary."

"But could you be mine?" he asked. "I'll be honest, Doc. I don't have anybody else."

"I can't."

"Come on, Doc. Please. I could use somebody like you on my side, I really could."

Dr. Thompson paused, staring off toward the wall for a few moments before sighing heavily, reaching into one of the front pockets of her lab coat, and producing a heavily creased business card, which she handed to him.

Lorietta Thompson, MD, PhD, it read.

"Call my office number if you really need to," she said. "I mean, really need to—like your arm just fell off onto the floor for no obvious reason. That level of need."

Isaac slipped the card into one of the photograph sleeves inside his wallet. "Got it," he said. "Only in the event of loss of limb. I promise."

"Good. So for the time being, keep your salt intake down, drink your two liters per day, and take the meds I gave you. Don't play around with this, Mr. Isaac. I'm serious."

* * *

Isaac's nightly visits to the vacant lot on Laumer Avenue became less and less frequent over time. One reason was lack of motivation. He'd repeatedly failed to lift the school bus in spite of his best efforts, so his drive to keep on trying was dwindling fast. But that wasn't the only reason. He was also afraid that if he kept taking the risk of leaving Tallah alone in the apartment at night, something legitimately disastrous might happen while he was away, something neither he nor she would ever be able to recover from.

While all of this was true—Isaac was genuinely worried about his daughter's safety in his absence, and the task of moving the school bus had absolutely become a source of frustration, a seemingly insurmountable obstacle in his mind—there was a third reason he'd quit going out for late-night practice sessions. A reason more difficult for him to acknowledge.

His interest in raising *objects* into the air was quickly giving way to another, more pressing interest.

Raising living things.

More than anything else, he wanted to lift *himself* off the ground, to experience the feeling of pure weightlessness. To take flight. That was the God's honest truth. He couldn't think of a better (albeit selfish) use of his power than that.

The problem was that he wasn't certain what effect it would have on his body if he were to break gravity's hold—Isaac couldn't even be sure that he'd survive the experience. Although almost six months had passed since the incident with the police officer, the memory of the pulverized SUV was still fresh in his mind, and since he was pretty sure that he had been responsible for said pulverizing (without even making a conscious decision to do so), he was genuinely afraid that he might accidentally do something similarly destructive to his own body.

Isaac needed to experiment first. So he decided to use the only test subject he had available.

The cat. Lando.

Isaac woke up late one morning in December, having already made the decision to skip out on work in favor of going through with the plan: *The plan to levitate the cat.* When he gave it even a few moments of serious consideration, the idea sounded ridiculous, not to mention morally and ethically questionable at best, and even though Lando wasn't his biggest fan (the cat was Tallah's, through and through), Isaac didn't relish the idea of inadvertently flattening him into a black doormat. The risk of seriously harming Lando seemed low—after all, it had been weeks since he'd put so much as a scratch on any object he'd raised, and why should this be any different? But Isaac still found himself feeling anxious as he called the cat into the main room, using a handful of its dry food nuggets as a lure.

When Lando finally sauntered in, Isaac didn't hesitate. Reminding himself that there was no meaningful difference between the cat and any other inanimate object, Isaac took control of its body and brought it gently (but quickly) off of the carpet before it had a chance to lock itself down with its front claws. Surprisingly, the cat spent a few moments staring vacantly straight ahead, its green eyes half-lidded, the way it often did when Tallah (and only Tallah) scooped it up for some attention. Lando appeared to be almost enjoying the experience, hovering somewhere around three feet up in the air. At that point Isaac was ready to declare the experiment an unequivocal success and set the cat back down on the carpet, but suddenly it started to struggle: first writhing its body in a corkscrew motion, then thrashing its limbs wildly. Hissing and spitting all the while.

Rather than giving up and letting the cat down, for some reason Isaac decided to see if he could calm it—or, more accurately, to see if he could *control* it—using his abilities. Isaac started with its four limbs. Slowly and painstakingly, he straightened each of its legs one by one as though posing a toy action figure. Once satisfied, he moved on to the cat's body, which was still corkscrewing madly around and around. He halted its twisting motion without any trouble whatsoever, realigned the animal's spine, then gently closed its mouth, ensuring that its tongue wasn't caught in between its jaws. Finally Isaac sat down on the carpet and watched the cat's nostrils flare open, its eyes dart wildly in every direction, and its abdomen rapidly expand and contract. It was effectively paralyzed.

He lost track of how long he sat on the carpet, transfixed by the sight.

Isaac had prepared himself fully for the possibility of failing—he'd thought long and hard about what he would do and how he would feel if the animal were to die or come up injured—but he realized that he hadn't prepared himself at all for the possibility of succeeding, and how that would feel. Experiencing the power of bending a living thing to his will, as dastardly as that sounded, was positively exhilarating. He'd focused so much on the fantasy of using this power to control his own motion that he hadn't stopped to consider the fantasy of using it to control the motions of others. To send them wherever he wanted them to go. To immobilize them completely, if he so chose. The possibilities hadn't been clear until he'd seen the animal helpless in front of him.

As Isaac continued to sit and watch, he heard the sound of a set of keys smacking the carpet somewhere behind him. He turned around and saw his daughter standing open-mouthed in the entryway by the front door.

* * *

Tallah had seen everything.

No amount of his explaining away the situation could dissuade her from the conclusion that she'd just witnessed her father making the family cat float in midair. It was hopeless. She was as stubborn as her father when it came down to *knowing exactly what she saw*.

Eventually Isaac gave up, went to the kitchen sink and poured a couple glasses of water before returning to the main room, sitting down at the card table, and gesturing for Tallah to join him. When she finally did, he nudged one of the water glasses closer to her hand.

They sat together and talked for what felt like a long time. He lost track after a while.

Against his better judgment, he decided to tell his daughter the entire story, starting from the incident with the police officer in North

Oakland. The only bit he left out was the part about repeatedly padding the readouts on the Quixit scales during his weigh-ins—Isaac didn't want Tallah knowing that her father had intentionally and regularly done the wrong thing over such a long period of time.

When he was finished telling her his story, Tallah was quiet—given what she'd just heard, it seemed appropriate to give her as much time to process as she needed, so Isaac stayed quiet too. Both of his daughter's hands were folded tightly around the water glass as though it might otherwise escape her grasp.

Isaac watched her. His eleven-year-old child, going on thirty-five. Such a tiny little thing—it was hard to imagine how so much trouble could spring out of such a diminutive frame. She had the same heart-shaped face, long thin braids, and liquid-black eyes of her mother (rest her soul), but the child's skin color—brown like a paper bag—was all from Isaac, for better or worse.

The child was smart as could be, by the way. Scary smart. Maybe she'd gotten that from him (he liked to think so), maybe from her mother, maybe from them both. He'd never been sure. Sometimes he felt as though her mind was something she'd built entirely on her own. The child was so fiercely independent and stubborn that, if there had been a way to physically connect a cloud of disparate neurons into a functional whole, she would have been the one to figure it out.

As Isaac watched her, he couldn't help but think about what he often did when he looked at his daughter, especially lately. He thought about how much she'd been messing up at school, at home—everywhere, all at once—and what he could do to stop her from sliding any further down that slippery slope.

Every so often, his thoughts were punctuated with questions like this one: *What in sweet hell is this child's problem?*

His daughter was a good kid deep down—he'd always known that to be true—but there were layers of molten anger swirling around her core, making it harder and harder (at least for him) to access the nucleus of her true disposition underneath, the stable and sound parts of her temperament. It was like a shroud she wore, the darkness. As she moved through her world—her elementary school, the corner store, her friends' houses—she always reminded him of a storm in the gathering stage. That phase when the gray skies are still building up their bluster. Seething. That was how Tallah always seemed, even when everything in her life—at least according to her—was going just fine. *Fine, Dad. Everything is fine.*

Isaac couldn't figure out exactly why his child was the way she was, though he suspected the most obvious answer: that it was the pressures of the world pushing down on her shoulders at too young an age. The fact that her momma had passed on before they'd gotten a chance to know one other, and he'd never had another woman in his life to help fill the gap. Or maybe it was because he'd moved her around from city to city too much when she was younger, or maybe it was something else that he hadn't done well enough as her father. But maybe it was all completely normal, just a natural sign that she was bumping up against those dreaded teenage years. It could have been all of the above, honestly—Isaac never knew the answer with any certainty.

What in sweet hell is this child's problem? That was definitely the question of the times.

"Shit, Dad," Tallah said, staring down at the water glass and shaking her head, an odd half-smile on her face.

"Hey."

"I'm sorry," she said. "But shit, Dad. I mean. *Shit.*"

"I know, all right? I know. The situation isn't easy to understand, let alone accept, but let's not forget that I'm your father when you're talking, so please keep things PG for me."

Tallah shook her head. "What am I supposed to say, Dad. *Wow?* Come on."

"I just don't want you using words like that, Tallah. Anyplace at all. But especially not in front of me. Okay?"

Tallah shrugged her shoulders by way of a response. She was showing off her finest expression of disdain—for everyone and everything, as far as Isaac could tell—the most prominent feature of which was her patented take on the classic *upper lip curl*. She used that expression to accomplish a whole host of seemingly contradictory goals: to draw people in, to put up walls, to broadcast indifference, to cover her fear, to seem wiser than she actually was. To put others in their place. It was the closest thing the child had to an actual Game Face, and like most Game Faces, it was all about protecting her fragile pride in the end. Unbeknownst to her, Isaac had actually seen her practicing that expression in the mirror on a number of different occasions, and even though he understood the reasons why she put it on, he still wanted to wipe it off her face every time she had the nerve to use it with him.

"Unbelievable," Isaac said. "Somebody who's cutting school as we speak *now* thinks it's a good idea to show attitude? I see how it is."

"You're cutting work."

Isaac snorted. "That's not even remotely the same thing, and you know it, Tallah. Don't you even start with that."

"It's the same to me."

"Look," he said. "When you're grown, you can cut work if you want to cut work. But you're a child. And children go to school. Period. That's all that needs to be said."

Tallah rolled her eyes, another one of her mainstays. "We don't even *do* anything. The teacher is just staring at her phone half the time, basically. She's got no control over the bad kids, so what am I supposed to do?"

"Which teacher?"

She shrugged. "All of them."

"I'm not worried about what other kids do, sweetheart. You go to school and you pay attention in class. That's what I care about. Can't you understand that?"

Tallah mumbled something that Isaac didn't understand. "What?"

"It's not like I even miss anything if I'm gone," she said loudly.

"Just go to school, Tallah. Honestly, I can't be out here trying to make money and simultaneously worrying about where you're at—

all right?" He reached across the table and put a hand on hers. "I know it's not easy," he added, softening his tone. "I get that. But I need this from you, Tal. Please, do it for the sake of us both."

Tallah didn't answer right away.

Eventually, she nodded. "All right."

"Thank you," he said, sitting back in his chair. He closed his eyes and rubbed his face with both hands. What in sweet hell was this child's problem?

They were both quiet after that. Tallah used a finger to draw designs in the condensation on the water glass as he watched.

It turned out to be kind of peaceful, actually, just sitting together quietly for a change. Between her schedule and his, they didn't often find time to spend together like this, and when they did, they often spent it arguing over trouble at school or at home—always trouble of some kind or another—rather than spending their time together just being.

"So show me," Tallah said.

"What?"

She smiled. "Show me what you can do, Dad. Come on."

"I thought I just did show you."

"Come on," she said. "Picking up the cat? I mean, that doesn't even count."

The cat. Isaac had completely forgotten about the cat.

The moment Tallah had walked in and interrupted his experiment with Lando, he'd lost control; the cat had dropped like a stone, and the second it hit the carpet, it was off like a shot.

Isaac pushed back from the table and stood up, jogged straight to Tallah's room, and dropped down to his hands and knees to peer underneath the bed, one of Lando's preferred hiding spots.

Isaac found him right away. The cat was huddled against the back wall, as far from the foot of the bed as it could possibly get. Lando stared at him with wide, wild eyes. Its body was shaking violently. As far as Isaac could tell from where he was, the cat was fine physically—but the poor thing looked absolutely terrified.

The sight of the animal's obvious suffering and the knowledge that he was the cause of it were too much to take. Isaac's eyes welled up; he covered his face with his hands.

Before long he felt Tallah kneel down beside him and rest her head lightly on his shoulder.

* * *

The weeks that followed were some of the best in Isaac's memory. He showed Tallah everything he was capable of. The abilities he knew about, and a few he hadn't yet discovered himself. Instead of spending every moment of his free time practicing alone, in seclusion, he spent the time utterly immersed in the wild, beautiful imagination of his only child. Seeing his abilities through her eyes. Exerting his sway anywhere and in any way she asked him to (within reason).

During those blessed few weeks, she was the undisputed architect of their adventures: going to the local gym and watching as she bench pressed three times her weight; heading to the Westgate Mall and triggering the Maximum Load alarm on the elevator whenever a skinny girl walked inside; driving up to Stinson Beach in Marin and discreetly affecting the roll of the tides. Making ants on the sidewalk line up in formation; forcing cars to pull over so his truck could blow by; boosting the canter of a long-shot horse at the local tracks (after placing a modest wager, of course). These were just a handful of the most memorable things they did as a team. They were nearly inseparable the entire time.

* * *

Isaac started bringing Tallah with him to the vacant lot on Laumer Avenue. He knew that he had no business doing such an irresponsible thing, keeping his daughter out so far past her bedtime, but they'd become so much closer on account of the time they'd spent together practicing that he just couldn't help himself; he wanted more of a beautiful thing. He rationalized the decision by telling himself that bringing her along was better than leaving her home alone, which was the truth—it *was* better. Of course, an even more reasonable (and parental) choice would have been to stop going out at night altogether, but he'd traveled too far down this transcendent path to even consider turning back.

During their first few outings, Isaac worked on raising the rusted-out school bus as Tallah whispered advice into his ear—pointing out patterns she'd observed in his successes and failures, advising him to try *this* instead of *that*—and while it was slightly irritating in the beginning, by the third day Isaac realized just how much his daughter could contribute to the process. To his actual development. He started listening to what she was saying, and with her advice, he was soon able to raise the school bus a couple feet off the ground (just enough to prove the concept; not enough to draw any undue attention) on every single attempt. After that, he worked for about a week on the fifteen-foot wall—the problem wasn't raising it; the problem was holding the structure together above the ground—until Tallah suggested that he *increase the gravity of a few cinderblocks in the center* to help keep the rest in line.

Her idea worked. Once he could successfully raise and lower the wall on command (and keep it from crumbling to pieces in the process), he moved on to the abandoned two-story building, by far the most difficult task he'd attempted thus far.

"It's the exact same thing as the wall," Tallah whispered. "Just more."

It was late one weeknight in mid-January, and they were huddled together near the empty dig site, staring up at the ramshackle structure in front of them. Its crumbling walls, shattered windows, and caved-in ceiling.

"Wrap the whole thing in *whatever you do*, like a net," she said. "And then you just lift the net."

"Sounds pretty easy."

"I'm not saying it's easy," she said. "I'm just saying you can do it. That's all."

Isaac looked up at the building. He could see his breath streaming out in front of him.

"You know it's attached to the ground, right?" he said.

She looked at him. "It is?"

"Um, yeah. It's connected by the foundation. That's part of the challenge—to rip it out. Basically, I need to uproot the building like a weed."

Her forehead wrinkled. "Like *weed?*"

Isaac stared at her for a few seconds in disbelief.

"Not *weed*. A weed," he said. "As in one single undesirable plant. Lord, have mercy. What the hell do you even know about weed anyway?"

"Nothing," Tallah replied, shrugging. "I've just heard about it. Everybody has."

"Mm hm. Well, that better be the truth, Tallah, or you and I are about to have a problem."

"It's the truth. Dang."

"Is it?"

"Yes. I said yes."

Isaac stared at her for a while. Her face could have been carved out of stone; it betrayed nothing about her inner thoughts, at least not to him.

"All right, then," Isaac said, returning his attention to the building. "We'll bookmark that topic for later. Right now, let's see what we can do to move this thing."

Tallah didn't respond. But he decided to leave well enough alone, for the time being.

Rubbing his hands together to warm up, he studied the target in silence, trying to work out the best strategy to solve a twofold problem: first, unearthing the foundation from around five feet of hardpack soil (with around fifty tons of *building* resting on top) and then, of course, lifting such an enormous mass into the air without disintegrating it. Eventually he turned around and picked through the pile of backfill, shoving dirt aside until he found a jagged chunk of concrete studded with a half-foot of rebar. He brushed it off, held it in front of Tallah, and turned it over and over in his hand.

"I've got an idea," he said.

"What?"

Isaac pointed toward the top of the building. "Like I told you, I think the best way to do this is to pull up from the top. Rip this monster from the earth. You know? But to do that, I need something *above* the target, something that can do the heavy lifting. And right now, as it stands, there isn't anything there that I can use."

"So what do we do?"

"So, I'm going to try something different, like an experiment," he said, holding out the chunk of concrete. "I'm going to use this."

She looked at his hand. Her nose crinkled.

"How?" she asked.

"I'm going to throw this rock-thing over the building. And at the exact moment it's flying above the roof, I'm going to lock the two together."

"The two what?"

"The rock and the building."

Tallah looked at one, then the other, going back and forth between them a couple times.

"Then I'm going to use the gravity of this," he said, holding up the piece of concrete, "to lift that." He nodded toward the building.

Tallah was quiet for a little while. She seemed to be evaluating the proposal on the table, giving it some real consideration, and by that point Isaac respected her opinion enough to give her time to come to her own conclusion.

"Would that even work?" she asked.

"No idea," he replied.

They spent some time discussing the specifics, and once they both felt comfortable enough to proceed, Isaac stood up, glanced around the lot to verify that they were alone, approached the building facade—covered with mold, the stucco fragmenting and flaking apart, the interior visible through countless gaps in the drywall—and took a deep breath. The condition of the building, coupled with its relative size when viewed up close, were enough to make him reconsider the entire ridiculous plan, but only for a moment. The truth was that he wasn't about to back down from an opportunity to take his abilities to another level, and he definitely wasn't about to back down from anything in front of his little girl.

Without another word, Isaac reared back and heaved the chunk of concrete, letting it fly, watching it sail up and over the eaves until it was roughly five yards above the rooftop's center line, at which point he reached out with his sway and took control, stopping it cold in midair. He let it hover there like a poor man's moon, just watching it for a little while. Then, as Tallah looked on, he quickly ramped up the attractive force of the concrete fragment while simultaneously lowering the downward drag on the foundation. Push and pull—it's the key to almost everything. Right away the earth underneath his feet began to tremble and he heard the sound of wood splintering, metal structures bending, connections popping loose, fibrous materials snapping, ripping apart. He took a few steps away from the building, pulling Tallah along with him, and continued drawing the structure upward, forcing it from above and from below in concert. Soon he could see an outline of the poured concrete slab in the dirt as the foundation began to emerge from underground, shedding a cascade of dust and rock and remnants of building materials as it surfaced. The structure rose higher. A series of pipes ruptured, sending thin streams of blackened water into the cavern left behind.

Isaac held the building in place for a few moments, staring up in disbelief at what he'd accomplished.

But then something went wrong.

Isaac heard his daughter's voice, high-pitched and insistent, coming from somewhere behind him, but he couldn't register what she was saying—his ears felt pressurized, as though he were rapidly ascending in an aircraft, and everything around him suddenly sounded muffled and distant. All at once, an overwhelming dizziness rushed over him. He felt like he was moments away from being sick.

Tallah clung to his wrist and shook his arm like a bullwhip. Everything in his vision slowly melted into darkness.

* * *

Isaac opened his eyes.

He blinked a few times to test whether his perception was real.

His surroundings were familiar to him, though his particular vantage point (lying on the floor, staring upward), combined with the dimness of the light from a single lamp, caused even the most recognizable items around him to seem slightly out of the ordinary, slightly artificial, as though he were dreaming about his own life rather than consciously participating in it.

But either way, dream or no dream, Isaac knew exactly where he was—in his own apartment, in the living room, down on the carpet—despite the fact that he had no memory of how he'd actually gotten there.

His head throbbing, he pushed himself up onto one elbow and looked around. It was nighttime—he could see a sliver of pitch-black sky through the window—but he wasn't sure of the time or even the date.

"Let yourself come back slowly," a woman's voice said. "Give it some time. Everything's okay."

Isaac glanced toward the kitchen entryway and saw somebody vaguely familiar, though he couldn't immediately attach a name to her face—her thin, bespectacled face.

Who is this person supposed to be?

"You don't recognize me, do you," the woman said, smiling lightly.

"No. I surely don't." His speech was slurred.

"I'm Dr. Thompson. We met at Urgent Care around a month ago. Is that summoning up any memories for you?"

Isaac stared at her, blinking.

"I helped you with your PMS issue," she added. "Your little 'monthly visitor.' Does that ring a bell?"

Isaac smiled.

Now he remembered. This woman was the doctor from Valley Med who liked to give him a hard time.

"Doc!" he exclaimed.

"Shh. Keep your voice down," Dr. Thompson hissed. "Your daughter finally went to sleep." She nodded toward the closed door to the master bedroom.

"Sorry," he murmured.

Dr. Thompson stared at him, shaking her head. Her disappointment was almost visible in the air between them like a fog.

"Look," she said. "I can only guess how you got yourself into this particular state, but my assumption is that you're either high or drunk off your rocker right now—either way, that's your business, not mine. But I need to tell you that you scared your daughter tonight, Mr. Isaac. You scared her. She's not the type to own up to it, but you did. I've been around long enough to know it for a fact."

"I'm not high or drunk," Isaac said, slurring.

"Right. You're clearly as sober as a priest. But like I said, it's not my business what you do. What I'm suggesting is that the next time you want to go somewhere and pass out on the street, why don't you put some forethought into it and hire a babysitter first. Don't take your daughter along with you for the ride. She doesn't need to see you like this. Trust me."

Isaac snorted. "See me like what?"

Dr. Thompson looked at him with obvious disgust.

"You realize that you just woke up from a stupor, laid-out on the floor, right?" she asked. "I'm going to give you enough credit to assume that's not your idea of stellar role modeling for a child."

"I don't think that's how it happened," he said, quickly pushing himself into a seated position—it made him feel dizzy almost instantly.

"Okay, how about this, then? Do you realize that the only reason you're inside your place instead of outside somewhere in a cold ditch is because your daughter called me, and between the two of us, we managed to half-drag, half-carry your stupid self back to my car?"

"She called you?"

"Of course," Dr. Thompson answered sharply. "You told her to, at least according to her, although I'm not sure how you managed to say anything coherent in the state you were in when I found you out there. But I suppose you don't remember any of that, do you."

Unfortunately, she was right—Isaac didn't.

In fact, there were a lot of things he couldn't remember about that night.

"You're a grownup, Isaac," Dr. Thompson continued. "Do what you want to do, but don't let it affect your daughter. I've been there before myself, which is why I'm bothering to tell you this. Your child cannot be a part of anything extracurricular you've got going on."

"I'm not doing extracurriculars," he said thickly. "You got me all wrong, Doc. I'm sparkly clean."

"Actually I don't think you are, Isaac. I really don't think you are."

Isaac rubbed his face. His skin felt like it was ready to slither right off of his body.

"You've got the wrong notion," he said. "It wasn't even like that. I just got sick is all."

"Whatever. And in any case, you've got your daughter trained real well, Isaac. She didn't snitch on you at all, not even a little bit."

"I told you. There's nothing to snitch about."

"Right. So I'm supposed to accept that you were *out on a walk*— in a vacant lot, after midnight—and you just happened to fall down in the process. For no reason."

Isaac shrugged. "If that's what Tallah said happened, that's what happened."

"Great. I've said what I need to say to you. I'm sincerely glad you're both all right."

Dr. Thompson went over to the sofa, gathered a tan overcoat in her arms, and headed for the door, walking right past him.

"Wait. Hold up," he said. "Give me a second. Please."

She stopped just short of the entryway and turned around.

Isaac climbed to his feet as quickly as possible and stood in front of her, swaying lightly.

"Thank you, Doc," he said, focusing hard on his pronunciation. "Really. I appreciate what you did for us. And I'm very sorry that I caused you all this trouble, making you come out here so late and everything. It was good of you." He sounded like a robot, but at least he'd been clear and concise.

Dr. Thompson stared at him.

"You're welcome, Isaac. But to be clear, the only reason I'm here at all is because of that little girl in there. She's the one reason. I want you to understand that."

"I hear you," Isaac said. "Okay? But still. I appreciate you doing what you did."

Dr. Thompson nodded, slipped on her coat, and left the apartment, closing the door behind her.

* * *

After that night, Isaac took a step back from using his abilities so freely, with such abandon. He needed to regroup, not only to repair the damage he'd done to his relationship with Tallah (as it turned out, Dr. Thompson had been right: he'd scared his girl half to death), but also because it was clear by the way his body had reacted when he'd raised the building off the ground that he'd reached a (hopefully temporary) upper limit to his capabilities. He needed to figure out whether he was limited by the mass of the object he was targeting, or whether his sway operated more like a battery that could be drained of its charge after a certain amount of use and therefore needed to be refilled through rest and recovery. Or maybe both were true. Or maybe neither. Isaac had no one to consult for answers, no precedent to study, no comparable situation he could use to make a reasonable inference—his only choice was to be more cautious, to pay closer attention to his body's signals during the process of breaking gravity.

* * *

"Make me fly," Tallah said one morning.

Isaac and his daughter were sitting together in their pajamas at the card table, eating pancakes and turkey bacon, a favorite of hers for reasons he'd never fully grasped. It was a Saturday in late February—the window was cracked open and he could hear the steady rainfall, once a mainstay of the winter season but now a cause for celebration in the Bay Area.

"You're ready for your wings, huh," he said, nodding. "I'd love to do that for you, sweetheart, but I can't. Not now. Be patient with me."

"Come on."

"I already told you. I need to try it on myself first. It's a safety thing."

Tallah shoved a forkful of food into her mouth. "Fine. Then *try it on you.*"

"I'm thinking about it. All right? I just need to figure everything out first."

That was the truth—Isaac really was thinking about it—but he was also stalling for time, which he was pretty sure Tallah already knew. He'd kept a close watch on Lando over the last month and the cat had seemed completely fine, absolutely normal, and as a consequence he'd grown more and more confident in the conclusion that there was no real difference between inanimate objects and living beings when it came to breaking gravity's hold. Isaac was confident, but he couldn't honestly say that he was certain.

"Landy's fine," Tallah said right on cue, her mouth still full. "You worry too much."

"And you sound pretty breezy for somebody who has no idea what she's talking about."

"I do know what I'm talking about. I've been paying attention," she said with a smile.

It was something to behold.

Tallah's smile was stunning, not only for the most obvious reasons—the way her cheeks lifted, the brightening of her eyes, her slightly crooked teeth lending just the right amount of *quirk*—but also for its relative rarity, a fact that nearly brought him to tears every time he thought of it.

"All right, then," Isaac said.

Tallah looked up at him. "Really?"

"I go first, though. Period. If I'm okay afterward, then it's your turn."

She hesitated. Her eyes were open wide; for a brief, heartbreaking moment she actually looked her age.

"What if you're not okay?" she asked.

"I will be." He smiled. "You worry too much."

A few minutes later Isaac was seated cross-legged on the living room carpet. Tallah stood in the entryway to the kitchen, watching closely, her hands busy tussling with one another.

"Ready?" he asked.

Tallah nodded.

"All right, then," he said. "Here we go."

Isaac closed his eyes, and within moments he felt his body lose contact with the floor and begin to drift into the air. Arms spreading wide, he opened his eyes, and as he rose upward he allowed his legs to unfold and relax until he approximated a standing position, roughly a foot above the carpet, with nothing but empty space beneath his feet. Tallah was staring up at him with an expression that any father would be grateful for: one that combined both love and admiration in equal measure.

The experience was overwhelming. Isaac had been somewhat prepared for the physical sensation of flight, having experienced its most fleeting forms—strapped into a seat on an airplane, on a carnival ride, bungee jumping once in Humboldt a few years ago—but he hadn't been prepared for this, the feeling of being *uncaged*. Slipping the invisible bonds that he hadn't even known he was restrained by until they were gone. The sudden, unexpected sense of ownership and control over his own body was physically staggering.

"What does it feel like?" Tallah asked in a near whisper. She was wearing the same adoring expression as before.

Isaac didn't stop to think. Still keeping himself afloat, he gently raised his daughter from the floor and drew her in closer, lifting her to eye level, and began to twirl her body around and around in wild pirouettes just underneath the ceiling—slowly at first, then faster and faster—as she laughed without restraint, throwing back her head, her long braids fanning out in perfect lines. Her eyes were closed, her arms were extended out to either side, and her back was arched like a ballet dancer's.

chapter three

Over six months had passed since the incident with the officer in North Oakland, and during that period Isaac had mastered the art of *drafting*—a word he used for the process of raising an object to a given height and holding it there, stationary, before setting it down in another place.

Any object.

Including himself.

He'd learned a few other, subtler tricks during that time as well: unlatching locked doors from the outside, driving the truck with the engine switched off, stopping the needle on their utility meter somewhere around midmonth, forcing the ATM to spit out a handful of extra twenties (nothing to feel too guilty about), putting together a simple meal without ever leaving the couch. Slowing down whatever happened too fast for his taste and speeding up whatever slowed him down. Shifting the balance, creating a more level playing field, at least as he saw it. He even discovered a way to create *persistent* effects— effects that would sustain themselves long after he'd moved on to other things. The secret involved his memory. As long as he didn't forget about an effect he'd created, that effect would persist until he chose to undo it. At least, that was the theory—it wasn't like he was subjecting any of his efforts to rigorous scientific scrutiny.

For the first time in Isaac's memory he felt a sense of power: an inborn power that couldn't be stripped away, that wasn't a function of another man's arbitrary whims, and that set him apart from—and above—everyone else that he was aware of. A power completely independent of the social order of things. A native power. He felt truly in control of his circumstances—truly safe from the raging violence of the world—perhaps for the first time in his thirty-some years on earth.

* * *

One Monday afternoon in the spring, Isaac was down in the warehouse at the Quixit facility, carrying a load of around twenty laundry bags in his arms (all at once) from his truck to the weigh scales, when the elevator doors opened unexpectedly and out walked Miss Leti Sanders. The one and only.

She stopped short at the sight of him.

"Damn," she said, her eyes widening.

Isaac immediately lost control of the bags—they slipped from his arms and toppled onto the concrete floor all around him. A few of the bags were heavy enough that they burst open on impact, spilling out clothing like the innards of a mortally wounded animal. The two of them stood silently for a few beats, staring at the mess he'd made. Regaining his composure quickly, he scooped up the closest unbroken bag, shuffled over to the scales, and set it down gently on the platform as Leti watched, evidently speechless. He held his breath afterward, waiting for her to announce that—like Tallah—she'd seen absolutely *everything*.

Eventually Leti shook her head. "We've got carts for that kind of thing, Ize. You know that, right?"

Isaac looked at her. "Sorry?"

"Carts." Leti pointed toward the far corner of the warehouse, near the cluster of yellow forklifts. He saw a few flatbed trolleys blocking an emergency exit by the stairwell entrance.

"Yeah. Of course."

"I mean, I know you've got those muscles going on and everything," she said. "But you need to use your mind, too. Think about your back. And your knees. Trust me—you should start now, while you're relatively young. Accent on *relatively*."

"Next time," he said, nodding. "Next time, for sure, I will." His head down, Isaac sauntered over to the pile, picked up another bag, and schlepped it to the drop-spot next to the scales.

He continued moving the load in silence.

Before long, Leti knelt down beside one of the ruptured bags and started scooping loose laundry off the floor and pushing it carefully through the rip in the plastic.

After that Isaac started to relax. Yes, Leti had seen him carrying the load, but she hadn't really *seen* what he'd been worried she had—namely, the ease with which he'd handled the weight. The level of control he'd exercised. He didn't want Leti Sanders to find out about the most recent developments in his life, mainly because he didn't want to do anything drastic to change their friendship—not only its deeper aspects, but also their casual banter, the easy back-and-forth that had always characterized their relationship. He knew that if she found out the truth about his abilities, all of that simplicity would disappear for good, replaced by tension and unease.

Or, maybe all of that wasn't true, and he just wasn't ready to share. He wasn't sure.

As Isaac hoisted the last bag (Leti had closed the tear with a strip of duct tape), he felt his phone vibrating in his pocket. He set down the bag and answered the call.

It was the principal at Tallah's school.

* * *

Isaac sped south on the 101 toward Lawndale Elementary, using his abilities to force the vehicles in front of him to swerve off onto the road shoulder and grind to a sudden halt, leaving a long line of bewildered-looking drivers and inflated airbags in his wake. He didn't care; he needed to get to his daughter as quickly as he could. That was the imperative. According to the principal, Tallah was being uncooperative in one of her classes—*demonstrating extreme levels of defiance, even for someone her age*, he'd told Isaac over the phone—and if she couldn't follow the instructions of campus security, the next step would be to call the police.

Isaac needed to be there, physically, to talk to his child face to face, before the situation escalated any further than it obviously had. He knew his daughter well. She was able to hear the sound of reason even in her angriest moments, but if she so much as sensed that somebody was trying to show her disrespect, to put a target on her back, to draw her into a conflict for no apparent reason other than to assert their own sense of dominance, she was bound to react—she felt compelled, almost obligated to respond in kind. It was much more of a reflex than it was a conscious decision on her part. To hear her tell it, she would rather die in those moments than allow someone—anyone, adult or otherwise—to strip her of her deep-seated pride.

Isaac brought the truck to a hard stop in a red-striped fire lane at the front of the main school building, threw open the door, and jumped out onto the sidewalk. He slammed the door and started running full-tilt toward the front office, only around thirty yards from the parking lot. As he approached the office doors, a young blonde woman in a blue pantsuit emerged, and the moment she caught sight of him barreling in her direction, she frantically snatched a handheld radio from her belt and began shouting something into the transmitter, her wide eyes fixated on his.

"No no no," Isaac said, slowing down to a walking pace and raising his hands as he got within earshot. "Please. My daughter goes here." He stopped moving entirely and stood at what he hoped was a reassuring distance, breathing hard, his hands held at shoulder level, palms out. "Please. I just need some help, that's all."

The woman stared at him, the radio shadowing half her face. Her thumb was cocked at an odd angle above the Talk button.

"I need to find my daughter," Isaac said. "Tallah Williams. Sixth grade. I'm not sure which class she's in right now."

The woman's expression suddenly softened and she lowered the handset; something he'd said seemed to have made a difference in her impression.

"You're Tallah's father?" she asked.

"Yes. She's my daughter. Can you help me find her?" Isaac was still struggling to catch his breath.

The woman put the radio up to her mouth, clicked the Talk button, and said "Cancel my last" into the transmitter. She re-clipped the radio to her belt.

"Come with me," she said.

The woman—she introduced herself as Ms. Billson—escorted Isaac to a group of low-slung, gray portable buildings toward the rear of the school campus. The moment he realized which portable was Tallah's, he swept past Ms. Billson, leapt up the metal stairs, and tore open the door.

The interior of the portable was larger than he'd expected, large enough to accommodate a full class of at least thirty students, but he spotted his daughter right away—and not only because she was the only Black child in the room. Tallah was seated at a writing desk in the far corner, staring straight ahead at the wall. The area around her had been cleared away. The neighboring desks had been pushed back to create an empty perimeter, a buffer zone, and a tall white man in a police uniform was standing directly behind her.

The officer glanced up at Isaac for a moment before looking down at Tallah again.

"Baby," Isaac said from the doorway. "It's me. Look at me. Please turn around, Tallah. Please."

Tallah continued to stare straight ahead as though Isaac wasn't there, as though none of the rest of the room's occupants—dozens of students and at least one teacher, not to mention the police officer himself—were there, either. She wore her most stoic expression, the one she put on when she'd exhausted every other option for dealing with the grownups in her life, the expression designed to let each and every one of them know: *you can do whatever you want, you can take everything else away from me, but you can't force me to look in your direction, to give you my attention, to acknowledge you, to blink.* He'd seen that same expression directed toward him, and he'd used it himself a thousand times before. He knew it all too well. In his mind, it represented the last bastion of the powerless.

The officer stared at him. Blue eyes, thin lips in a straight line.

"Are you her father?" he asked.

"I am. What happened, officer?"

"A lot. Your daughter needs to learn how to listen, first of all. And she needs to start acting right for her teachers here. This situation could have been avoided. It shouldn't have gone this far to begin with."

"I'm sorry. Look. Whatever happened, she didn't mean anything by it. Please. She's sorry, trust me. Tell him how sorry you are, Tallah, okay? Go on."

Tallah didn't respond—she didn't even seem to register his presence. Isaac walked further into the room, keeping his hands high and visible. He felt the eyes of everyone in the room boring into him.

"Sir. Stop," the officer said. "I need you to stay put and be calm."

Isaac stopped walking.

"Just let me talk to her," he said. "Tallah. Talk to me, sweetheart."

"Sir. *Don't.* Your daughter has gotten as many chances as we can give. I'm sorry, but right now, she's being taken into custody for failure to comply, and believe me—it's the last thing I wanted to come out of this, but it wasn't my choice. It was hers."

"Come on," Isaac said. "Under arrest? She knows she messed up, but she's just past ten years old. She's got no business being arrested."

The officer turned toward him and dropped a hand to his belt.

"Sir. I'm not going to tell you again," he said. "Stay where you are."

Isaac stopped. He hadn't even realized that his body was in motion. The idea of his child being taken into police custody was almost more than he could handle.

Isaac took a deep breath.

"Sir. I understand," he said. "You're just doing your job. But please, officer. You know how kids can be sometimes. Right? Do you have any kids? If you do, you know how they can be when their minds aren't set right. It happens."

The officer ignored him. He turned his attention back to Tallah.

"I need you to get up," the man said.

Tallah was motionless. Seemingly untouchable. Blank. She didn't give any indication that she'd even heard the officer's command, much less any indication that she planned to comply.

"Get up," the officer repeated sharply. "This is the last time I'm asking."

"Tallah," he said. "Go on and get up, like the officer told you to. It's okay. Just get up, baby. We can figure out the rest later. You're not giving anything away by doing what this man is telling you to do."

"Get up," the officer said, dropping a heavy hand onto Tallah's shoulder.

At that moment, without warning, his daughter came to life.

She shoved the officer's hand away, and when he tried to put it down a second time she twisted around in her seat and began to fight ferociously—pushing, clawing, punching, screaming as though it were a matter of life and death—until the officer finally backed away. Chest heaving, his cap on the floor at his feet, the man stood still for a few moments, staring down at Tallah with his eyes wide and his teeth bared, before descending on her again, this time with both hands at the ready. He grabbed a fistful of her hair at the scalp and wrenched her head backward, then took hold of her collar with his other hand and physically dragged her body out of the desk, upending it entirely. As she writhed violently in his grip, he wrestled her to the floor and flipped her over onto her stomach, pushing her face into the carpet in an effort to regain control, screaming for her to stop struggling, to stop resisting, to *comply*. He dropped a knee onto the middle of her back, reached around to the back of his service belt for a long plastic zip-tie, and managed to loop it around one of her wrists as she flailed her arms wildly.

For a few moments Isaac watched the scene in disbelief. And then he snapped.

Without thinking, without any semblance of a plan, he charged headlong toward the officer with both fists clenched, unconsciously using his sway to send everything in front of him—desks, a wooden easel, a TV on a rolling stand, an overhead projector and, God help him, the bodies of *children*—scattering randomly to either side, slamming into the portable walls as he flew by. He parted everything in the room almost biblically, clearing a path forward in a matter of seconds. The officer looked up at Isaac with an expression of abject terror as he frantically scrabbled for the service weapon at his waist, snatched it from its holster, leveled it, and fired in one lurching motion.

Isaac reacted without even breaking stride, instantly ramping up the weight of the projectile by countless orders of magnitude, bending its trajectory so that it struck the floor at his feet with a *whump* and rattled harmlessly across the carpet like a glass marble.

Before the officer had a chance to fire another round, Isaac drafted the man into the air, letting him hang there almost insect-like, immobilized, while Tallah scrambled to her feet. Once Isaac was sure she was clear, he slowly walked the last few steps to reach the officer, focused on the gun in his hand, and weighed the weapon down until it slipped from his grip and embedded itself a couple of inches into the floor. Then he let the man fall in a heap.

To his credit, the officer climbed to his feet almost immediately, regarding Isaac with a terrified—yet resolute—expression. Isaac didn't hesitate for a moment. He didn't pause to think.

He put his hands on the man.

The officer crumpled to the floor at Isaac's touch, his legs bent at impossible angles, crushed underneath his own body's sudden, unnatural weight. Pale splinters of bone burst through the heavy fabric of the man's pant legs, blood pouring in rivulets from the perforations onto the carpet.

While the officer screamed in agony behind them, Isaac paused to make sure that none of the children had been seriously injured, then took Tallah's hand and walked with her to the door.

* * *

It wasn't until they made it back to the apartment that Isaac truly understood the severity of what he'd done, the extent of the crimes he'd committed, and the gravity of the likely consequences. He had seriously injured a police officer—the most hallowed of hallowed professions—a grievous enough transgression for any citizen, regardless of their circumstances, but for somebody like Isaac it was a capital offense. He had brashly committed one of the gravest errors a Black person in the United States could possibly commit: he had dared to touch an untouchable class. He'd wounded an enforcer of the status quo, and he'd survived.

A rabid, feverish search was probably already underway, with dozens of cops in the streets baying for his blood like a pack of scent-whipped dogs, and once they finally caught up to him and cornered him in a hole somewhere, they would do everything in their power to ensure that the encounter ended in violence. If he wasn't killed outright while being taken into custody, he would experience an unfortunate but fatal injury while being transported in the cargo area of a police trawler, or he would unexpectedly succumb to a preexisting medical condition at some point during questioning, or he would inexplicably commit suicide while sitting in lockup, awaiting trial.

Worse still, Isaac had assaulted a police officer using an inexplicable ability that no one would understand, much less accept, and because every classroom at Lawndale was equipped with live security cameras (he'd been told as much at the start of the school year), soon everybody in the free world would see exactly what he was capable of.

Within the next ten minutes, Isaac had packed all of their necessities into two battered black duffel bags: one for Tallah and one for him. He'd made the decision to run, at least for the time being. A small part of him was still considering turning himself over to the authorities and trying to make things right as best he could, but that wasn't an option until he found a safe place to put his daughter. If he were to be taken into custody now, he knew good and well that Tallah would be sent directly into the hands of Child Protective Services, especially given the high probability that the police wouldn't accept his peaceful surrender to begin with, but instead would find ways to escalate the situation so that *they didn't have a choice but to put him down*, leaving his daughter orphaned. And the thought of his daughter being absorbed into the churn of the social services system was absolutely devastating. He couldn't allow it.

Unfortunately, Isaac could only think of one place Tallah could go. He had no blood relatives to speak of, so he was going to have to ask Leti Sanders, his only friend in the world, for help.

Once the bags were packed, Isaac went to the bedroom; Tallah was lying face-down on the bed, motionless. He knocked two times on the door jamb.

"Sweetheart. We need to go."

Tallah didn't move. Her body was positioned above the sheets but her face was buried in a pillow, her braids splayed in every direction.

"We need to go, baby," he said, knocking again. "I'm sorry, but we can't stay. It isn't safe here."

She shifted slightly, but stayed silent.

"I'm serious, Tallah. We need to go." He approached the bed, took hold of her heel, and shook it lightly.

Tallah said something into the pillow, but her words came out muffled.

"What?"

"I don't want to," she said, lifting her face for a moment before plopping back down.

"Well, it doesn't matter what you want right now. You have no choice." He clapped his hands. "Come on. Let's go."

Tallah slowly turned over and propped herself up onto one elbow. She wiped both eyes with the back of her hand, then wiped her nose with the heel of her palm. Even from the doorway, he could see that the pillowcase was wet.

Isaac sat down on the edge of the bed next to her. They didn't have time for all this, but he needed to make time, just a little.

"How's your back doing?" he asked, trying to sound calm.

Tallah sniffed and wiped her nose again. "My head doesn't feel good. My back's all right."

Isaac took his daughter's chin gently in his hand and studied her face, tilting it to one side, then the other. There was a purplish bruise underneath her left eye and an angry-looking scrape—from the carpet, no doubt—on the apple of her cheek. She closed her eyes.

"I know I messed up," she said, nodding.

"Hey. Don't do this now. It's all right."

"No. I know I messed up, Dad. I know I did."

"Listen," Isaac said. "I understand how you feel, sweetheart. I do. But we don't have time to think about any of that right now."

"I'm sorry." She opened her eyes; they looked glassy. The tears were steadily building.

Isaac leaned in close and gathered her in his arms, being careful not to press his shoulder against her face. She burst out crying.

"Shh. It's okay," he said. "We'll be all right."

"I couldn't *think*. I tried." She sobbed, gasping after every other word.

"I couldn't think either, sweetheart. I understand."

Isaac held her for a long time—much longer than he should have under the circumstances. It wasn't prudent, but he didn't stop himself.

Eventually she stopped crying, her breathing slowed down, and she fell asleep, stretched across his lap, her mouth slightly open. Isaac stared at her face. The dried tear tracks and the bruising. As he watched her sleep, he heard a noise coming from the direction of the living room. It sounded like someone was standing outside the front door of the apartment, shifting from foot to foot.

Isaac shoved Tallah off of him and shot to his feet.

"What's wrong?" she asked, her eyes wide.

"Shh."

Isaac cocked his head. He heard the sound again.

"Dad?"

He ran to the closet and tore open the door.

"Get in," he said, pointing. "No matter what you hear, stay quiet and don't move. Go."

The front door to the apartment suddenly burst open, sending a jagged shard of the wooden frame pinwheeling into the living room.

A squad of at least ten officers wearing black helmets and body armor swarmed through the broken entryway, their compact rifles raised to shoulder level.

Isaac had just enough time to slam the door to the bedroom before the officers let loose with their semi-automatics, littering the particle board with bullet holes, tearing the material to shreds, spraying composite fiber tufts into the air like downy seeds. He threw himself face down onto the carpet and covered his head with both arms.

The volley abruptly stopped, and a man with a raspy voice shouted something that sounded like commands, but Isaac wasn't sure whether they were directed toward him or toward the other officers in the squad. Either way, he couldn't let himself wait. He rolled over, climbed to his feet, and moved to one side of the shattered door, staying in a crouched position.

"Officers?" Isaac called through a gap in the panel. "I've got nothing on me, and I'm not a threat to anybody. All I want to do is to turn myself in with peace. All right?"

He waited for a response, but none came.

"Hey. I'm coming out," he said. "You hear me? Nothing but peace, officers."

Staying hidden against the wall on one side of the opening, Isaac turned the knob, pulled open the remains of the door, and let its wobbly momentum carry it all the way to the wall bumper. He straightened, took a breath, and stepped into the entryway. As he moved into position, he was already visualizing the effect he was about to produce, the influence he planned to wield over these unfortunate men.

Before the cops had a chance to react, Isaac whipped them off their feet and rocketed their bodies straight upward into the plaster ceiling with a thunderous *whump* and then released them, letting their limp bodies plummet back to the floor in a shower of drywall, stucco fragments, loose body armor, and assault weapons. It was over in a matter of a second—two at the most. When the dust settled, he could hear the sound of sirens in the distance, loud voices in the apartment building's courtyard, and the groans of the officers in front of him as they tried desperately to recover, to regain their bearings, to crawl toward the nearest fallen gun.

Ignoring all of it, Isaac turned around, approached the closet door, and knocked twice. He noticed that the door hadn't been closed all the way; it was resting against the metal strike plate.

"It's me, baby," he said. "We need to go. Now."

Isaac listened for a response.

"Tallah?"

He opened the door slowly, deliberately. Tallah must have been terrified, and he didn't want to make things worse by barging in like a bull.

"Everything's all right," he said as he entered the closet.

Isaac looked around, but he didn't see her.

He shoved his clothes aside—pants, shirts, and jackets— sending plastic hangers clattering to the floor.

Tallah wasn't there.

Panicking, Isaac left the closet, dropped down onto his stomach, and frantically searched under the bed, yanking out long plastic bins full of winter clothes, a box of old CDs, a broken flat- screen monitor. He leapt to his feet, ran to the master bathroom beside the closet, and ripped down the shower curtain, sending the metal tension rod clanging into the bathtub below. He tore open the cabinets underneath the vanity, emptying them of towels, washcloths, hotel shampoos, and cleaning supplies, even though he knew in his heart that Tallah couldn't possibly fit into such a confined space.

She was nowhere to be found.

Isaac returned to the bedroom and stood near the entryway, his mind racing. Keeping one eye on the downed officers, he tried to recreate the sequence of events—the SWAT team breaching the front door, the sustained volley of gunfire, the almost instant incapacitation of the entire team—but none of it got him any closer to figuring out where Tallah could have gone in such a short period of time.

Isaac scanned the room helplessly. That was when he noticed a small, open window just above the bullet-ridden headboard.

The window screen had been torn to create an opening.

Isaac burst outside through the shattered front door into an open-air courtyard at the center of the apartment complex. A few picnic tables, lawn chairs, and rusted barbecue pits surrounded a bone-dry swimming pool with cracked blue tile. The sun was on its way down—it had already fallen below the level of the building's rooftops—creating a dim atmosphere in the atrium.

Across the courtyard, three or four uniformed officers had already spotted him from behind the cover of a few thick-trunked potted palms, their weapons drawn but pointed downward at the patio. They looked authentically surprised, as though they hadn't been expecting him to come out alone—or perhaps had expected he would only come out on a coroner's gurney.

When Isaac saw the officers, he immediately stopped running and stood frozen near a low wrought-iron fence surrounding a group of planter boxes.

"Hold up," a voice shouted, echoing. "Nobody do anything. Just hold steady."

Isaac scanned the courtyard. Between the dim lighting and the acoustics, he couldn't pinpoint the owner of the voice.

Before long, he saw a man casually step out from a covered entranceway around twenty yards to his left, holding one hand up in the air as though trying to hail a taxi. Isaac recognized him right away: his tall frame, his squared-off jaw, his jet-black, slicked-back hair. It was the same plainclothes police officer he'd tangled with on Claremont Avenue in North Oakland. The man was even dressed roughly the same—a tight black t-shirt, loose-fitting jeans, and a belt full of potential pain and suffering—only this time, he wore a gray ballistic vest to top off the ensemble. Once the man had Isaac's attention, he raised his other hand to match the first one, giving the appearance of full surrender.

"It's all right, Mr. Williams," the man said, walking slowly in his direction. "Everything's good here. At ease."

The officer said a lot more than that, but Isaac had stopped listening to him—his mind had gone to another place entirely. He was busy using his influence to create a first (and only) line of defense: a crudely fashioned *gravity updraft* between himself and the group of officers, like a barrier made of pure dynamic lift, a shield of vertical wind. If Isaac created the effect correctly, it would mean that anything they decided to throw his way, from bullets to tear gas canisters, would encounter the updraft first—this aegis of air—at which point the object would be caught in a kind of gravitational geyser and catapulted upward to some undefined height (Isaac hadn't thoroughly tested this effect, so who knew for certain?), but hopefully somewhere in the vicinity of kingdom come.

When he'd finished, he wasn't able to see the effect, but he could feel the gravity updraft oscillating in front of him, almost like the thrumming bass from a stereo speaker.

The officer stopped walking and stood near a row of blue and white deck chairs near the empty swimming pool. He lowered his hands to his sides.

"My name is Gates," he said. "I'm just here to have a conversation with you. Okay? No stress, no BS—just talking is all."

Isaac snorted. "So now you want to talk," he said, almost spitting it. "Now you want to listen to what I'm trying to tell you. Now you're ready to hear me."

"I am," Gates said. "I really am ready, Mr. Williams."

As far as he could tell, the man's response was completely

sincere. Isaac stared at Gates, surprised by the level of anger he felt—not only at the memory of their last interaction, but at the contrast between that interaction and this one. He was also surprised by his level of fear. The fact that he could *still* be afraid of this officer, of all the officers, in spite of his tremendous power and the numerous ways he could use it to hurt them irreparably, made him even angrier.

"I can't help but notice that you're a lot more civil right now," Isaac said. "Compared to last time, I mean."

Gates shrugged. "Different circumstances, you know? Things just change. All the time, they're changing." He snapped his fingers a few times. "Quick as a wink. What can I say? You got to keep up with the flow."

"Different circumstances," Isaac said, nodding. "Yeah. They are quite a bit different now, aren't they. Speaking of which, this is San Jose, last I checked. Shouldn't you be up in Oakland right now?"

Gates' expression darkened for a moment, but then he managed a thin-lipped smile.

"Got transferred, man," he replied, shaking his head. "It happens sometimes. Like I said: *changes*. And what about yourself? What brings you all the way down here to the beautiful South Bay?"

Isaac didn't answer right away. This back-and-forth, faux-casual banter was wearing thin. He knew that every word coming out of Gates' mouth was part of a larger power play he was running, whether to distract him, weaken his resolve, convince him that they were friends, or to project a lack of fear. In the end, everything Gates said to him was about establishing some measure of control.

"Nothing in particular brings me down here," Isaac said. "This is just where I stay now." He gestured to the door behind him. "I mean, this is where I used to stay—that's probably closer to the truth at this point, thanks to you all."

"So that must mean you're planning on heading off to somewhere new," Gates said. "Easing on down the road, I suppose. Is that the plan?"

Isaac glanced at the officers positioned near the trees—they hadn't moved and their weapons were still lowered. He glanced over his shoulder to check what was left of his front door. Thankfully, there was no sign of the assault team he'd left incapacitated in the living room, at least not yet.

"Sounds about right," Isaac replied.

Gates looked up toward the sky as though contemplating something weighty, but Isaac wasn't buying it. He knew it was all part of the show, something to keep him occupied.

"Change can be a good thing," Gates said, nodding. "It sure can be. But when I make a change in my own life, I always want to be sure I don't leave anything precious behind when I decide it's time to uproot myself. Maybe that's just me. But the last thing I want to do is change the only good thing I've got going for myself. So before I make any big decisions like this one, I always ask myself—am I a hundred percent sure that I've got everything I need before I hit the road?"

It only took Isaac a moment to cut through the man's BS, to understand his actual meaning. Gates was talking about Tallah. Somehow he knew that she was missing.

"Listen," Gates said. "This situation you're in? It's going to get a whole lot more complicated, the longer you let it drag on and on." He pointed toward the door to his apartment. "That team in there was just the tip of the fucking spear—a very long and very sharp spear. The video of all those antics you pulled at the school has only been seen by the department as far as I know—all internal, just a handful of people—and already you got fucking SWAT thrown at you as the opening salvo. Think of it like an appetizer. So consider this for a minute. What happens when that video leaks online and everybody out there in the world sees it? Think about everybody—everybody in law enforcement and beyond—who will be gunning for a piece of you then. Believe me when I tell you, it won't be easy to manage, even if you really can do all the tricks we saw you do on that video."

Isaac didn't respond. All he could think about was Tallah and whether she was safe.

"By the way," Gates said. "Between you and me. How in the

hell did you do all that shit anyway? Redirecting bullets? Making pigs fly? Please, do tell."

"You forgot crushing SUVs."

Gates pointed at him. "Exactly. I mean, *fuck me.* The footage wasn't great inside that classroom, to be honest—pretty grainy, actually—but even so, it's abundantly clear that you're pretty goddamn capable."

"Where's my daughter?" Isaac asked.

"That goddamn SUV," Gates continued, ignoring him. He was smiling and shaking his head as though recalling a fond memory. "You have no idea how long I spent trying to puzzle that one out. I'm almost glad you did what you did today—no disrespect to Chauncey, the man you very foolishly took out of action down at Lawndale—because at least now I know what tin-canned my fucking truck. At least I know."

"Where is my daughter," Isaac repeated.

"I hear you, man, I hear you. Just calm down. I was getting to that," Gates said. "So, one of my guys found your little girl wandering back there somewhere behind the building and picked her up. Dumb luck, if you ask me." Gates stopped looking at Isaac and turned toward the group of officers. "No offense, Julian," he called out. "But that was some dumb luck, you little bastard, you know it was."

Gates looked back at Isaac. "Anyway. She's safe with us now— a damn sight safer than she'd be if she was running around wild next to you, I might add. So don't worry about your little girl. Worry about *you.* Worry about making the right life decision for yourself, one that will increase your chances of seeing your child grow into adulthood."

"And what would that be?" Isaac asked. At this point, his mind was reeling. He was simply trying to buy himself some time.

Gates looked puzzled. "What would what be?"

"What is the decision?" Isaac asked. "The right decision, if you were me."

A small part of Isaac—a part that he hated—was hoping that Gates would give him an answer he could actually use, a strategy that would end the unmitigated disaster currently in progress.

"That's an easy one," Gates replied. "Or, at least, it's easy to say. Not necessarily easy to get done. But in either case, here it is—you need to come quietly and turn yourself in. Predictable that I would suggest this, I know, but that doesn't change the truth of it."

Gates shrugged his shoulders casually, as though they'd been discussing the best spot to grab takeout for lunch rather than the direction of Isaac's life. The man wore a Win Some, Lose Some expression that made Isaac want to bury him neck-deep in the soil.

"Bottom line, you broke the law," Gates continued. "Several of them, in fact. Not to mention several bones, by the look of Chauncey's legs." He shook his head. "As a father, I can almost understand why you did what you did. If I saw the things you saw—which I never would, by the way, because my daughter knows how to fucking listen to authority—I'm not sure what I would do. But the reason doesn't make a difference. You did it. Period. Which means that you've got to pay the price. Like it or not, that's what happens when you decide to go your own way—they send us in." He waved toward the other officers. "They send in the hammer, and then we go to work on you."

Gates stopped talking and stared at Isaac as though expecting a response of some kind, most likely unequivocal agreement. The truth was that Isaac had only been half-listening during the man's speech. He was busy thinking about Tallah—where they might have taken her, and how he could get her back without hurting anyone else.

"So, returning to your question," Gates said. "What should your decision be? That's easy as pie. You need to do your fucking time, Mr. Williams; that's what your decision should be. Come along like a man, do your fucking time, and maybe you'll get out before your daughter's twentieth birthday party starts. Like I told you, it's easy to say, and not so easy to do. But believe me, you don't want to go the other route with this."

"And how do I know I'll survive if I run your route?" Isaac asked.

Gates stared at him like he'd asked him to solve a math problem.

"Survive? What the fuck you mean survive?"

"I mean keep breathing," Isaac said. "How do I know I'll be treated like a human being?"

"Because I'm telling you."

Isaac snorted. "Listen. I just got fired on by ten cops wearing full-on riot gear," he said. "They came into my apartment *hot*. Started snapping off shots at me on goddamn sight. No warning, no nothing. So yeah, I guess I'm looking for a little more than just your reassurances about my welfare."

Gates shrugged. "What do you want to hear, man? Just give me your wish list. I'm not about to promise anything I can't deliver—that's just not me—but if I can do it, I will."

Isaac wasn't sure how to respond. As he saw it, he only had three options—perhaps the only three options that had ever existed in the blood-soaked chronicles of humanity.

Battle, submit, or run away.

Crossing swords felt like the best choice of the three, at least in the heat of the moment. Or, if not the best choice, the most viscerally satisfying one. Giving himself over to his anger wholly and with abandon, like wading into torrential floodwaters and allowing the currents to carry you crashing over anything in their path, transforming your body into a bludgeon. Becoming an instrument of ruin. Part of Isaac wanted nothing more than to ride atop his towering rage and lay waste to everyone and everything that had ever blocked his progress, ever done him any harm, intentionally or otherwise, but he knew that going to war wasn't an option he could seriously consider. He'd never been a pacifist to speak of—in fact, he'd demonstrated time and again that he had no problem with the concept of violence if absolutely necessary—but he was a father first and foremost, and a single one at that. Which meant that his primary duty, above all else, was to be there. To live. And Isaac knew that if he started rampaging on a bunch of cops, powers or no powers, he wouldn't be long for this world.

And on top of all that, Isaac honestly didn't want to hurt anybody else, not even police officers, unless he had no other choice, and he didn't want to break any more laws than he'd already broken. So he made his decision, right then and there. He would only fight if he had no other option. And if he had no other option, he would do whatever he had to do—but no more than that. Which left him with the other two options on the table.

To surrender or to run.

As much as he hated to consider it, surrendering still felt like the right decision—the morally right one. That didn't necessarily mean that he should do it, but it *did* mean that he needed to give it real consideration. Turning himself over to the police and facing up to what he'd done, whether justified in his own mind or not, might send a powerful message to his little girl: you can fight for what you think is right, even if it means breaking the law in the process, but you need to be ready to face the consequences when you're through.

But surrendering would also mean something else. It would mean that Tallah would have to live her life without a father while he served whatever sentence they handed down, which given what he'd done over the course of the past few hours, would be a considerable stretch—again, assuming he even survived being taken into custody. Either way, he wouldn't be around to raise his daughter, which was all that mattered.

Isaac just couldn't allow that to happen. Which left him with the last, best option on the list. To flee.

If Isaac decided to cut and run, it would mean finding out where the police had taken Tallah, forcibly removing her from the situation, whatever it was, and relocating to another state, another city, another job, another school—another life—yet again. That alone would be hard enough, but accomplishing these tasks while poor, notorious, and Black would add a layer of difficulty that he wasn't certain he could manage.

Bottom line, once the footage of what he'd done in that portable classroom went public, Isaac would instantaneously become the most infamous person on the planet, recognizable on a global scale, and would likely have a sizeable bounty on his head. Which meant that most of those hunting him would be doing so with the goal of seeing him captured or even worse. In fact, he realized that he'd been kidding himself by imagining that the United States was even an option for him anymore. At a bare minimum, he'd have to leave the continent of North America, and more likely the entire Western Hemisphere. Even then, he'd never feel truly safe. His only chance—unless everyone somehow assumed the video footage was fake, which was a possibility, albeit slim—would be to use his powers at a frequency and scale he'd never considered before.

So, out of a collection of three godawful options, Isaac made his choice. He was going to run, for better or worse. He would take his chances on the road with Tallah and avoid all conflict unless pressed into a corner.

Watching Gates' face, Isaac prepared himself. But before he could make a move, he felt a cold piece of metal pressed firmly into the back of his skull. It was the muzzle of a firearm—he'd experienced the feeling before, and it made an indelible impression every time.

"Don't you move," a voice said. It sounded like the same raspy voice he'd heard from one of the officers inside the apartment. "Do not move."

"Okay," Isaac said. "Relax. I'm not moving."

"Shut the fuck up," the officer snapped. He was so close that Isaac could feel the man's breath against the back of his neck. "When I tell you, you're going to reach backward with your hands, toward me, keeping your arms completely straight. You understand?"

Isaac didn't respond. He needed time to think.

The weapon pressed harder into the back of his head.

"Hey. Asshole. Do you hear me?" the man said. "Nod your fucking head."

There wasn't time. Almost any course of action Isaac took would result in either the breaking of more laws, or getting a bullet in the brain, neither of which were high on his list of goals. He had only one relatively asinine alternative rattling around inside his head. So he went with it.

Isaac leaned forward into the updraft.

chapter four

Isaac woke to the deafening sound of the wind. His body was turning over and over. He managed to open his eyes and saw that he was falling from the sky.

The ground beneath him was so distant that it looked like a topographic map. Tracts of land reduced to basic geometric shapes. Bodies of water reduced to blue daubs, mountain ranges reduced to pencil sketches. Entire municipalities reduced to simple gridlines.

Isaac tried to scream. The air was rushing into his throat and lungs with such force that he couldn't produce a sound. He could barely breathe. All of his survival instincts had been replaced by sheer, unbridled panic.

He let himself fall. He wouldn't have called the decision *surrender*, but that was the only proper word for it. On the most basic level, he'd given up. He closed his eyes and thought about his daughter's face, and it was then that he remembered who he'd recently become. The control that he was now able to wield over the world. He'd forgotten it so quickly. So much of his life had been lived without a sense of control that it still felt foreign to him, like a newly transplanted limb might feel to an amputee.

He didn't have much time. His clothes whipping violently, his body wheeling, Isaac directed his sway toward the impossibly feeble gravity of his own body mass and reversed it, then immediately *increased it*, effectively transforming himself into an object of repulsion rather than attraction. Pushing everything away in a radius instead of drawing it in. Dispersing entire cloud formations instantly as he whisked by.

Isaac waited, terrified—it was all he could do. The only way to know for certain whether this idea would save his life would be to let himself fall dangerously close to an instant, crushing death.

As he plummeted closer and closer to earth, the landmarks beneath him began to take shape, reveal their detail, and become recognizable. He convinced himself that he might actually be able to see the approximate location where his body would impact if something went horribly wrong: somewhere between 1st Street to the west, 8th Street to the east, Empire Street to the south, and Taylor Street to the north.

Suddenly he felt himself slowing down. It was gradual at first—barely perceivable—but over a short period of time he went from plunging uncontrollably to sinking fast, from sinking fast to drifting slowly downward, until he reached an equilibrium between push and pull that left him hovering in midair, in limbo, maybe a thousand feet above ground, as though he'd been rejected by the very planet itself.

* * *

Once Isaac found a way to return discreetly to terra firma (in Fremont, no less—some fifteen miles from the launch point at his apartment), he ditched his cell phone in one of the salt lagoons near the Dumbarton Bridge, stopped by an ATM and withdrew an absurd amount of cash (with the help of his abilities, of course), and took the 181 bus back to San Jose, where he checked into a grubby motel on the Alameda near downtown and paid for a few nights in advance.

By the time he got himself settled in the room—consisting of little more than a bed, a TV, a nightstand, a phone, and a toilet—it was almost nine at night. Absolutely exhausted, he took off his shoes, pulled back the sheets, and lay down on the mattress with his hands behind his head. He stared up at the ceiling, thinking about Tallah—where she was, how she must feel, what he would need to do to get her back—and within a matter of a few minutes he drifted off.

The next morning Isaac made the mistake of turning on the television. He was everywhere.

At least half of the available TV stations were airing some form of special report detailing every deed he'd done over the past eighteen hours—with video footage to accompany every claim—starting with his confrontation with the officer in the portable classroom and ending with his body, by all appearances, *launching into the stratosphere*.

It caught him completely off guard, seeing himself through the lenses of so many different cameras. The truth was that he'd only expected to see footage of the single, precipitating incident in the portable classroom, certainly not the melee that took place in his own apartment, and not even the showdown with Gates in the atrium courtyard afterward. Bottom line, he had grossly underestimated the level of surveillance in common areas, but he'd also overlooked another key factor, obvious in retrospect: body cameras. He'd completely forgotten about the body cameras worn by the police.

Because of all those recording devices, there was video evidence of every single time he'd broken the law—both the laws of the city and the laws of gravity itself—since he'd first rolled up in his truck and parked in front of Tallah's school. In fact, even *that* had been videotaped; there must have been a camera on a light pole in the parking lot as well.

Some of the newscasters wondered aloud whether the whole thing was nothing but an elaborate hoax, the result of a series of clever camera tricks or modifications to the footage during post-processing. Other news stories tried to provide logical, natural explanations for the phenomena captured on film, with some even postulating that he was high on PCP at the time, which apparently would've given him the strength to toss ten grown men straight upward into the ceiling without physically touching them, as well as leap high enough to actually leave the camera's frame of view. Whatever the explanation, the underlying message was consistent across every channel he turned to: an African-American male named Isaac Williams had injured multiple police officers during the performance of their lawful duties, and therefore needed to be apprehended and brought to justice, posthaste.

After showing several minutes of video footage, one of the news reports showed a frame grab of Isaac's face—angry, wide-eyed, and unmistakably Black—beneath the words "Wanted by U.S.

Marshals" in bold red lettering.

Isaac called Leti Sanders using the phone in the motel room.

"Who's this," she said. She sounded annoyed already, which didn't bode well for the conversation he wanted to have.

"It's me. Don't hang up."

Leti didn't say anything. Isaac heard a rustling sound for the next few seconds—it sounded like she was going somewhere, and in a hurry.

"Dammit, Isaac," she whispered. "You can't be calling me like this. Period. But especially not here, not now. I need this job."

"I know, Let. I'm sorry."

"I've seen the news, Isaac. I saw what you did—all that mess you made. What the hell were you thinking?"

"I *know*, okay? I need your help," he said. "Please, Let. I don't have anybody else to ask."

"Hold on."

Isaac heard more rustling; she was on the move again. He heard the sound of a door opening and closing.

"What, Isaac. What do you want?"

Isaac hesitated. He wasn't sure exactly where to start.

"I need to get the hell out of here. Out of town, out of state, out of everything," he said. "Someplace gone. I'm not sure where yet."

"Stop. I don't even want to know what you're up to. If they ask me where you're headed, which they probably will eventually, I don't want to have to lie to somebody."

"I'm not asking you to lie," he said.

"Good. Because I would lie for you if I could, Ize—you know that—but I just can't right now. I'm sorry. I've got too much going on in my own life to get caught up with somebody else's problems, even yours."

"I get that."

"I'm glad that you do."

"And I'm so glad that you're glad, Leti. I really am. So now that everybody's glad, would it be all right if I talked for a second?"

"Yes," she said. "Sorry."

"Do you still know that girl down at the courts? The social worker. Azalea? Aretha?"

"Alana," she said. "Yeah. Why?"

"It's Tallah," he said. "She's in custody somewhere. They took her last night and I need to know where they're keeping her."

"How's Alana supposed to know that?"

"She isn't. She's supposed to figure it out. Make some calls to the right people. Text somebody. Hell, I don't know. Something. Will you just ask her to help me, please?"

Leti didn't say anything.

"Hello?" he said.

"I heard you."

"So will you help me out or not? All I need is information, Let, that's all. There's nothing illegal about a little knowledge."

All he heard was silence on the other end for what felt like a long time.

"Leti. Yes or no."

"Yes," she replied. "Yes. Of course I'll help."

"Thank you. Just call me back at this number when you know something. If I'm out, leave me a voicemail."

"Okay. But Ize."

"Yeah?"

"That video the cops put out," Leti said. "All of the videos I saw online. Those tricks they showed you doing."

She hesitated for a few seconds as though struggling to find the right words.

"Was all that really you?" she asked. "I mean, I know it was *you*. But was it really you doing those things?"

"No, Leti. It was my stunt double."

"I'm being serious," she said. "Was it real or not?"

"Was it real?"

"Yeah. I mean, the whole thing looked fake as hell. Like special effects."

"It wasn't special effects," he replied. "It happened. Trust me."

Leti paused.

"So that was actually you?" she asked.

Isaac didn't answer right away.

When Tallah had found out about his abilities, it had been oddly simple—she'd actually seen what he could do, not through a video file playing on a screen but *in person*, with her own two eyes, leaving significantly less room for doubt. Discussing it with her afterward had been relatively easy because of the event she'd just observed firsthand, because she was his daughter, and because of her age. She was young enough that the idea of magic existing in the world might still have been a slim possibility somewhere in her mind.

The situation with Leti was far different. First of all, she was older and wiser. Based on conversations they'd had, Isaac knew that she'd witnessed and experienced a lot in her lifetime, more than any one person should be forced to see or endure. Second, she didn't actually watch him use his powers, at least not in the truest sense. And third, although he felt connected to her, she wasn't exactly family. Bottom line, he wasn't sure how to tell her what he was capable of.

"I can do things," he said.

It was the best he could come up with.

"Things?"

"The SUV from before. The one I told you about. That thing with the shopping cart running up the road. It was me—I mean, I didn't know it was me at the time, but it was. And then it went on from there. Everything you saw on the tape."

Leti didn't say anything.

"I wanted to tell you—"

"So why didn't you, Ize?" she asked. "I could've helped you make sense of what was going on."

Isaac snorted. "Tell you how, Leti? 'Oh, by the way, I can make gravity do what I tell it to.' Is that what I was supposed to say?"

"Why not?" she asked.

"Because I was still trying to figure it out myself," he said. "I don't know, Leti. What does it even matter? I'm telling you now."

"So how did it happen?" she asked. "The power. How did you get it?"

Isaac thought he heard a twinge of jealousy in her voice. Or maybe it was longing—that might have been a better word for it.

"I don't know," he replied. "Honest to God, Leti, I don't."

* * *

At midday Isaac left the motel and went outside into the sun. It was a calculated risk.

He knew that he was a Wanted man (with a capital "W"), and that multiple law enforcement agencies were likely scouring the Bay Area to track him down, but, strangely enough, that was precisely the reason why he needed to leave the relative safety of his room. He needed some new clothes. Anything would have been better than what he was wearing (*the exact same clothes he was wearing in the video seen by millions of viewers, the one where he performed actual magic to defeat a horde of cops*), but he also wanted something that would deflect at least some of the suspicion that seemed to follow him around wherever he went, whether he was a fugitive from the U.S. Marshals or was heading to work at Quixit Incorporated.

In short, he needed a suit and tie. It wouldn't stop a hail of gunfire, but it might make the authorities look elsewhere long enough for him to do what needed to be done.

Still dressed in his work uniform, he walked quickly down Race Street with his face lowered. He took a left on San Carlos and slipped into a cramped second-hand shop as a crowd of day laborers milled around a couple of food trucks in a vacant dirt lot across the way.

A female employee—white, around his age, with short black hair—looked up from where she was sitting by an old cash register, reading a fashion magazine.

"Hi," she said. "Can I help you find something?"

Her voice sounded pleasant enough. But as she stared at him, Isaac couldn't help noticing that her mouth was pinched closed, her blue eyes seemed wider than the situation called for, and her brow was deeply furrowed—she looked decidedly unsettled. He couldn't figure out whether she'd recognized him from the news, whether she was taking in the dirty, rumpled appearance of his uniform, or whether he was simply witnessing the normal level of concern that shopkeepers seemed to display whenever he entered certain stores.

"Thanks," he said. "I'm good."

Isaac looked around for a few moments. There wasn't much to see. The entire store consisted of a dozen racks of clothing, a few shelves full of kitchenware, and some worn-out athletic equipment (tennis rackets, skis, and a snowboard) leaning against the wall.

"Actually," he said. "Where do you keep your men's clothes?"

The woman nodded toward the back of the room.

"Fifth rack on the right," she said.

"Thanks."

Isaac spotted a clothes rack brimming with men's button-downs, slacks, and dark suit jackets on hangers. He headed in that direction, moving deeper into the store and further from the exit. Committing himself. When he reached the rack, he turned so that he was facing the front checkout counter and started browsing through suit jackets, sliding plastic hangers along the metal rail, occasionally glancing up at the clerk. She didn't seem to be paying him any mind; she was busy staring at her phone—not typing anything (as far as he could tell), just casually swiping at the screen with a forefinger once in a while.

Eventually Isaac settled on a navy-blue suit jacket, a white button-down, and a pair of charcoal-gray slacks. Nothing fit perfectly, of course, and he couldn't find a single necktie anywhere, but the outfit was good enough, far better than the one he was wearing at the moment, anyway. It would have to do. He draped the clothes over one arm and approached the front of the store, laid everything down on the counter, and pulled out his wallet as the woman checked the tag on the suit jacket and typed a few keys on the register.

"Find everything okay?" she asked, checking a second tag.

Isaac studied her face. Over the course of his visit, her expression had changed from deeply concerned to completely disinterested, which was a comfort.

"I did, thanks," he replied.

The woman held the white shirt up high, shook it out, and turned it toward the light. For a moment, the shirt looked almost ghostly, like an apparition she'd managed to catch with her bare hands.

"This is nice," she said matter-of-factly. "It'll look good against your skin tone."

Isaac paid the bill and left the store with the clothes in a black plastic bag tucked under his arm. Heading up San Carlos Street, keeping his face lowered, he scanned the roadways, then the sidewalks, alternating between them as he passed storefront after storefront. An old-fashioned tailor's shop. A used car dealership. A Starbucks. An Ethiopian restaurant.

When he reached the corner of Race Street, a black and white police cruiser passed him on the left, slowed down, then immediately pulled a sharp U-turn across a solid double-yellow line as he watched, completely paralyzed. For a brief moment he held out hope that the cop was responding to a different call, something unrelated, and that the vehicle would continue on its way, but he had no such luck—the cruiser rocketed directly toward him, cutting across oncoming traffic, sending oncoming vehicles swerving to avoid a head-on collision. With blue and red lights flashing, the car screeched to a halt around ten yards ahead of him. Both front doors swung wide open.

Isaac didn't wait. He turned and sprinted back the way he came, his arms pumping, the bag of clothes swinging in his fist. The sound of his footfalls on the concrete echoed underneath the storefront awnings. When he reached the entrance to the second-hand store, he abruptly cut right, bolted across the street to the dirt lot where the food trucks were parked, and continued running past the trucks, past the startled day laborers, heading toward a chain-link fence on the other side of the field, fighting his way through the tangle of dry sedge weeds in his path.

Soon Isaac heard the low droning sound of a helicopter overhead. Without warning, a single round of gunfire rang out. The bullet struck about five feet ahead of him, kicking up a cloud of dust and sending him reeling off to the right, his arms oaring wildly for balance. A second shot came almost immediately after the first—again, striking the ground in front of him with a *thwap*—as he continued to stumble forward. Another shot came. Then another. Spaced a few seconds apart, always striking a yard or two ahead of his feet, the shots seemed like they were meant to deter him more than they were to eliminate him, but there was no way of knowing for certain, and he couldn't exactly stop to clarify.

He needed to protect himself. Out of desperation, he used his sway to weave a force—a repulsive force—in an arc above his head: a gravity canopy, for lack of a better term. In theory (since he'd never actually tested this particular effect), if an object were to come into contact with the shield, that object would be redirected roughly back the way it came. But who the hell knew for sure? All Isaac could do was hope for the best and keep running as quickly as he could.

Soon he heard the familiar crackle and squeal of a loudspeaker coming to life above him.

"Stay where you are," a man's voice boomed down, godlike, from overhead. "Drop your weapon and lie facedown on the ground."

My weapon?

Isaac ignored the officer's commands and continued running— within seconds, another shot rang out, striking a clump of dead brush to his left with a jarring hiss. Then another shot came. Then another. He couldn't keep going on like this. Whatever he was doing, it clearly wasn't working.

The truth was that he had no semblance of a plan—he wasn't

fleeing toward any destination in particular. He was simply running aimlessly, instinctively, praying that his pursuers wouldn't or couldn't track his movements. But it had become clear in short order that he wasn't going to escape by simply retreating. He was going to have to make this problem go away.

Isaac stopped running and raised his hands above his head, still gripping the black plastic bag in his left hand, as the police chopper dipped to a lower altitude—not all the way to the ground, but close enough to whip the dust into a blinding flurry all around him.

"Drop the weapon," said the voice from above. "Lie down on the ground and lock your fingers behind your head."

Squinting through the dust, Isaac turned and looked back over his shoulder. Three police cruisers had jumped the curb and were bumping their way across the vacant lot in his direction, a virtual sand storm erupting in their wake. They'd reach him in moments. If he was planning on doing something, he was running out of time to decide what and act on it. As he watched the vehicles approach, he began to call upon his sway again, preparing to do exactly what he'd been trying so desperately to avoid: namely, to confront the authorities directly using a violent energy that they could neither comprehend nor control, giving them even further motivation—and justification—for hunting him down.

"Drop the weapon," the voice boomed from above.

Isaac looked up, shielding his eyes with a forearm. The helicopter was hovering around fifty feet above his head. He reached out with his influence.

Immediately the chopper plunged at least twenty feet straight down before pulling up at the last moment and leveling off, the engine whining and rattling as it labored frenziedly against the weight of its own chassis—the weight that Isaac had just increased by roughly a factor of ten. He heard a loud, bright *ping*, and a column of black smoke began pouring from somewhere near the tail. Pitching and wheeling, the chopper descended in a spiral, dropping at the same steady rate as a common elevator car, until it impacted the ground at an angle, on a single landing skid. The rotor blades whipped furiously into the earth, sending plumes of dust skyward in a fountain of grayish-brown, before snapping cleanly in two and casting a jagged length of black carbon fiber toward the street. The chassis leaned precariously to one side, held steady for a moment, groaning, then crashed to the earth, shattering every panel of glass onboard from front to rear.

As the dazed occupants struggled to climb out of the ruined cabin, Isaac turned his attention to the trio of police cars still on approach. The vehicles were barreling over the uneven terrain, pitching from side to side, their sirens wailing. He didn't wait. He quickly multiplied the weight of all three cruisers at once, effectively transforming them into oversized plow blades, driving their front ends deep into the earth and leaving their rear wheels spinning helplessly in the dust-choked air.

Isaac made his way back toward the motel. He took a roundabout route, balancing the need to get out of the open quickly with the need to ensure that he wasn't being followed. When he finally arrived, exhausted and covered in sweat, he fumbled with the card key at the door, dropping it twice before finally slotting it into the lock with a trembling hand. He shoved open the door and stumbled into the room.

He suddenly felt like he'd come down with a serious flu. Something was wrong. He dropped the bag of clothes, lurched into the bathroom, fell onto his knees, and dry heaved violently. One, two, three, four times in quick succession, with barely enough time to take a breath in between. His nose began to bleed, dripping steadily onto the porcelain, onto the gray linoleum, onto his clothing. Dizzy and feverish, he spat into the toilet, then rested his forehead on the edge of the bowl for a while, pinching his nostrils closed while simultaneously trying to catch his breath.

Eventually he managed to climb to his feet, grab a handful of tissues from the box beside the sink, and stagger over to the mattress, where he collapsed in a heap on top of the sandpaper bedspread. His head was pounding—it felt as though something inside his skull was desperately trying to break free. He couldn't tell which way was down and which way was up anymore.

* * *

Isaac woke to the sound of a phone ringing. Eyes still closed, he fished around in his pants pocket for his cell before remembering that it was gone, tossed into the marshes near the Dumbarton Bridge. He reminded himself where he was: in a motel room. He was lying on a bed in a San Jose motel room, and the phone he was hearing was the one that belonged to the motel, not him. Still groggy, he opened his eyes, rolled over gingerly, reached for the phone on the nightstand and fumbled with the handset, his fingers uncooperative and stiff. By the time he managed to pick up the phone from the cradle, it was too late—the ringing had stopped.

It had to have been Leti calling. Or at least he hoped it was. He was desperate to find out whether she'd gotten any information about Tallah's whereabouts.

He sat up on the edge of the bed and tried dialing Leti's number, but had to hang up and start over a few times because of his sudden, inexplicable lack of basic hand-eye coordination, not to mention his piss-poor concentration. At last he got it right. The phone rang only once before connecting.

"Isaac?" Leti said.

She sounded nervous, which made him feel even sicker than he already did. All he could imagine was that she'd learned something about Tallah that he wouldn't want to hear.

"Did you just call?" he asked.

"I did."

"Do you know where she is, Let? Tell me you have something."

Leti didn't respond right away.

"Hello?"

"I'm here," she said. "And, yes, I do have something. But I want you to hear me out—all the way. It's not good news, Isaac, I won't lie. But I need you to listen."

Isaac couldn't believe that Leti was drawing this out, teasing it now for a *big reveal* later, but what was he going to do? She was holding all the cards.

"All right," he said. "I'm listening. Go on."

"I talked to Alana like you asked, and she found out where they're keeping Tallah, at least for the moment. It's an open secret, evidently—they're not even trying to keep her whereabouts under wraps. But Alana kept telling me over and over that they could move her at any time. Any time, Ize. You need to keep that in mind."

"Where, Leti? Just tell me."

"She's being kept in a federal building," Leti said. "In San Francisco. It's one of the skyscrapers in the Civic Center Plaza downtown."

"A federal building?"

"A building run by the U.S. government. Yes."

"I know what federal means, Leti. Why the hell is she there?"

"Just hear me out, okay? I haven't even started getting to the worst part," she said. "This particular federal building houses the FBI's San Francisco field office, which takes up the entire thirteenth floor. They're keeping Tallah there so they can talk to her, but according to Alana she slept there last night as well—in some kind of on-site dorm room they have for the crisis response team. Anyway, it doesn't matter. The point is that she's there, Isaac."

"Unbelievable."

"Unfortunately, there's more," Leti said. "Sorry to report."

"There's *more?*"

"I'm sorry. But the FBI is only one tenant out of many. I did some reading online, and that same building also houses a branch of the U.S. Marshals and the Drug Enforcement Agency. The place has twenty-one floors—it takes up an entire city block."

"Fantastic. Is that everything?"

"Almost," Leti replied. "Because it's a government building, it's got the Federal Protective Service guarding it. They're part of the Department of Homeland Security, Isaac. These aren't mall cops riding around on scooters chasing shoplifters. This is closer to a military unit."

Isaac gave himself a few moments to digest the veritable cornucopia of atrocious news that Leti had just force-fed him.

"The FBI, the Marshals, and the DEA," he said. "Plus the DHS running security, just to top it all off. Is that a fair summary?"

"Yes."

"Lord, have mercy."

"Yes," Leti said.

"All right, then. Anything else I need to know about? Don't tell me. There's a moat, right? A moat filled with a bunch of damn—what. Alligators? Piranhas?"

"Just one more point you need to know," she said. "This building is a monster, Ize. Everybody's there. You've got the FBI on the thirteenth floor, like I mentioned. The Marshals on the twentieth. The DEA on the top floor—the twenty-first. But you've also got the U.S. Attorney's Office, the District Courts, a branch of the IRS, the damn Passport Agency, for God's sake. They've even got their own post office branch in the basement. Fitness center, cafeteria, medical clinic, credit union, everything. It's like a city in and of itself."

"Get to the point, please. I don't need a list of amenities."

"I know you don't, Isaac," she snapped. "My point is that this place is crawling with workers, all the time, at any given moment, top to bottom. From maintenance workers to office workers. Cooks, clerks, custodians, cashiers, you name it. They may not all be trained to kill you on sight, but you can bet that a good number of them would recognize your face and immediately call on somebody who is."

Leti was absolutely right. Isaac was at a loss. It wasn't shocking that Tallah was being kept under lock and key—he knew the police weren't just going to let her off at the curb somewhere—but he had expected her to be placed in a temporary foster shelter or group home, *maybe*. At worst, a juvenile detention center. It wouldn't have been easy to spring his daughter from any of those places without causing collateral damage, but it would have been doable.

But an FBI office? Freeing Tallah from an entire floor full of irate Special Agents without hurting anybody sounded like an overwhelmingly difficult challenge, even if the rest of the building were empty, and even if he were at full strength. But it felt especially farfetched given that the building would evidently be packed with eyewitnesses, and given how he felt at the moment: lethargic, achy, nauseous, and weak. He could barely fight his way to the phone. How could he possibly fight his way into an office of the FBI?

"What are you thinking?" Leti asked.

"I'm not sure what to think right now."

"Well, then. How about some unsolicited advice. From a friend."

Isaac knew that tone all too well. Leti was ready to tell him something else he didn't want to hear.

"No, thanks. I'm good."

"You should think about turning yourself in, Isaac," Leti said quietly. "Just think about it. I'm serious. The things you've done—the police aren't going to forgive and they're not going to forget. You know I'm right, Isaac. You know I am."

"Yeah. I know you are."

"So maybe you need to face up to it. You know? Serve out your bid before it gets any longer, and then go home to your daughter and put this behind you. Not because it's the right thing, but because it's the quickest path back to normal."

"You want me to turn myself in," he said.

"I want you to think about it."

"After everything I've done? After everything they've *seen* me do? If I let them take me now, I'll never be free again."

"I know it looks bad," Leti said. "But do you really think you can run, Isaac? Is that your plan? Because they will never leave you alone, never allow you to live a normal life, never stop hunting, wherever you may try to hide yourself. I believe that to be true with all my heart, Ize. The way I see it, you have a choice between two very bad options, and surrendering seems less painful than the alternative."

"And what happens to Tallah while I'm locked up, Let? Have you thought about that detail?"

"I'll take her," Leti said without hesitation. "She can come stay with me. Okay? She'd be part of the family, same as one of my own. No different."

Isaac couldn't manage a response. He was too taken aback. The truth was that Leti may have been shining him on—simply offering to take Tallah as a way of making the idea of surrender seem more palatable, as a way of easing his mind so he'd make the choice she obviously wanted him to make—but he doubted it. Leti wasn't one to lie, at least not to him, especially when it came to a matter as serious as his daughter's care.

So, assuming that her proposal was real, Isaac was left wondering: could he actually say yes? Would he really be able to hand Tallah over to Leti on a long-term basis? He knew that she was a mother and a grandmother, and had legally adopted her daughter's only child at her daughter's request, but that was all he knew. Not only was he completely unaware of her parenting philosophy and approach, but he'd never even seen her interact with *any* child, much less his own. At the same time, he didn't have anyone else in his life—no one he loved, no one who loved him, and no one he trusted—other than Leti Sanders.

"Isaac?" she said.

He cleared his throat.

"I couldn't let you do something like that," he said quietly. "I appreciate it. But I can't."

"Why not?" she asked.

"Look. If I was going to trust anyone in this world with my only child—anyone—it would be you, Let. But I'm not willing to be thrown into some hole over this. I'm just not. I know that I did wrong, and I didn't mean to hurt anybody, but this is my daughter we're talking about. Was I just supposed to stand there and watch while a grown man beat my baby to the ground?"

"I understand that."

"If you do, then you understand why I have to go after her," he said.

chapter five

Isaac put on the clothing he'd purchased from the second-hand store—the navy suit jacket, the white button-down, the gray slacks. Miraculously, the plastic bag had protected them from the worst of the dust and dirt; they were barely even rumpled. He sat on the edge of the bed with his hands folded in his lap and stared out the window awhile. It felt like he was having an almost out-of-body experience, as though he'd just returned from an overseas trip across a dozen time zones.

The sun was swinging low over the rooftops. It was late afternoon, which meant that he'd slept for at least three or four hours. Crashing hard in the middle of the day wasn't typical for him, even when he wasn't working, but it was clear that he'd needed it in the worst possible way after tangling with the police. Whatever his problem had been when he'd staggered into the motel room, he was feeling better now, relatively speaking. The pounding in his head, the nausea, the vertigo, the weakness—they'd mostly passed. He touched his nostrils lightly and looked at his fingertips. The bleeding had stopped, too.

It was time. He needed to go. If he waited any longer, most everyone at the so-called *Phillip Burton Federal Building and U.S. Courthouse* in San Francisco would start heading home for the day, which—strangely enough—ran counter to what he was planning. Crowds, he thought, might actually work to his advantage.

Isaac got to his feet, went to the bathroom, and washed his face, watching the runoff turn pink as he cleaned out his nose. He dried himself with a hand towel and stared at his reflection for a while, evaluating the lines etched into his brow and around his eyes, the areas along his jawline that had slackened over time. He was in his mid-thirties, which wasn't old by most measures, but there was no question that the years—or said differently, his particular set of experiences over the years—had taken a certain toll.

And so had gravity.

The relentless, implacable downward pull of gravity had influenced the appearance of everything from his skin tissue to his posture, and not in particularly flattering ways, at least according to feedback he'd gotten from the dating pool. Reversing these effects, even temporarily, could make him look years younger than he actually was—so much so, in fact, that he might suddenly look like another person entirely.

Isaac decided to start with the bend in his back. When it came to improving posture, he'd always been told to pretend that a string was attached to the top of his head, pulling him straight up toward the ceiling, which would (somehow) cause the various elements of his skeletal structure to fall into their proper places via a wondrous process that no one seemed able to explain, a magical chain reaction of biomechanics. This procedure was easier said than done, of course, but he was fortunate enough to be able to rely on something more than just his core musculature to accomplish the task. With some help from his influence, Isaac lifted his body weight by the slightest degree, which allowed his neck to straighten, his shoulders to relax and align, his hips to move into a neutral position, and the arches of his feet to rise. He practiced a number of times, lifting and lowering, until he could adopt his new posture more or less at will and hold it as a persistent effect.

From there, Isaac moved on to the most difficult task at hand: modifying his face.

Leaning over the sink basin, studying himself in the mirror, he got to work—lifting, smoothing, rounding, refining—giving himself the equivalent of a gravitational makeover. Over a short period of time, his brow lost its furrows, his eyes lost their crow's feet, his mouth lost its laugh lines. His cheekbones appeared higher, his jaw more angular, his chin more squared. The procedure wasn't perfect—after all, he was pioneering a new field of cosmetic surgery, and he wasn't using anything as exacting as a scalpel blade. The excess skin that he'd pushed and prodded and rearranged, though minimal, had to move somewhere, so he ended up with a bit of swelling at the base of his skull, right above the nape of his neck, neatly covered by his hair. It easily passed for a normal irregularity in the shape of his skull—the small knot was barely noticeable, even when he was expressly searching for it.

When Isaac had finished with his face, he arranged his body into its new and improved posture and stared at himself in the mirror, completely dumbstruck. He looked almost the same as he did when he was twenty-one years old. Or, said more accurately, he looked like a twenty-one year old stranger who could (hopefully) pass for the person he used to be.

He'd managed to correct the asymmetries, improve the proportions, and erase most of the obvious flaws of his true face— many of which had contributed to his unique appearance—making him look almost like a sculpture modeled roughly after an image of his younger self, as though someone had fashioned a replica of him based on a hazy memory. There were *suggestions* of his real identity in the contours of this new face, but it was by no means an exact reproduction. Which meant that he'd accomplished exactly what he'd set out to do.

As he stared in the mirror, the tears started coming down almost immediately, in spite of himself. It was foolish and untimely as could be, and he knew it. But how was he supposed to prepare himself properly for such an experience? Seeing himself transformed almost instantly into a much younger man was like receiving a desperate message directly from his past, reminding him that he'd already burned through decades of his life with nothing tangible to show for it, no place where he could feel safe, no marker to plant in the soil, no mountaintop he could claim to have ever climbed, no family other than an eleven-year-old child who had no other choice in the matter. Nothing to mark his passing—to declare that *he was here*—other than the scattered tracks of somebody who'd spent a lifetime on defense. Reacting. Stranded in a state of survival. Over the years he'd played all his cards the best he could, made his most well-considered moves, taken the risks he believed were worth the price, and searched for the most promising ways to surmount the obstacles in his path, but he'd still never amounted to much of anything in the world. And the sight of his own face at an age still filled with possibility and potential served as a reminder of just how much he'd lost since that time in his life, how far he'd truly fallen, and how vastly different his life was now in comparison to what he'd once imagined it could be. The rush of memory was more than he could manage. In fact, the only thing that kept him standing upright was the thought of his child: Tallah definitely hadn't been a part of his plans when he was young, but she would never be on his list of regrets. Far from it.

Isaac took a deep breath, wiped his eyes, checked the mirror one more time, and left the motel room without looking back, leaving the card key locked inside on the nightstand. Whether he succeeded or failed in what he was about to attempt was irrelevant; either way, he wouldn't be returning to this place.

Outside, in a Vietnamese restaurant parking lot along the Alameda, Isaac stole a car for the first time in his life. A silver Toyota Camry. An older model—maybe early 2000s. Boosting it was easy. Not because he was innately talented at using a pry bar to unlock a car door, cracking open a steering column, and hotwiring the ignition. It was easy because he didn't have to do any of those things to accomplish the task.

All he needed to do was apply a little sway to the situation.

Trying his best to project a casual vibe, Isaac lifted the manual lock button and opened the door without using a single tool or laying a finger on the frame. He eased himself into the driver's seat, shifted the transmission into neutral, and—without switching on the vehicle's engine—quietly rolled out of the parking lot and continued up the road.

He drove the stolen vehicle in the direction of his apartment complex. It wasn't by choice. He needed to retrieve a couple of items from a shoebox inside the chest of drawers in Tallah's bedroom—

items that would, in theory, help him slip into the federal building unrecognized: a Mississippi driver's license and a *Biloxi Sun Herald* press pass.

It was the one he'd used during his first job as a journalist in Biloxi when he was fresh out of undergraduate school at Blue Cliff. That piece of laminated plastic from the *Herald* was one of the few personal effects that he'd managed to save when Katrina touched down, and he'd held onto it for all these years mostly to remind himself of the time in his life when he'd been the most proud of the work he was doing. He'd considered himself a true newspaper man back then, as quaint as that might sound. Granted, most of what he'd done was small-town stuff—researching obituaries, monitoring road closures, covering public interest events—but he'd also researched and written a handful of stories that had made a real impact on the (albeit small) community of Biloxi, Mississippi. He'd published pieces about an embezzlement scandal at the school district offices, illegal dumping by a paint company up north, and racial profiling by the Harrison County police department. He hadn't *changed the world* with any of his reporting, but he'd made some kind of positive difference, at least he liked to think he had. The press pass served as a lasting memento of those times, as well as a form of motivation to push him back into the field one day, something he'd always hoped to do eventually but had never felt he could.

Both the press pass and the driver's license—each of which showed a picture of a fresh-faced, twenty-two-year-old version of himself—were tucked inside a plastic badge holder with a black nylon lanyard attached, which was in his shoebox full of keepsakes inside the bureau. It would take him all of thirty seconds to retrieve, assuming the police had left the scene—which they probably had, given that twenty-four hours had passed since the SWAT team incident.

If the cops weren't lying in wait for him in the apartment (and he could find the press pass and ID), the plan moving forward was simple—or, as Detective Gates would put it: simple to say, if not simple to do. Isaac would drive up to San Francisco in his new stolen ride and use his official-looking credentials to enter the federal building through the front doors—just walk his ass right in. If he was questioned by security at the entrance (highly unlikely in his mind), he was ready to lay out a story that he was in town temporarily to cover a court case on the tenth floor involving a fictional Mississippi expat named Beau Arrington (a name that sounded sufficiently Southern to his ear). But he was confident that even the most zealous guards at the gates would simply be checking IDs and manning the metal detector, not asking each individual about the reason for their visit. The challenge would be to try and look like he belonged, a task that would be made much easier by the fact that he would be wearing both the clothing and the face of a young, ambitious reporter out on assignment. But he would need to sell it. In fact, his act would need to be so convincing that the guards would fail to notice that he happened to share the exact same name as the most wanted man in the Bay Area, not to mention the fact that the dates on the license—both the issue date and the expiration date—were slightly antiquated, to say the least.

After gaining access to the federal building, Isaac would simply take the elevator to the thirteenth floor, where the FBI branch offices were located. From that point, he had no idea what would come next. All he knew was that he wouldn't have the luxury of holding back. He would need to let loose with everything inside of him.

The first thing Isaac did when he reached the apartment complex was to keep right on driving by. He passed by the front entrance and circled around the block, subtly scanning for signs of a police presence (there was nothing obvious), then repeated the process three or four more times before finally parking along the curb toward the back of the building, where he'd stashed the truck yesterday. (There was no sign of the truck—most likely it had been impounded as evidence.) He exited the car, straightened his clothes, and started walking toward the front entrance. Trying his best to project an air of legitimate purpose, of belonging.

Without making a conscious decision, he'd already modified his bearing, his stride, and his facial expression to broadcast what he'd come to believe (through years of trial and error) were signals of civility and normalcy in the eyes of the general public. Projecting a safe and reassuring presence. Although he was practiced at the art of adapting himself in this way, it was still frustrating—even now—to feel as though he had no real choice in the matter, especially when his focus should have been on more important things than making himself palatable to the world at large. He hated the fact that his mind contained a dedicated block of memory reserved for just this very purpose. He couldn't help but wonder—what greater purpose could that area of his mind have served, in an ideal world, if it had been freed?

The front doors to the apartment complex had been propped open. Isaac climbed the three stairs and stepped through the entryway, walked down a short, dimly-lit hallway past the elevator, past the wall of silver mailboxes, past the leasing office, and exited through a second door into the grayish light of the building's atrium. Casually looking around, he made his way across the open-air courtyard, entered the pool area, and sat down on the cleanest-looking deck chair he could find. A group of Latino folks—a family of five, by the looks of them—had claimed one of the barbecue pits, and a boy around Tallah's age was grilling some kind of meat that smelled incredible, a painful reminder of how long it had been since he'd eaten anything substantial. An older man, presumably the boy's father, glanced in Isaac's direction but otherwise showed no signs of recognition—he took this as a sign that his youthful facade must have been convincing enough, but he couldn't be certain. It was possible that the man simply hadn't caught up on the latest news cycle, and that he would have recognized Isaac instantly if he had. As it was, though, the man seemed more occupied with his loved ones than with playing bounty hunter and chasing fugitives on the run. Isaac sat back in the chair, took out his phone, and tried to look (casually) busy, his eyes periodically darting toward the barbecue pits, toward the exit, toward the yellow barrier tape crisscrossing the boarded-up door to his former apartment. He waited.

There was no sign of the police, or anyone else for that matter. No news crews, no crowd of gawkers, no one other than a normal family enjoying a mild spring evening outdoors. He'd expected more, honestly. More activity, more chaos, more interest, more *something*. It was hard to shake the feeling that the relative calm in the courtyard was somehow a bad sign, too good to be true, but he didn't have the luxury of indulging his sense of caution at the present.

He decided it was time. He stood up, pocketed his phone, and crossed the courtyard toward the apartment, taking a short, winding footpath lined with potted palms and decorative planter boxes. He looked over his shoulder to be sure he wasn't being watched, then used his influence to quietly loosen the sheets of plywood that kept the door in place. After the door was freed, he quickly moved it aside and slipped through the opening, replacing the barrier once he was through.

The inside of the apartment looked like the site of a bomb blast, calling to mind the all-too-common images of cafes, coffee bars, theaters, schools, and places of worship shattered by men and women with automatic firearms and improvised explosives packed against their bodies. The ceiling had all but fallen inward, the furniture had been upended or broken apart, and the carpet was covered in at least six inches of debris—shreds of paper, splintered shards of wood, plaster fragments, broken glass, and bullet casings. It was clear that someone (the police, a group of random opportunists, *someone*) had absolutely ransacked the entire apartment, ripping apart the sofa cushions, spilling the contents of every drawer, emptying every cardboard box, turning out the pockets of every article of clothing. Searching high and low for God knows what—clues to his whereabouts, evidence to use against him in court, a piece of the puzzle that might help explain his abilities, random souvenirs from a real-life criminal at large, inspiration for news stories, personal effects to sell at an auction online. All of the above.

There was no way of knowing for certain, and it hardly mattered now.

Isaac stood in the entryway and listened for any signs of life, but all he could hear was the distant sound of rush-hour traffic and an airliner passing overhead. He waited. The air in the room still smelled vaguely of burnt gunpowder and stale perspiration. Once he was confident that he was alone, he made his way carefully to the master bedroom.

Stepping through the broken doorway, he saw more of the same ruin: the queen-sized mattress had been slashed and gutted, the nightstand was resting on its side, and the tall chest of drawers had been split apart by what he could only guess (judging by the score marks in the wood) was some form of hatchet. There wasn't time to survey the damage. He dropped to his knees and started shoving aside piles of loose clothing, foam batting, and even broken glass with both hands, digging through the wreckage, searching for the shoebox with his keepsakes inside.

After a few moments of fruitless searching, Isaac heard a rustling sound coming from underneath the bed frame, a frenzied scrabbling, and before he had a chance to react, a dark object shot out toward him and collided with the side of his leg before settling next to his feet. It was the cat. Trembling violently, it curled its body into a ball and buried its face into Isaac's pant leg. He'd never seen it so terrified before, not even after he experimented on it in the living room. The fact that Lando had sought him out spoke volumes about his well-being—normally, the cat wouldn't have given him the time of day unless food was involved, so he knew the animal must truly be distressed if it was viewing him, of all people, as a source of comfort.

Isaac stroked Lando's head for a few moments before returning to the task at hand, combing through the thick layer of debris on the floor, sweeping his forearms across broad swaths of the carpet to clear more space. Eventually he found the keepsake box—an old Air Jordan shoebox—crushed under a broken section of the bureau. His high school and undergraduate diplomas, a stack of around fifty rubber-banded photographs, a few homemade Father's Day cards, and the plastic badge holder were still inside, by the grace of God.

His *Sun Herald* press pass was visible through the clear plastic window, an image of himself from almost fifteen years ago staring back at him. His Mississippi driver's license was tucked directly behind the pass in the same pocket. He looped the badge holder around his neck, tucked the nylon lanyard underneath the collar of the dress shirt, gathered the cat in his arms and stood up. He went into the closet and dug out the pet carrier—nothing more than an ordinary-looking duffel bag with a mesh zip-top and a shoulder strap—from the heap of items on the floor, then wandered through the apartment, picking out what he needed from the wreckage of his former life. He was able to line the carrier with a soft kitchen towel. The last of a bag of cat food went into an old Tupperware container. Once the cat was inside the carrier, he shouldered it and headed for the front door of the apartment.

Outside, Isaac found himself face to face with a KNTV news crew: a white woman wearing stage makeup and holding a microphone with the NBC logo on its handle, a bearded Black man balancing a camera on his shoulder, and a third person—a young Latina with short hair and thick, blue-rimmed glasses—typing on an iPad as she walked.

Isaac's stomach dropped. If anyone was going to be up to speed on the latest news cycle, it would be this group of characters: they'd probably been looking at his (old) face for the better part of the last forty-eight hours. These were exactly the kind of people that he had to be able to deceive if he was going to survive.

"Hey there," the white woman said, her face brightening. "Can we get in and shoot for a little while?" She pointed a red-nailed finger toward the apartment. "Hoping to get a little more B-roll. I'm guessing we'll need, what, like five minutes at the most?"

It was looking like Isaac had passed the first test.

"No problem," he said, moving the plywood barrier aside (with his hands, not his abilities) and stepping out of the doorway to make space. The woman didn't move. She stared at him with her large head slightly cocked.

"Are you with the police?" she asked.

Isaac was ready for this question—or, if not for this exact question, for the idea of being questioned. He smiled in a way that he hoped looked casual but, in reality, felt tight-lipped and forced. He immediately wished that he'd practiced a few facial expressions in the mirror before he'd left the motel room.

"I'm out here for the story," he said, holding up the press pass, careful to cover his full name with his thumb. "Same as you all."

The woman peered through the doorway. "Who let you in?" she asked. She was holding the microphone in front of her chest as though she was expecting to deliver a live broadcast at any moment.

"I did," he replied.

"You did?"

Isaac shrugged. "You gotta do what you gotta do, right? I'm trying to make a name for myself."

"That's the right attitude, as far as I'm concerned," she said, nodding. "Anything for a story. I understand completely."

"Exactly. I guess I'm just a young and hungry up-and-comer," he said.

* * *

Isaac pulled onto I-280 and headed north toward San Francisco. For the first twenty miles it was slow-going, but traffic started to thin out around the city of Palo Alto, the point at which the landscape on either side of the roadway opened up into rolling yellow foothills backed by acres of coastal redwoods all the way to the horizon.

He was pushing the stolen Camry as hard as he could while keeping with the flow of traffic. He'd broken the pin on the steering lock, so the wheel felt loose and wobbly in his hands; it was vibrating almost uncontrollably as he tried to keep pace with the fastest vehicles in front of him, weaving his way past the slower cars, moving from lane to lane. He didn't have much time. If he was going to reach the federal building before the end of the workday, he needed to hurry. No security guard was going to believe that a reporter was showing up to cover a court case at six o'clock in the evening. Did court cases even happen this late in the day?

Isaac was starting to realize just how asinine this idea really was. There were so many obvious flaws in his so-called plan that he seriously wondered whether his mind had been compromised by a combination of exhaustion, anxiety, and whatever health issues he'd been experiencing from the use (overuse?) of his abilities.

The only reason he wasn't abandoning the scheme altogether was that the main alternative—using his sway to wage a direct, frontal assault against the building and all its occupants—while tempting, didn't seem possible given his need to keep Tallah safe, his own pretty strong desire to survive the experience, plus his determination to minimize casualties among the people whose job it was to bring him in (or bring him down). Not to mention how he felt—a lot less than a hundred percent, suffice it to say. He just didn't see a way to *go hard* against what amounted to four small armies (the U.S. Marshals, DEA, FBI, and DHS) and come out on the other side with Tallah intact, with the body count low, and with a heart still beating inside his chest.

He'd considered another strategy as well—waiting until nightfall, flying up the side of the building like a bat, and breaking open a window somewhere on the thirteenth floor. That would no doubt leave him with fewer adversaries to worry about, but he knew that breaking a window to the FBI's office would inevitably set off some type of high-tech security alarm, and he couldn't picture himself stumbling through unfamiliar hallways with a siren blaring in his ears, desperately trying to find Tallah before the cavalry arrived, heavily armed and ready to gun down an intruder on sight. Not to mention his problem with flight—lifting himself off the ground took a lot out of him, even on his best days, and he needed to preserve his sway to deal with whatever resistance he encountered *inside* the building; he couldn't show up to the fight already depleted. In the end, he decided to move forward with the original idea, and if he couldn't pull it off, he'd just have to improvise.

As he approached an exit for the city of Millbrae, he glanced in the rearview mirror: there was a CHP officer riding a motorcycle close behind. He had no idea how long the cop had been there.

Isaac checked the speedometer. The needle was pointing at zero. With the engine turned off, the gauge wasn't getting any power, a fact that he was already aware of but had forgotten in his moment of panic. Within seconds, the red and blue beacons on either side of the motorcycle's front headlamp started flashing.

Isaac spat out a curse.

He considered using his influence to turn the officer's ride into the equivalent of a ship's anchor, but trying to flee now would only draw more law-enforcement attention to the scene, effectively transforming him into the Grand Marshal of a cop parade on its way to San Francisco. He couldn't allow that to happen. He needed to keep his mind right, let this thing play itself out as much as possible, and— only if need be—take care of any problems as quickly and quietly as he could.

Isaac pulled the car to the road shoulder, stopping alongside a tall brick sound wall with a mass of ivy tendrils spilling down its face. The officer eased the motorcycle to a stop, flipped the kickstand down, and dismounted, removing his helmet and setting it down on the saddle. The man casually approached the passenger's side of Isaac's vehicle, still wearing his mirrored shades. No pistol drawn, no defensive posturing, no tactical maneuvering. Just normal walking, with a little bit of authoritative swagger added in for good measure. The officer's relatively nonchalant manner, coupled with the fact that he hadn't waited for backup to arrive (and hopefully hadn't called for any), went a long way toward easing Isaac's mind. He hadn't been recognized. The vehicle he was driving hadn't been reported stolen, at least not yet.

This was a simple traffic stop. And although he knew as well as anyone that a simple traffic stop could quickly escalate into something complicated, he needed to behave like a typical driver who'd made an innocent mistake.

The officer—a squat white man with a clean-shaven head—stood by the passenger's window and knocked a couple of times with a black-gloved fist. Keeping his own hands spread open and visible, Isaac carefully reached across the cabin and rolled down the window with the manual crank. The commotion of the highway came flooding into the vehicle's interior, amplified by the nearby sound wall. He suddenly realized that he wasn't feeling very well—nauseous, dizzy, and light-headed—and the exhaust fumes pouring in from outside weren't helping matters any.

The officer leaned into the frame of the open window. "Afternoon, sir," he said.

It wasn't the greeting he'd been expecting—in fact, he hadn't been expecting a greeting at all, other than a brusque demand to produce some paperwork.

"Afternoon, sir," Isaac replied.

"Do you have an idea why I stopped you today?"

Because I'm a fugitive? A fugitive wanted for assaulting multiple police officers, burying three cop cars, downing a helicopter, and now I'm driving a stolen vehicle? While Black?

"I'm guessing that I was going too fast?"

"The speed limit along this corridor drops from 65 to 60," the officer said. "It's unexpected. We're trying to get more signage to that effect. But in any case, you were clocking around 75. That's a little bit heavy-footed, young man."

Young man. That was a good sign.

Isaac nodded. "I wasn't paying enough attention—my mind was someplace else. Sorry."

The officer patted the bottom of the window frame with an open hand. "Understood. But regardless, I need to see your license, registration, and proof of insurance, please," he said.

Isaac had to do what the man asked. What real choice did he have? Slowly and deliberately, he reached into the pocket of the badge holder around his neck and produced the Mississippi license.

The officer lifted his sunglasses to the crown of his head and held the license up to his face, but he only glanced at it for a moment.

"Mississippi, huh," the man said, looking at him.

Isaac wasn't exactly sure how to interpret that statement.

"Right. The Hospitality State," he replied.

The Hospitality State? What are you saying?

"I don't hear it," the officer said. "In your voice, I mean. I wouldn't have pegged you for a Southerner by hearing you talk."

"Yeah. I get that a lot. I think it's because I moved around quite a bit as a kid. I don't think I ever had enough time to pick up an accent from anywhere."

"So you're in town for the GDC, I suppose?"

Isaac had no idea what the man was talking about.

"Pardon me?"

"Sorry. It seems like everybody I run into lately is here for the Game Developers Conference. It's running up at the convention center this week," he said. "I've started making assumptions at this point. If I see anybody from out-of-state, especially somebody young, I just assume they're here for some Silicon Valley conference or another."

"Of course," Isaac said. "Yes. Exactly. I'm here for the GDC, but I'm not actually a developer himself, in the coding sense. So I'm in town for the conference, yes. I'm just not a *participant* exactly. I'm here to cover the event. Media stuff." He held up the press pass.

Lord, he was either coming off like a liar or an absolute basket case, one or the other. Maybe even both.

"Right on," the officer said. "I was able to take my son to the Moscone Center on a guest pass Monday, on opening day. He's crazy into gaming. I play a little bit as well."

"Right on."

The officer smiled.

"I see you've got a little baby of your own, don't you," the man said. "I know how that is. Believe me."

Again, this cop had completely lost him.

"I get it," the officer continued, shaking his head. "You couldn't let yourself leave home without her, could you. We have a springer spaniel at home, and I'm the exact same way about him. He's too big for a plane, though. But still. If I could, I'd take him everywhere. Hell, I'd put him on the back of the bike with me if the job allowed for it."

Isaac suddenly understood. The officer was talking about the cat. Lando's carrier was sitting in the back seat on the passenger's side, near where the cop was standing, and the cat must have been visible through the mesh top.

Isaac smiled. "Exactly," he said, nodding. "That's my little road warrior back there. If I go, he goes. That's the rule."

"So he travels well? I mean, you hear all kinds of things about how cats can be." The officer rolled his eyes. "Ornery devils."

"Absolutely," Isaac replied. "Yeah, my little guy travels just fine. For a cat, I mean."

The officer didn't respond. Isaac stared up at him like a student in class, wondering whether he'd given the proper response.

"Well, all right then, Mr. Williams," the man said. "I just need to take a quick look at your registration and proof of insurance, please, and then you can be on your way."

Isaac panicked. He realized all at once that he had no idea where the documentation was (if it existed at all), whose name was printed on it, and whether or not it had expired.

"Sir?" the officer said. "Are you with me?"

"I'm sorry," Isaac mumbled. "Yes. Of course."

Isaac reached toward the glove compartment, the most logical place to find the registration and proof of insurance, but as he started to lift the latch he hesitated, absolutely terrified of what he might find inside (A pistol? A stash of heroin? A severed human hand?).

"Mr. Williams?" the officer said.

Isaac froze, his fingers resting on the lever, and looked up at the man's face. Surprisingly, the cop was pointing at his own nose.

"You're bleeding, Mr. Williams," he said, pulling a handkerchief from his back pocket.

Amazingly (out of sympathy?), the officer let Isaac go. It was a relatively unfamiliar feeling, the relief he felt at being given a warning by someone with the authority to mete out punishment. True, he'd had to shed his own blood to get it, but still, it had happened. Isaac understood that some folks could regularly get away with things like speeding—the little trespasses that don't rise to the level of sin in most people's eyes—but not him. He'd never had the knack for slipping under the radar.

After the officer left, Isaac stayed in the car for a long time with his head tipped back and the handkerchief pressed against his face, listening to the last of the rush hour traffic, the chassis rocking gently back and forth with the force of each vehicle passing by. He tried to quiet his mind, but he couldn't stop ruminating on how quickly everything good in his life had fallen apart. In the span of just two days, he'd lost his only child, his apartment, and (assuming the management at Quixit had access to a TV or smartphone) his employment. And judging by the way he felt at the moment, his health wasn't very far behind. It was as though a second storm had swept through and taken everything he'd tried so hard to build since the coming of the first.

Eventually Isaac lowered the handkerchief, checked his nose in the rearview mirror, and tossed the bloody rag onto the passenger's seat. He needed to move on. Not to San Francisco, but to somewhere safe where he could recuperate. He'd given up on the plan to free Tallah, at least for the night. There wasn't enough time to reach the federal building before it closed its doors to the general public, and in any case, he was feeling too sick to move the vehicle two feet in that direction, much less to stage a rescue mission against 10,000-to-1 odds. It didn't feel like a choice. He needed to find a place to hole up, lick his wounds, and rest until tomorrow, when he would try this seemingly futile exercise again.

The cat began to mewl from inside its carrier in the back seat.

"Shh," Isaac murmured. "It's okay, Lando. You're okay."

Isaac managed to roll the Camry to a hole-in-the-wall motel, this time in Millbrae, around fifteen miles south of San Francisco. The room was almost identical to the last one—a bed, a TV, a nightstand, a phone, a toilet, and not much else—unless he was hallucinating the entire thing and he hadn't actually left the motel on the Alameda, which seemed like an actual possibility given how he felt. He stumbled inside and closed the door, unzipped the duffel bag so Lando could run free, and peeled off his dress clothes, stripping down all the way to his boxers. He went to the bathroom, drank as much water from the tap as he could stomach, crawled onto the bed, and got under the sheets. By the time he'd gotten settled, his heart was hammering as though he'd just finished running a series of sprints.

There was no denying it: his health was getting worse. In fact, he was starting to worry that it didn't make a difference how he used his sway or how much rest he took in between each use. More and more, it appeared that *the very act of using his abilities* had been taking a toll on his body over the past six months. If so, it meant that he'd been slowly wearing himself down, using himself up, and that he might not have much more time left if he continued down this same path.

Breathing heavily, he reached over to the nightstand and picked up the handset from the phone cradle. He dialed Leti's number.

"Who's this?" she demanded.

For a brief, absurd moment, Isaac wasn't sure how to answer the question.

"It's Isaac."

"Excuse me?"

Isaac cleared his throat. His mouth felt dry and constricted, as though his tongue had thickened from dehydration.

"It's me," he repeated. "Isaac."

Leti didn't respond right away. He heard the sound of a young child's cackling laughter in the background, followed by the sound of a door closing, after which the laughter went quiet.

"Where the hell are you, Isaac?" Leti hissed.

"I'm still kicking around a little bit. Don't you worry about me." His words were slurring again.

Leti paused.

"You've got to be kidding me. Are you drunk right now?"

Clearly, he needed to pull himself together.

"No," Isaac answered. "I just don't feel right—that's all. Anyway, it doesn't matter. Listen. I'm sorry to be asking you again, but I need your help, Let."

"Okay," Leti said. "Don't be sorry. Just tell me what you need. If I can do it, you know I'll do it." She sounded like a mother talking to her wayward child—both worried and weary simultaneously. "Just tell me what it is."

Over the next half hour, Isaac told Leti everything that he needed her to do. The conversation took that long, not because his list of needs was so extensive, but because the few things he needed were so profoundly serious, and his ability to communicate them so impaired. To start, he made a request of Leti that he had absolutely no right to make, the single most significant request that could possibly come from a father: he asked her to take care of his only child once he was gone.

More specifically, he asked her to come to Millbrae the following morning and wait in the motel room while he took a quick jaunt up to San Francisco to grab Tallah from the FBI offices on the thirteenth floor of a heavily guarded federal building—in spite of being seriously afflicted himself. Assuming he was successful (which seemed more and more unlikely by the minute), he would either bring Tallah to the motel room (if he had any strength left) or he would find somewhere safe as far from downtown SF as possible, at which point he would contact Leti and ask her to come pick up Tallah and take her home.

"What about you?" she asked.

"What about me."

"You said I should come to the city and get your girl. But what about you? Where will you be?"

"I don't know," he replied. He felt drowsy all of a sudden. It was becoming a struggle just to keep himself awake. "If we make it to that stage, everybody will be looking for the two of us—her and me, together—which means she'd be better off if I stayed away for the time being."

"*If* we make it to that stage?"

Leti sounded upset, which would have been touching if he hadn't been so exhausted.

"Look," Isaac said. "I need to tell you, Let. Something bad is happening to me—real bad. Everything I've done over the last six months, or maybe everything I've ever done, period—I think it's all coming back around. Circling to find me." He paused, yawning. "Karma or something like that. My body feels like it's starting to shut down, Leti. I think I could be dying."

"So *stop*. Turn yourself in and do your stretch like I've been telling you to do. This wouldn't be the first time somebody went to prison, Isaac. It's been done before. You wouldn't be the first."

"I know," he murmured. "You're right about that. You're right about everything. But I need my daughter with me, Leti. I need her."

"I get that, Isaac. I get it. And your daughter needs you, too. She needs you alive."

"Exactly. She needs me," he said, his eyes closing. "That's why I'm going to snatch her from that building tomorrow. Lucky thirteen, baby. I'm going to get her out of there. And after I do that, I'll stop, Leti. I promise I will. I'll get Tallah and we'll go somewhere safe and then once I'm sure everything is all right, I'll stop. I won't use this power again, I swear to God, Let. I won't. Not for anything."

"What about school, Isaac?" Leti asked. "What about her friends? What about a normal life for her? How are you going to provide anything of value to a child, living on the run, looking over your shoulder all the time?"

As much as Isaac hated to admit it, Leti had a good point. She had a few of them, actually.

"I'll figure all that out once she's free," he said.

"And what if you don't make it out of that building, God forbid? I'm supposed to just, what—raise your daughter as my own for the rest of her life? Be her mother? Is that what you expect from me, Isaac?"

"I'm so sorry for all this, Let. I really am."

"Oh, cut the BS," Leti snapped. "If you're so damn sorry, then end this thing the only way that makes any sense. Do you deserve prison for defending your child? No. Is it fair? Of course not. But you don't get to stop parenting on account of fairness."

"Okay, but—"

"People go to jail, Isaac," she continued. "People with kids. *Parents.* If it happens, then you keep right on being a father as best you can from inside a six-by-eight cell. You don't get to just end your own life and toss the responsibility onto somebody else's shoulders."

"But you told me you would." Isaac was starting to sound like a child himself.

"Of course, I told you I would. But that was when we were talking about losing your freedom for a matter of years, not losing your life. Lord have mercy, Isaac. Why don't you just stop and admit to yourself that this isn't even about Tallah—this is about preserving your precious fucking manhood, and nothing else."

That woke Isaac up a little bit.

"What did you say?"

"This is all about you, Isaac," Leti said. "Cops took your daughter—something that belongs to you, in your mind—and you don't like that very much. So now you're heading off on your own personal bullshit crusade to get her back. Even though you know good and damn well that you'll never get that child out from under the FBI, your pride won't let you accept defeat and turn yourself in—which any fool can see is your only real play here. But never mind reason. You'd rather charge in there, sacrifice yourself valiantly in a losing battle with some blaze-of-glory thick-headedness, and then leave me to pick up all the pieces when you're through."

Isaac didn't respond right away.

Was she right? Is that what he was doing?

"Bullshit," he said.

"That's fine, Isaac. You have all the power here. You have the luxury of doing whatever you want to do, because you know that I'll be there for your little girl in the end, one way or the other. Because I care for you, and—by extension—for her, even during the times when you make me wish to God that I didn't."

"Just make sure you're here tomorrow morning, Leti. Why don't you start with that."

"Go to hell, Isaac."

"Okay. It's settled, then. Thank you," he said. "Oh, and one more thing. I really hope you like cats. Do you like cats, Leti? Tell me that you're a cat person."

All he heard was silence on the line.

"Leti?" he said.

She'd hung up on him.

chapter six

The next morning Isaac woke up early, dressed himself in the suit jacket, white button-down, and gray slacks, looped the press pass around his neck, and left the motel room, placing the Do Not Disturb sign on the door handle and slipping a small piece of motel stationery in between the latch assembly and the strike plate to keep the lock from catching.

He ate breakfast at a diner across the street from the motel. Two eggs over medium, sausage, home fries, and wheat toast. Coffee, black—plenty of it. Afterward, he was feeling better than he had in a long while. He ditched the Camry a few miles from the motel (he couldn't afford to expend his influence pushing a vehicle around) and walked to a local copy shop, where he set out to do something he should have done years ago but had convinced himself was only for the well-off. He wrote out a will.

It wasn't nearly as difficult as he'd thought it would be. Using a public workstation opposite the cash register, he found a sample Word template online that included a provision on "naming the guardian of the decedent's children." Most of the text was boilerplate—standard stuff. All Isaac needed to do was fill in the blanks and print out the final document.

If a Guardian is required for any minor child, I nominate, as my first choice, Leticia Berryessa Sanders, to serve as Guardian.

Isaac took the will to the front counter, asked the two clerks to sign as his witnesses, folded the paper, and slipped it into the breast-pocket near his heart. One of the clerks, an older white man with a short gray beard and a fringe of salt-and-pepper hair around his head, watched Isaac with an odd half-smile on his face until he was finished.

"It's not my business," the man said. "But you seem pretty young to be thinking about—whatever—*estate planning*. Don't get me wrong. I applaud your forethought. But I have to ask—what's that about? I'm just curious is all. If it's too personal, I totally get it, no problem."

Isaac looked at him. The clerk was right: it was none of his business and it was personal. But the man seemed well-intentioned enough, and the sad truth was that talking to someone—even a perfect stranger asking about his last will and testament—sounded pretty good at the moment.

"I'm sick," Isaac replied. "And I have a daughter at home who I need to do right by. That's the whole story." He shrugged.

The man gave him a look of genuine sympathy and shook his head. "I'm sorry," he said. "Sorry to hear you're sick, and sorry I asked about your business."

"It's all right."

"No, it isn't all right. I should've known better," the man said. "Of course you have something serious going on—why else would you be in here making a will?"

"Really, it's okay—I appreciate the concern. Have a good one." Isaac headed for the door.

"You too," the man said. "Take care of yourself out there."

Isaac caught the BART train running from Millbrae to downtown San Francisco. As he stood in the aisle, hanging onto a grab strap while the train car swayed rhythmically on the tracks, he watched the other passengers embarking and disembarking—business riders, pleasure riders, rich riders, poor riders—and wondered what each of them was thinking and feeling, whether they noticed him standing there, and if they did, whether they wondered about his thoughts and feelings or whether they were simply uncomfortable, or curious, or indifferent, or disgusted, or a dozen other possible responses they could have to his presence in the car. For a fleeting moment, he even wondered whether any of them could somehow perceive how afraid he was at the moment and guess at the reason behind it—did anyone sense the nature of what he was about to do? Could anyone predict, just by looking at him, the assortment of criminal acts that he was minutes away from committing?

Isaac got off the train at the Civic Center Station, walked up Golden Gate Avenue for a few blocks, sweating on account of his nerves (in spite of the fifty-degree spring weather in the city), and when he got within eyeshot of the front doors of the Phillip Burton Federal Building and U.S. Courthouse—a twenty-one story gray monstrosity near City Hall—he stopped in his tracks and stared.

Five—no, six—overgrown men with dark-blue body armor and snub-nosed machine guns strapped to their shoulders were flanking the glass-front entrance on either side. One of the guards held a leash with what looked like a two-hundred-pound German Shepherd on the other end; the dog was sitting bolt upright, its ears rigid and sharp as twin blades. And this was *outside* the building. He could only imagine the level of security waiting for him on the inside.

But, strangely enough, the small army of guards wasn't the worst part. The worst part was a simple sign posted near one of the doors: a professional-looking placard made of white foam-core board. The sign had been propped up on a metal easel with three telescoping legs.

CLOSED TO THE PUBLIC, the first line read.

And underneath that:

NO PRESS

Lord, no.

Isaac couldn't let himself panic. He needed to act. Staying in character as *the intrepid young reporter* out on assignment (and feeling as though he had nothing to lose by trying), he hurried across the concrete plaza in front of the building and approached one of the guards, a young Black man with deeply pockmarked cheeks and sad-looking eyes. The man visibly straightened his posture and shifted his rifle a few degrees higher as Isaac got closer.

"Excuse me," Isaac said.

The man nodded his head by way of a greeting. Isaac had been hoping for a little more congeniality off the bat, but there was no going back now.

"What's the situation with *no press*?" he asked, gesturing toward the sign. "That's a mistake, right? You can't really be trying to stop the information flow like that."

"Sorry," the man said.

Isaac waited, but soon it became evident that the guard had nothing more to add.

"So we're just *out*?" he asked. "No love? That's it?"

The man shrugged.

"Come on," Isaac said. "What happened?"

"They don't tell me anything. Just no press," the guard replied. "No press, no public. We're badging everyone in."

The guard had managed to string together a series of words, which felt like progress, even though the words themselves weren't the ones Isaac wanted to hear.

"Can't you help me out, man?" he asked. "I've got this story that needs telling—you have no idea. I came all the way up from Mississippi to get it right. Please."

The man shrugged again. "I don't decide. Sorry," he said.

At that point, another guard—a hulking white man with pale, freckled skin—stepped forward. Wilson, his name tag read. He was smiling.

"What's your business with us today, sir?" Wilson asked brightly. "You got a case on the docket?"

Isaac held up the press pass.

"I'm covering a story," he said.

The man frowned and shook his head. "Not today, you're not. I'm sorry, sir. It's employees-only this morning. If you're on the docket, you get a pass. If you're affiliated with outside legal counsel, you get a pass. But that's about it. Otherwise, you've got to have a job here if you want in."

"How long?"

"How long, what?"

"How long will it be closed for?"

Wilson shrugged.

"Until further notice. That's all I know."

Isaac sat on a concrete park bench on the opposite side of Golden Gate Avenue for at least an hour, watching the federal building and trying to decide what to do next. If he hadn't already outed himself as a member of the (fake) media, he could have tried to convince the guards that he was part of a court case—either a member of a legal team (harder to convince them) or a defendant (probably much easier to convince them)—but it was too late for that now, and at any rate, he probably wouldn't have been able to sway them in either direction, regardless, given their state of high alert.

Using subtlety seemed hopeless. He was going to have to take a more emphatic approach.

It was getting close to the noon hour. All around him, the plaza was steadily filling with well-groomed men and put-together women holding cardboard coffee cups and taut paper sacks with deli logos on the sides, walking alone or together in pairs, all of them looking around for something relatively simple: a place to sit and eat lunch outside for forty or fifty minutes of their day. As he watched the crowd (the world?) pass him by, he experienced a sense of longing that was almost incapacitating—a yearning for a completely different life—but he knew that no matter what he did from that point onward, no matter how fiercely he fought, he would never enjoy the kind of life that these people took for granted every day: a life of safety, exemption, and normalcy. If he'd ever had a chance at that kind of existence at all, that chance was gone.

Isaac spent some time watching the good people of downtown San Francisco going about their business, his sense of resentment deepening. It wasn't directed toward anyone in particular, but toward everyone and everything in equal measure. He was positively seething, a word he'd used to describe his daughter at various points in time but which now applied equally well, perhaps even better, to him.

Before long he had to force himself to turn away and focus on something else. He stared at the sky, overcast and gray, and scanned the stark, rectangular facade of the building itself, seemingly impenetrable. He watched the cars in their endless stop-and-go routine on Golden Gate Avenue and wondered where the drivers were headed, what they were thinking about, and whether any of them had no destination at all and were simply driving aimlessly up and down whatever road lay straight ahead.

After a while he caught sight of a white bus trundling up Larkin Street to his left—a prison bus. The kind with a thick chassis that looks vaguely armored, a couple of fence-like partitions in the interior to separate prisoners from guards, and a series of slits along the sides where the windows of a normal bus would have been. The bus stopped at an intersection, turned right onto Polk, then immediately took another right turn into a narrow driveway that ran alongside the federal building, almost like an alley. The bus pulled up next to a set of double-doors on the side of the building, and Isaac heard the sound of the air brake system releasing its pent-up pressure. The sliding hinge door on the side of the bus folded open, but no one came out.

It gave him an idea.

Isaac scrambled to his feet, visibly startling a group of women sitting on the edge of a dry fountain basin, sprinted down Golden Gate Avenue to the intersection, and headed up Larkin until he reached the corner of Polk Street, near the curb cutouts where the bus had pulled into the alleyway. He stood behind a cinderblock retaining wall and peered around the corner, still breathing hard. Nothing about the situation had changed. He could see the rear of the bus—a swing-handle latch on its back door, metal screens covering the back windows, and bold, black lettering just below the roof that read, PRISONER TRANSPORT. STAY BACK.

There was only one explanation for a bus full of prisoners pulling up to the Phillip Burton Federal Building and U.S. Courthouse:

these men were about to go inside and stand trial. He couldn't be certain, but he also couldn't think of any other reason they'd be here. He waited, trying to work up the nerve to move forward.

His plan was simple, at least in theory. He would make his way into the federal building by passing himself off as young, Black, and in chains. It was sadly perfect—the one disguise that everyone would accept without a single question. It would be the closest he could possibly get to being invisible.

Isaac watched the bus for at least ten minutes as it sat idling near the side entrance to the building, dark exhaust pluming from its tailpipe. The building's double doors looked pretty well fortified: thick metal panels, multiple locking mechanisms, and two security cameras mounted on the eaves.

The rumbling of the bus's engine abruptly cut off, and the chassis went still. He couldn't wait any longer; he needed to act.

Using the minimum amount of influence necessary, Isaac ramped up the weight of the left-front wheel until the tire burst under the elevated pressure, sending the metal rim crashing down onto the asphalt and leaving the vehicle listing noticeably to one side. Seconds later, two uniformed guards spilled from the side door of the bus, their weapons drawn, and hurried around front to see what the hell had just happened.

There was no way of knowing how many guards, if any, were still inside the vehicle—its narrow, tinted windows were covered with black security grates, making it impossible to see the interior clearly—but he'd decided to move forward and be prepared to use his powers to deal with anything unforeseen. He crouch-walked to the tail of the vehicle, used his sway to pop the latch, and quietly opened the door, revealing a secure compartment with a single padded seat (empty), presumably used by one of the guards to keep watch over the prisoners from a rearward position. Directly in front of him was a floor-to-ceiling chain-link wall with a locked gate separating the back compartment from the rest of the prisoners, most of whom seemed to be craning their necks, trying to get a clear look through the narrow side windows. No one stood up, so he assumed that everyone must be tethered to their seats.

Isaac quietly closed the rear door of the bus. Staying low, he took a moment to scan the main compartment through the gaps in the chain link. Around thirty men wearing standard-issue orange jumpsuits were seated in the body of the bus, around half of its full seating capacity. No guards had been posted among them, at least none that he could see. At the far end of the main compartment, past the rows of prisoners, was *another* floor-to-ceiling chain-link wall with a gate leading to a *third* compartment up front: the driver's area. Inside the driver's compartment, he could see a third guard standing halfway down the steps, leaning out of the bus and yelling something to the other two guards outside, both of whom seemed to be busy trying to wrap their minds around what had gone wrong with the tire.

Isaac didn't have much time. He popped the lock on the security gate, opened it, and stepped into the main compartment, closing the door behind him. A few of the men seated in the rows closest to the back of the bus turned around to look over their shoulders, their eyes widening at the sight of a stranger on board.

"What the fuck," one of them said.

At that moment, Isaac came to two important conclusions. First, he realized that a good number of these men wouldn't hesitate for a moment to call attention to his presence, to shout for the guards, if they perceived it was in their best interest to do so—or if they *just got the urge* for some reason that he'd never understand. Secondly, he realized that if he was going to take the place of one of these men, to pass himself off as another person, he would need to quickly evaluate the face of every man to find the closest match. It wouldn't need to be exact—Isaac seriously doubted that these guards had spent enough time with any of these men to become familiar with their faces—but he needed to be reasonably close.

He made the decision to address both issues simultaneously.

Using his influence, he took control of every single prisoner on the bus at the same time and gently but firmly steadied each tongue, closed each set of jaws, and angled each body until he could make eye contact with every man from his position at the rear of the bus. The compartment went silent. He glanced up to check on the third guard— he had exited the bus and was standing near the side door, talking into a handheld radio.

Isaac looked over his captive audience.

"I'm sorry," he said quietly. "I wouldn't be putting you in check like this unless I had to." He meant that.

"One of you is about to be set free," he continued. "You'll trade clothes with me, leave this bus, and run. But I won't force anyone to do anything. Whoever it is will volunteer for the chance."

Isaac paused, staring at the face of each prisoner. The level of hatred he saw in the eyes of some of those men was palpable, but he ignored it. He didn't have the time or the energy to worry about anybody's feelings at the moment. As he searched for a reasonable match, he had to remind himself several times that he looked different than he did normally—that he was searching for a match to his new face, rather than to his old one. He was looking for a young Black man around twenty-one years of age with light brown skin, a clean short haircut, and a thin muscular build. Somewhere around about five foot ten or so.

Around half of the inmates were Black—but out of those, only five were the right age, build, and skin tone. Another three non-Black men were close enough that he thought he could probably pass for any one of them, but that was all. Eight options out of thirty. As for the non-options? Isaac turned them all back around to face the front of the bus, leaving the eight (lucky?) candidates facing him, then forced the eight men to close their eyes.

"If your eyes are closed right now, you need to listen," he said. "In a moment, I'm going to let go of you. Give you control over your own eyes again. If you want to volunteer for what I'm asking, open your eyes. But if you want no part of this—which would be the wise choice, by the way, given what I'm about to do in your name—keep them closed."

He looked at the men, each in turn.

"All right," he said. "I'm asking you now. Who's looking for the opportunity to run away from all this? Knowing that if you get caught, not only will the escape add real time to whatever sentence you've already got riding on your shoulders, but so will all the crimes that I'm about to commit using your identity. My crimes will become your crimes. So, knowing all that—who wants the chance anyway? If you do, open your eyes. If you don't, you know what to do."

Isaac watched as six men kept their eyes closed, while two men opened them. One of the two volunteers was a young, light-skinned Black man, and the other was more challenging to categorize—maybe Afro-Latino? Isaac turned the other six around in their seats to face forward again.

"I'm going to release your tongues now," he said to the two men. "Do not raise your voice. Do not call out for anyone. When I ask you a question, answer quickly and quietly and then shut your mouths."

He looked at one face, then the other. "Blink if you understand me," he said.

Each of them blinked once.

"All right, then," he said.

Isaac decided to address the young Afro-Latino man first.

"What's your name?" he asked.

"Nesto. Man, you gotta let me move. Please. I'm going claustrophobic in here right now."

"All right, Nesto. Calm down," Isaac said. "I need to ask you what you did to end up on this bus, on your way to a federal courtroom. And tell me the truth, Nesto. I don't want to have to hurt you right now."

"Robbery, man," Nesto said. "It was B and E on a bank. All right? B and E."

"And did you hurt anybody during the robbery, Nesto?"

"No, man. No. Maybe a couple guys got roughed up a little bit.

But that's all. Can I go now, please?"

Isaac ignored him and turned to the other man.

"What's your name?" he asked.

"Deron," he answered.

Isaac could see beads of sweat forming on the man's brow, just below the hairline.

"All right, Deron. What did you do to end up in here?"

"Nothing."

Isaac stared at him.

"What did you do," he repeated.

"I mean, I was part of something, but it wasn't me doing it, per se. So nothing, man. All right? Nothing."

Isaac glanced up toward the front of the bus. The first two guards were standing together near the busted wheel on the driver's side, staring down and having what looked to be a heated conversation, while the third guard continued to pace back and forth near the side-door, barking into his handheld radio.

Isaac stared at Deron.

"What was the *thing* you were part of, then?" he asked. "Just tell me, Deron. I don't have time to be playing around with you right now."

"It was drugs, okay? Drugs coming in by boat off the coast. I wasn't even knowing what it was at the time. I got caught up. Period. The end."

"Can I go now?" Nesto said, his eyes darting back and forth. "Hurry, man. Come on."

Isaac had heard enough. He closed both of their mouths and held their tongues in place. He could only let one of these men go, and there wasn't time to weigh the decision properly—a decision he didn't even have the right to be making in the first place. He just needed to choose somebody and move forward.

"I'm sorry, Nesto," Isaac said. "It's not personal or anything like that, all right? I'm sure you're delightful. But I'm going to let Deron go."

Nesto's eyes narrowed, which was the closest Isaac was going to get to understanding the man's thoughts on the decision, since he had lost the ability to speak for the time being. He turned Nesto around to face the front of the bus like the others, and looked at Deron.

"I'm about to let you go," Isaac said. "And when I do, you're going to take off those peels you're wearing and hand them over. I'll give you the jacket and pants I've got on. And then you run the hell out of here, Deron. Don't you look back."

Without another word, Isaac popped the man's restraints, returned control of his body, and took off the suit coat as Deron crouched in the aisle and started tearing off the jumpsuit.

"Hurry up," he said. "Move."

In less than a minute's time, Isaac was zipping himself into a set of prison oranges while Deron was busy tucking the white dress shirt into the gray slacks. When Deron finished, he pulled on the navy-blue suit coat, opened the gate to the back compartment, and exited quietly through the rear door of the bus, closing it behind him.

Isaac took Deron's seat in an otherwise empty row and picked up the restraints from the floor: a standard set of handcuffs and a length of cable, almost like a thin bike lock, attached to the seat base. The cable lock was supposed to be threaded through the links between the two cuffs, limiting the wearer's range of motion, preventing him from fully standing. As Isaac looked over the restraints, he realized something: in his haste to free Deron, he hadn't managed to unlock the cuffs and the cable. He'd broken them—both of them. Irreparably. The metal teeth of the cuff ratchet had been stripped smooth, making it impossible to secure, and he'd snapped the cable near its built-in locking mechanism, leaving the braided wire interior exposed on both ends. As he tried to assemble the broken restraints into something passable, the third guard—a heavyset white man— reentered the bus, opened the glovebox, and started fishing around for something. The man was getting ready to come back to the main compartment. Isaac could tell. There wasn't much time.

He released his control over the prisoners' bodies—he'd been holding them steady this entire time—but he kept every single mouth closed and every single tongue in check. He needed them to hear what he was about to say.

"Look here," he said quietly. "I'm about to give you back your voices—everybody's in here. But I'm telling you right now, each and every one of you: watch what you say. If I hear anybody talking about me, talking about Deron, talking about Nesto, or talking about anything else they've seen or heard since I got on this bus, I'm about to start breaking bodies in here. Trust me on that. Nod if you can hear me." He looked around and saw everybody's head—even Nesto's—nodding vigorously.

At that point, the guard snapped the glovebox closed, approached the barrier separating the driver's compartment from the main compartment, unlocked the gate, and stepped through, closing it behind him.

"We got a little problem, fellas," the guard said. "Long story short. The front tire blew out, right? Simple enough. But when it blew, it blew *big*. Big enough that the wheel dropped down to the street, the front axle broke, and the entire undercarriage crashed out. And now we've got a leak—maybe multiple leaks—somewhere in the fuel line. Which means we've got a lot of gasoline spilling out underneath the bus. A lake's worth, pretty much."

The guard paused, as if for effect. No one said a word. In fact, no one even seemed to move a muscle, with the exception of Isaac—he was furiously trying to reassemble his restraints into something passable without drawing the guard's attention. He managed to get the cuffs around his wrists and hold the swivel-arms closed by pressing them against his thighs, but the cable lock was hopeless. He'd threaded it through the links between the handcuffs already, but beyond that, there was nothing he could do.

"Anyway," the guard continued, "we need to unload and get you guys inside for showtime. Let's go. Look alive."

Isaac glanced up. The other two guards had entered the driver's area and were about to pass through the gate into the main compartment. He'd run out of time; there was nothing left for him to do but wait.

Starting from the front row and working their way back, two guards worked together to untether each inmate and escort him outside, still handcuffed, to an assembly point near the building's double doors, where the third guard stood watch, a shotgun at the ready. Isaac watched as all of the inmates in the rows ahead of him were removed from the bus and led one by one to the side entrance. After around ten minutes of waiting it was his turn to go.

The guard who approached him was a tall Black man with a name tag that read Sergeant Wilkins. Without even glancing at Isaac's face, Wilkins crouched down to unfasten the cable lock from the seat anchor between his knees. When Wilkins got his hands on the frayed end of the cable, he looked up at Isaac, his eyes widening.

"You did this?" Wilkins asked. He looked almost excited by the prospect.

"Nope. It must've broke when the bus hit the street," Isaac replied.

Wilkins stared at the cable for a moment, nodding, then got to his feet. "So you noticed it," he said. "You knew it broke?"

Isaac nodded.

"For real?" Wilkins asked. "So you were aware, but you didn't do anything about it. Is that what you're saying?"

Isaac shrugged. "What was I supposed to do?"

"Well, shit," Wilkins said, shaking his head. "If you put me in your exact situation—broken lock, nobody around—let me tell you what I'd do: I'd be fucking gone. Poof." He snapped his fingers. "But then again, I'm no bitch. And clearly, you must be a bitch, Mister—" He paused, pulled an iPad from under his arm, and typed for a few seconds. "Mister Deron Coates. Clearly you must be a little bitch, Mister Coates, because in a situation like this one, a little bitch would either (a.) tell a C.O. about the broken lock, or (b.) do nothing. And since you did nothing at all—you, my friend, are a bona fide little bitch.

Grade A."

Isaac didn't respond. He stared straight ahead, keeping his wrists pressed tightly against his thighs. Wilkins shook his head, muttered something about bitches being bitches, and yanked the cable from the links between Isaac's cuffs, grabbing hold of his upper arm. Isaac kept his wrists pinned against his stomach as Wilkins strong-armed him down the aisle, through the barrier gate, and out the side door.

Two out of the three guards—Wilkins, plus the heavyset white one that Wilkins called Mills—brought the group of inmates inside the federal building and, with the help of four members of the Federal Protective Service, escorted them into a heavily fortified stairwell. Shoulder-to-shoulder in pairs, the group climbed all the way up to the tenth-floor landing, where they stopped in front of a gray metal exit door with a black-domed security camera mounted above the top rail. Mills, who had been holding up the rear, edged his way to the front of the group until he was standing with his back to the gray door, facing them. His skin was bright pink and coated in a sheen of sweat.

"All right, fellas," he said. "For those of you new to this, we're about to enter a hallway directly outside the U.S. District Court for Northern California. Your job is to wait in the hallway until your case is called, at which point you'll walk inside, meet with your counsel, and proceed with the hearing. That's it. Questions."

Mills looked around, seemingly at every face. He was still breathing hard from the effort of the climb. "Good," he said. "When we get into the hall, I'll need everybody to stay quiet while you wait. No chatter, no cursing, no hollering. Shouldn't be a problem—this is a quiet group we've got today."

Sitting on the tile floor in a long line along the wall, the group waited in the hallway outside the courtroom for a couple of hours while nine or ten inmates were cycled through the courtroom in reverse alphabetical order. From time to time, Isaac caught one of the inmates glancing warily in his direction, but otherwise no one moved, at least not that he saw, and no one spoke a word.

Apart from the inmates on the tile, the two guards who'd gotten off the bus, and the four-man security team, the hallway was abandoned. A couple of vending machines, a water fountain, two restrooms, and a row of elevators at the far end, next to a window—that's all there was. The judge had clearly reserved a few hours on her schedule to give them her undivided attention.

As Isaac waited for his name to be called (first name Deron, last name Coates), he frantically tried to devise a reasonable plan to remove himself from this chain gang as inconspicuously as possible. The FBI field office was on the thirteenth floor, which meant that he needed to somehow slip away from the other inmates, take the elevator or the stairs another three floors higher, and make his way to the field office without bringing the entire Federal Protective Service down on top of his head in the process. While wearing a bright orange jumpsuit. He had no idea even how to start. The only thing he knew for sure was that, whatever he chose to do next, it would involve using his influence. With emphasis.

After another hour, Isaac's nose started to bleed. He didn't even feel it. By the time he'd realized what was happening, the front of his jumpsuit was spattered with deep red blotches.

"What the hell," Wilkins barked, storming across the hall to stand over him, glowering. "Aw, man. That's some nasty shit, inmate. Pull yourself together."

Isaac brought his cuffed hands to his face, keeping his wrists pressed together, and pinched his nostrils closed. He tilted his head back until it touched the wall.

Wilkins continued to stare down at him with obvious disgust. "I know you did that to yourself on purpose, man. Trying to get out of your big day in court by bleeding a little bit, right? Well, that's some bitch shit right there if I've ever seen it. Weak as hell."

"No."

"Damn right, no," Wilkins said. "As in, no way in hell you're missing court. What you're going to do is suck that blood back and man up."

He kicked Isaac's leg firmly with the toe of his work boot.

At that point, Mills came over. He glared at Wilkins for a moment, then crouched down in front of Isaac.

"You all right?" he asked quietly.

Isaac nodded, still holding his nose. He could feel a warm rivulet running down his left forearm and dripping from his elbow.

"Damn," Mills said. "You really turned the faucet on, didn't you. Are you injured?"

"He's fine," Wilkins said. "I'm telling you, Mills, you need to quit this bullshit babysitting routine of yours. It's embarrassing."

Mills paused for a moment before climbing to his feet, taking a step closer to Wilkins, and looking him directly in the eye. Mills must have been six inches shorter, minimum, but that didn't seem to faze him in the least.

"Like it or not, the job calls for us to determine whether this inmate's health is at risk. In any situation. Period," Mills said. "That's what we do. So if you've got some kind of problem with that, then you can piss off back to the bus and wait there until I'm finished."

Wilkins didn't respond. He stared at Mills with a murderous expression on his face. Mills turned his attention back to Isaac.

"Get up," he said. "Come on."

Isaac did what he was told. Keeping his head tilted back and his nostrils pinched closed, he slowly got to his feet. Mills took hold of his upper arm.

"What the hell are you doing, man?" Wilkins asked, shaking his head.

"My job," Mills said. "I'm taking this man to get himself cleaned up." With his hand firmly planted on Isaac's arm, Mills steered him down the hall in the direction of the elevator at the far end.

"All right. Wait," Wilkins said. "Hold up, now. Hold up."

Mills stopped and turned around.

"Look," Wilkins said. "I'm sorry, okay? I got this. Let me do it."

Mills paused. "Really?" he asked. "You're sure about that?"

"That's what I said, didn't I? I got this. Damn."

The men's restroom was located at the end of the hallway, down a short corridor next to the elevator. One hand gripping Isaac's shoulder, Wilkins pushed open the restroom door, leaned in, and looked around for a few seconds before yanking him through the entryway and shoving him toward the row of sinks. Isaac stumbled forward, still holding his nose (and his cuffs), and came to a stop in front of one of the vanity mirrors.

Isaac caught a glimpse of himself.

Even with his hands in the way, he could see enough of his face—his eyes, brow, and jawline—to be surprised by it. He hadn't had time to get used to his new appearance; in fact, he still looked like a complete and utter stranger, especially now that he was dressed in prison orange.

Wilkins was watching him from the entryway, keeping the door propped open with his boot. "What the hell's your problem?" he asked. "Wash up, inmate. Get it done."

Isaac didn't move.

"Hey," Wilkins said, slapping the door with an open hand. "Get your ass into that water and sanitize yourself. Now."

Isaac turned around to stare at him, his hands still cupping his nose. Wilkins' eyes widened for a split second—a flash of genuine surprise—but then he smiled broadly. By all appearances, he seemed absolutely delighted with Isaac's decision to disobey direct orders.

Nodding his head slowly, Wilkins stepped out of the entryway and let the door swing closed behind him. He drew a tactical baton from a loop in his belt and brandished it like a saber, advancing toward Isaac.

"Remember," the man said. "You chose this. It was your decision to take a hardheaded route, not mine."

Isaac let Wilkins take a few steps before he dropped his hands away from his face, bringing them down to waist level. The cuffs swung open, slipped off of his wrists, and fell onto the tile with an echoing clatter. Wilkins stopped dead in his tracks.

"Oh, shit," he said.

Before Wilkins could take another step, Isaac snatched the man clean off his feet, drafted his flailing body into midair, and held it in place around six feet above the floor, carefully folding his frame into a fetal position like a poseable figurine—knees to chest, chin tucked, arms wrapped around the shins. As Wilkins started to cry out, Isaac locked his jaws closed and steadied his tongue. The man grunted a few times before going silent, his nostrils visibly flaring with every breath.

Isaac took a few steps closer until they were face to face. Wilkins' eyes were darting wildly in their sockets.

"I need to take your clothes," Isaac said quietly.

Wearing Wilkins' dark blue guard uniform, Isaac bolted out of the restroom and sprinted down a short corridor past a bank of payphones and a janitor's closet, coming to a stop at the entranceway to the main hallway. He could see the elevator doors to his right, but he couldn't reach them without being exposed—he would need to step out into the hallway and risk being seen by the guards (and the collection of inmates) assembled at the opposite end.

He glanced around the corner, catching sight of Mills, the four-man team of FPS agents, and the line of orange jumpsuits seated along the wall. No one seemed to be concerned about his or Wilkins' whereabouts or even looking in his direction, but he needed to maximize his chances of remaining unseen, so he quickly used his sway to target the heavy wooden doors leading into the courtroom—the doors that were only a few yards from the spot where everyone had gathered. There wasn't time for subtlety or finesse: he simply tore the doors open and slammed them shut again. A resounding *boom* echoed throughout the hallway like a pealing roll of thunder.

Isaac didn't wait to see the reaction it elicited. He stormed into the hallway, scrambled to the elevators, and pounded the call button. Darting glances over his shoulder, he waited until the doors trundled open and then slipped inside, lunging out of the entryway and pressing his back up against the sidewall.

chapter seven

Isaac slumped against the wall of the elevator car, his head swimming. He was feverish and anemic, nauseous and sluggish. The sweat was pouring off of him as though he'd just run a mile while sick with pneumonia, which was about how he felt.

Given the state of his health, Isaac wasn't sure how much longer he could hold Wilkins where he'd left him—in one of the bathroom stalls, perched on the toilet, wearing nothing but a white t-shirt and bright red boxer shorts, unable to move a muscle or speak a word. At the time, Isaac thought that he'd be able to keep him there for a good while—at least long enough to get a decent head start before the man could sound the alarm—but now Isaac wasn't sure anymore. Even though he'd tried to use his abilities sparingly at every step, he was struggling to divide his focus between one location and another, to hold in his memory everything he'd altered. It was all he could do to keep himself from collapsing on the spot.

The elevator slowly rose. Level 13. Isaac spat on the floor and wiped his mouth with the back of a hand.

The elevator doors opened directly into what looked like the waiting area of a doctor's office. Two plush couches, a row of padded armchairs, a TV monitor showing a video about the operations of the FBI, a table stacked with magazines organized by areas of interest. Or was it organized by the gender of the target audience? Or was it alphabetical, by title? He wasn't sure.

Why do I care about this so much?

Clearly his mind wasn't working the way it should have been.

As Isaac tried to leave the elevator, the doors began to close—sensing an obstacle, they jolted open again, rattling on their metal rails, startling him. His legs nearly gave out.

"Sir?" a woman's voice said. "Are you okay?"

Her voice sounded mechanical, robotic.

Isaac looked up and saw a middle-aged white woman with short black hair and reading glasses staring at him from behind a thick slab of what he could only assume was bulletproof glass. She was saying something else, but he couldn't understand it; her voice was burbling through a small speaker built into the window itself. He suddenly felt as though he'd stumbled into a credit union branch. The woman paused and stared at him with her head cocked.

"Sorry," Isaac said. "I didn't catch that." He tried to smile but immediately stopped himself once he remembered how awkward it had felt the last time he'd made the attempt.

"What is the problem you are responding to?" she asked, over-enunciating every word.

"The problem?" he asked. "What do you mean?"

Isaac thought he saw one of her eyebrows raise, but it was difficult to tell through six inches' worth of paneling.

"Well, you're not with building security," she said. "Wrong uniform. But clearly you're with law enforcement in some capacity, right? And when one of you guys comes around to pay us a visit, it's generally not to spread tidings of good cheer. So I drew a conclusion: there must be a problem. It's called the power of making inferences. That's one of the reasons why the FBI is so amazing."

Isaac chuckled a little bit at that. His laughter was primarily an attempt to remain in character (a guard might laugh at that kind of thing, right?), but he also found the quip categorically funny. His head suddenly felt slightly clearer; he'd probably accidentally released Sergeant Wilkins without even realizing it.

"You're right about that," Isaac said, nodding. "I'm not here to talk about rainbows, unfortunately."

The woman smiled. She had a very large, oddly pleasant-looking gap in between her front teeth. "No worries at all. Who are you here to see?" she asked.

"I don't have an appointment with anyone in particular, actually," he replied.

The woman frowned. "I see. Well, that means you need to talk to the duty agent, then." Her tone was flat. Final.

"Duty agent?"

"Yes," she said. "The agent on duty. The duty agent."

Isaac wasn't sure he liked the sound of that. Bottom line, he needed access. Real access. He needed to make his way behind the bulletproof glass, into the actual offices—cut his way deep into the heart of the operation with scalpel-like precision—if he was going to find Tallah without causing too much pain and suffering in the process. Isaac didn't claim to know anything about the organizational structure of the FBI, of course, but he wasn't confident that a *duty agent* was going to get him where he wanted to be. The role sounded too much like an administrator or spokesperson.

"Let me guess," Isaac said. "The duty agent is the unlucky one who has to deal with all the eccentrics who walk in here, right? Conspiracy theorists and whatnot? Is that what he does?"

"She. *She* is the unlucky one. At least for today. And yes, the duty agent handles all unscheduled visits to our office, for whatever reason, eccentric or not."

"Look. I'm not here to report an alien sighting," Isaac said. "I'm not trying to tell anybody my thoughts on who did what on the grassy knoll. You can take me seriously."

"I do take you seriously, sir."

Isaac tapped the badge pinned to his shirtfront. "Doesn't this mean something though? Come on. Shouldn't I get the chance to talk to somebody with some rank, as a professional courtesy maybe?"

"The duty agent's name is Special Agent Trujillo," the woman said. "She's a rock star, don't you worry—she can help you. I promise."

Isaac couldn't wait around much longer. At any second, an alarm was going to sound and the Federal Protective Service would flood every floor of the building en masse, trying to track him down. He needed to push forward, whether he had a decent plan or not.

"All right, I hear you," Isaac said, approaching a metal security door next to the bulletproof window. "I'll talk to the duty agent, then—no problem. Open the door, please."

The woman shook her head.

"You can talk all you want from exactly where you're standing, sir," she said. "My name is Special Agent Trujillo. I'm the duty agent."

It only took a few minutes' worth of discussion with Trujillo to conclude the obvious: she was going to make him jump through a thousand hoops before she even thought about letting him through that metal door. The woman started off by asking for some basic information—his name, his address, his employment information, his reason for visiting—all of which Isaac blatantly fabricated on the spot (and none of which would hold up when she inevitably asked to see his ID). As the minutes passed, he was becoming more and more convinced that he'd gone as far as he could go without using his sway offensively—even violently if need be. He decided to give himself just a couple more minutes to try and persuade Trujillo to let him through the security door, and if the power of persuasion didn't work within that period of time, then he'd have to rely on another power altogether.

A minute passed with more of the same. Trujillo pointed to a line of plastic document holders on his side of the bulletproof glass.

"Go ahead and fill out the IRQ-5535 form," she said. "It's an interview request form—nothing too complicated. The main point is to detail the reason for your visit, and to be as specific as you can."

A form?

That settled it. Isaac needed to act. His mind was racing through his options, but in spite of the relative brevity of the list, he couldn't latch onto a train of thought that led to a particular one. He still felt disoriented and scattered. Lost. How would he make his way past the security door, for starters? It would be quicker to break it down with brute force, but would it be wiser to take control of Trujillo herself and convince her to let him in? Which would require the greater expenditure of his dwindling energy? As Isaac tried to devise a plan of attack, he absentmindedly paged through the various stacks of forms, halfway searching for the proper one. There had to be at least five or six documents to choose from. It was ridiculous.

"No—not that one," Trujillo said, her voice buzzing through the speaker. "The one in back. One more over. Exactly—that one."

Isaac pulled out a copy of the IRQ-5535 form and stared at it without really seeing any detail. It looked like a white haze—almost as though he was staring at a thick fog through a miniature window pane.

From behind him, Isaac suddenly heard the elevator make a bright chime, followed by the sound of the doors rattling open. He'd run out of time.

Gathering his focus, he turned around and saw a squad of three security officers in full body armor step out of the elevator car in a triangle formation, rifles raised to shoulder level. They fanned out, taking (presumably) strategic positions throughout the waiting area as though storming an enemy structure during a time of war.

"Hey." It was Trujillo's voice coming from behind his back, but it didn't sound amplified any longer. "Listen to me, okay? Right now, if you're thinking of anything—anything at all—other than lying down on the floor and putting your hands behind your head, I want you to clear it from your mind. Just stop now. It's okay to just stop."

Isaac glanced over his shoulder. Trujillo had opened the security door, slipped into the room, and was now pointing what looked like a nine-millimeter handgun directly at his face. It suddenly occurred to him that she'd probably never believed any of his nonsensical ramblings for more than a minute or two, at best. No— she'd probably called for security at the first hint of deception using some kind of panic button, which meant that she'd been stalling, waiting for them to arrive, ever since that moment.

"Just stop, okay?" Trujillo said quietly. "It's okay to be done with this. You haven't done anything that can't be walked back."

Isaac smiled a little bit; he couldn't help it.

"But I have, Special Agent Trujillo. I really have. That's the problem."

"Bullshit," she said. "Look, I don't know what put you behind bars originally, but this? You'll be hit with a misdemeanor absconding charge. That's no more than a single year tacked on. That's it. One year. You're still young—three-sixty-five is nothing you can't handle."

Trujillo seemed authentically concerned—not necessarily about his well-being, but about controlling the situation at hand, keeping it from spiraling.

"I'm sorry," Isaac said. "I really wish I could stop. I want to."

"You can."

"I can't," he said. "I'm sorry, Special Agent Trujillo."

Without another word, Isaac went on the attack. Almost instantly, Trujillo and every member of the three-man security team collapsed to the floor like wooden puppets whose strings had been snipped mid-performance. It was over in a split second. The silence of the room was broken by the sounds of dazed groaning. Somewhere, someone was gasping for air.

Isaac quickly approached Trujillo and knelt down next to her body, near her shoulder. Her glasses were askew and her brown eyes were open wide. Pinned to the floor under the insurmountable weight of her own clothing, she appeared to be struggling to take a simple breath. He eased the weight on her torso, but left her limbs stuck fast where they were—her pose reminded him of a child in the middle of making a snow angel. Her chest visibly expanded, and he could hear the rush of air into her lungs.

"I'm sorry," he whispered, and he meant it.

Once the woman's breathing had settled into a normal rhythm, she looked up at him with half-lidded eyes. By all appearances, she was drifting into unconsciousness.

"You won't make it," she murmured, shaking her head back and forth almost imperceptibly. Her eyes were wet. "Whatever you're trying to do. You won't be able to."

Isaac got to his feet, slipped through the steel door near the bulletproof window, and entered what looked like a security control room. A handful of monitors streaming video feeds from various cameras, a wall-mounted rack holding a semi-automatic rifle, and the desk where Trujillo had been seated in front of the glass, evidently reading through an open case file. On the far end of the room was another reinforced steel door, apparently locked.

Isaac stared at the monitors, one after another. The first showed a view of the main lobby just inside the building's entrance. A few people were casually milling around, either coming or going, but that was all—no real activity to speak of.

The next monitor showed a split-screen view of the interior of each elevator car, six of them in total. Three out of the six cars were crammed with multiple teams of FPS security officers, armed with what looked like military-grade assault weapons. The footage was grainy, but he was pretty sure he saw Sergeant Wilkins among them, decked out in an ill-fitting uniform that he must have borrowed from a particularly unlucky colleague.

Wilkins or no Wilkins, one thing was certain: Isaac couldn't allow these guards to reach the thirteenth floor—there were too many of them, and they were too well-armed. He needed to slow them down using the minimum amount of effort, so he did exactly what he used to do with Tallah at the Westgate Mall: he triggered the Maximum Load alarm on every elevator unit, one by one, watching the screen as each car jolted to a halt and the men inside began wandering around, bewildered-looking, searching for a way to escape. The tactic wouldn't hold them off for very long, but it would buy him some time, which hopefully would be enough.

The third monitor showed a view of the FBI waiting area just a few yards from where Isaac was standing. He could see Trujillo and the bodies of the three guards lying motionless on the floor. It was difficult for him to watch. Every instinct screamed at him to return to the waiting area and make sure everyone was still breathing freely, but he couldn't; there wasn't enough time.

The last monitor—the largest one—showed a wide-angle, overhead view of the inside of the FBI offices themselves. A broad, open floorplan with windows along one wall and wooden desks scattered throughout. No cubicles to divide the space into sections; just a single, common area with a hallway at the far end leading to somewhere the camera couldn't reach. He could see dozens of agents hurrying this way and that—the thrum of activity reminded him of the trading floor on a stock exchange, only with a lot more assault rifles involved. He watched as one of the agents—a burly blonde man wearing a blue FBI windbreaker—racked the slide on a pump-action shotgun and charged into the rear corridor, out of the field of view.

The FBI clearly knew that Isaac had arrived. However, he had no reason to believe that they knew (a.) his actual identity, (b.) the reason he was standing outside their front door, or (c.) the fact that he wasn't planning on waiting for them to come out and say hello.

Isaac approached the second metal security door, the one that he believed would eventually lead him to the unsettling scene he'd just witnessed on the video monitor: *namely, the floor full of heavily armed FBI special agents in a state of high alert.* There was a numbered keypad on the wall next to the handle, and next to that, a small video monitor showing footage of a hallway that he could only assume was located on the other side of the locked door. The hallway looked empty—nothing but a long corridor with fluorescent tube lighting ensconced in the ceiling. No agents were standing there waiting for him to emerge, at least none that he could see on-screen.

Since Isaac didn't know the code to unlock the door, and he didn't think Trujillo would be particularly forthcoming with this bit of information, he did the only thing he could think of doing: he ramped up his influence and used it to push. Driving his energy forward, repelling everything in a focused arc. Shoving against the door with his sway. Immediately he heard the sound of wood splintering, plasterboard cracking, metal structures flexing all the way to their stress limits and rupturing. Within seconds, the entire door—along with the frame, as well as a good three feet of the *wall* on either side—burst free and hovered, still under his control, into the hall on the other side of the entryway. He marched close behind, dust and debris trailing in his wake.

Holding the fragmented section of the wall aloft in front of him, and peering around its edges periodically to find his bearings,

Isaac made his way down the hall toward a closed door at the opposite end. It should have been effortless, managing such a modest weight—he'd handled objects several orders of magnitude heavier only weeks ago—but it was a struggle to maintain control over the slab and keep himself upright at the same time. He was fading fast. Even then, he knew it was true, but he couldn't allow himself to stop.

At around the halfway point, Isaac heard a *click-clack* and saw the door at the end of the hallway swing open. A pair of agents wearing sleek body armor and black helmets and holding clear ballistic shields stormed out, knelt down on either side of the entryway, and without hesitation or warning, opened fire with the automatic rifles at their shoulders, a deafening report reverberating through the narrow space.

A swarm of bullets thudded into the thick of the slab, pinging off of the steel door panel, sending tufts of building material drifting through the air like snow, littering the tile with fragments of his makeshift shield. Bits of drywall, metal shavings, concrete nodules, tangled lengths of wire. His ears ringing, teeth gritted, Isaac kept pressing forward, and when he got within a reasonable range, he heightened his influence and propelled the broken wall toward the agents, watching as it hurtled through the air, spinning, seemingly in slow motion. The two men didn't have a chance to react. The impact sent their bodies sprawling backward as though they'd been struck by a speeding vehicle. They slammed into the wall and slid limply to the floor as the slab crashed down nearby. Their ballistic shields, utterly useless against such a colossal mass, clattered on the tile, wobbled for a few seconds, and went silent.

Isaac didn't hesitate; he pressed on. Stepping past the two agents, he pushed forward through the doorway, leaving the hall and entering the area he'd seen in the monitor moments earlier: the auditorium-sized office space of the FBI's San Francisco branch. Immediately he found himself face to face with around fifty special agents. Some had taken cover behind desks, while others were standing with their feet spread apart and handguns drawn, but each of them—to a person—wore an expression that could only be interpreted as one of fear or confusion. He saw no trace of the cocksure swagger he'd somehow expected to encounter.

When he saw what he was up against, he quickly ducked out of the doorway and crouched behind a polished wooden panel emblazoned with the blue-and-yellow FBI insignia. Department of Justice, it read. Federal Bureau of Investigation. Fidelity, Bravery, Integrity.

"I've got no weapons on me," he called out. "I didn't come in here to hurt anybody. You hear me?"

Isaac waited. There was no response.

"There's a child here with you," he said. "She's a young girl—"

His voice unexpectedly broke, and he had to stop himself. His eyes were welling up with tears.

He cleared his throat. "I want you to bring that girl out here and send her over to me. Once you get that done? We're gone. No more problems, no more pain for anybody in here."

Isaac waited again. All he could hear was muted chatter, none of which he could decipher from his position behind the wall.

"Hey," he shouted. "Somebody better talk to me. I'm not playing with any of you right now."

"All right," a man's voice said. "All right. We hear you."

"So bring her out, then," Isaac said. "Tallah Williams. After that, she and I will be up out of here. Gone. End of story."

"I understand, sir," the man said. "My name is Armstrong, and I'm the—"

"I don't need to know all that," Isaac snapped. "All I need is for you bring out Tallah Williams and send her over here. Do it now."

"It's not that simple."

"Well, it better get that simple," Isaac said. "Or it's about to get real complex for you people. I don't think you understand."

Isaac heard more muffled voices, quickly followed by the sounds of hurried movement. Light footfalls, fabric rustling, gear rattling. The barely audible clicks of firearms in motion. The sounds were growing progressively louder with every second that went by.

Someone—a small group—was bearing down on him, converging on his position in what felt like a coordinated, lightning-quick assault.

Isaac didn't stop to think. He scrambled to his feet, stepped out into the open, frantically targeted *everyone*, and let loose. All of the influence that he'd been holding in reserve—everything inside of him that he'd been too afraid to expend out of a sense of self-preservation—he unleashed in a wave.

Every man and woman in the room instantly fell into violent convulsions and then rose from the floor at once—their heads thrown back, mouths wide open, their arms outstretched to either side, their feet pinned together at the ankles—and remained suspended in air around halfway to the ceiling. Weapons slipped from limp fingers and clattered on the tile. It looked as though a mass crucifixion had just taken place using invisible scaffolding. The room was silent.

"Which one of you is Armstrong?" Isaac asked quietly.

Nobody answered. He heard sniffling and moaning, but nothing that resembled a coherent response. At that moment he realized that he'd ratcheted open every set of jaws, wrenching every mouth as wide as it would go, and he'd kept every tongue firmly fixed in place. These poor souls couldn't have spoken an intelligible word if they'd tried.

He relaxed his control for a moment. "Which one of you is Armstrong?" he repeated.

"I am," a voice said. "I'm Armstrong."

Isaac turned and saw a short, sturdy-looking white man suspended in the air above an L-shaped desk at the back of the room. His chin was quivering and the fingers on his left hand twitched spasmodically every few seconds.

"Tell me where she is," Isaac said. "Please. I just want to take her home, that's all. I don't want to hurt anyone."

Armstrong's eyes were wheeling around in his skull.

"Tell me," Isaac said. "It's okay."

"She's in the breakroom, I think. I'm not sure."

"I don't work here, Special Agent Armstrong. I don't know

where that is."

"Down the hall." Armstrong's eyes darted to his left, toward a side corridor. "Down the hall."

His head throbbing, heart racing, Isaac made his way down the corridor, ripping open every door along the way—a couple of empty offices, a conference suite, an interrogation room with a metal table at its center—calling out for his daughter. As he approached the final door, he saw the handle rotate downward and upward again, after which the door slowly swung open to around the halfway mark, its hinges whining in protest.

His daughter peered out into the hallway. Her brow furrowed.

"What do you want?" she demanded.

Lord, help me. She doesn't recognize my face.

"It's me, Tallah," Isaac said. "Listen to my voice. We need to go. Come on."

His daughter didn't move.

"Tallah," he said sharply, snapping his fingers. "We need to get out of here. Now. Let's go."

Tallah stared at him for a few beats. Her brow relaxed and her mouth dropped slightly open.

"Dad?" she said quietly.

Hand in hand, Isaac and his daughter hurried back down the corridor to the main office area, at which point Tallah dug in her heels, dragging him to a halt.

"*Holy shit,*" she whispered, staring up at the bodies in the air. He felt her grip change almost instantly from claw-like to yielding.

"Tallah. We don't have time for this—we have to go."

"Yeah," she said quietly, still staring as though enraptured. "Yeah. All right."

"Tallah," Isaac said. "Move your feet. Come on."

"I am. Why do we even need to—"

"Shh," he hissed. He put a hand on her shoulder.

"Do we really have to—"

"Dammit, Tallah," he snapped. "Be quiet for a second."

Isaac paused with his head cocked, listening.

He heard echoing voices. Heavy footfalls from what sounded like combat boots, and the rattling of tactical equipment attached to duty belts. The sounds were coming from the hallway up ahead, where he'd leveled the two agents with the broken slab of the wall only a few minutes earlier. Someone—almost certainly the army of FPS guards from the three elevator cars, plus an irate Sergeant Wilkins—was only seconds away from coming through the door into the back offices.

They needed to find another way out. Isaac took Tallah's arm by the wrist.

"I need you to do what I do," he said.

She looked at him. "What?"

"Just run," he shouted.

Releasing his control over the group of agents suspended above them, Isaac yanked Tallah to the right and sprinted parallel to the doorway, using his sway to bulldoze a path through the rows of heavy wooden desks, sending them airborne, cartwheeling end-over-end in either direction. As the limp bodies of the agents plummeted to the tile on every side of them, smacking the tile like a wave of suicides, Isaac targeted one of the floor-to-ceiling windows directly ahead and shattered the pane outward, sending a cascade of tempered glass chips bursting into empty space. He could hear the rattle-crack of gunfire at their backs as he towed Tallah, screaming, to the edge of the broken window and—with the wind howling in their faces—leapt blindly through the jagged fissure into the open sky, dragging his daughter along with him.

They fell together, the way family always seems to. By around the seventh floor, Isaac was able to slow them down using the same method he'd used when he slowed his own descent after his encounter with Gates. Sheer repulsion. But this time he had to figure out how to repel the world around him while still holding fast to his only child.

Cradling Tallah in his arms, he took them down toward the Civic Center Plaza and a throng of astonished spectators. People pointing, capturing video with their phones, yelling what sounded like obscenities. As they approached the ground, Isaac realized that he was coming in too quickly, and because of his current condition—weakened, dizzy, and nauseous—he wasn't able to decelerate. Over the final ten feet, his mind gave out completely and they plummeted, Tallah screaming in his ear, to the concrete plaza below.

The moment they landed, he heard a sharp, wet snap, and he knew that he'd broken his leg. High up, somewhere between his knee and pelvis. The pain was almost blinding. He cried out—he couldn't stop himself.

He tried to climb to his feet, to find Tallah among the swarming crowd, but he staggered, lurched forward and collapsed, his vision dwindling away to black.

chapter eight

Isaac heard familiar voices. A casual back-and-forth banter, comforting somehow, even though he wasn't a part of it. The feeling reminded him of times when he was a child, lying face-down on a fold-out cot in the front room on a Saturday morning, drifting in and out of sleep while his momma and Auntie Freedie worked on breakfast in the kitchenette—dark coffee, applewood bacon, corn cakes, sweet potato hash with Tabasco mayonnaise—at the same time as they worked on the countless sister issues left over from when they were little girls: loss, abuse, neglect, abandonment, and a series of betrayals and petty slights, perceived or otherwise. Isaac didn't know about any of those things at the time, of course—as he grew up a little bit, he came to understand that there were some heavy matters being considered over the stove, but that was all he knew. Even when they were busy debating the most difficult topics from their childhood, and even when things got as hot as the stovetop coils themselves (which they definitely did on occasion), Momma and Freedie had a knack for making their arguments seem, from the outside at least, like plain *talk*. But by the time they'd finished with their plain talk, they were always the better for it. It made them closer, all that time spent in the kitchenette together. You could just tell with a single look.

Isaac opened his eyes. He was laid out on a brown leather sofa in a space he'd never seen before: a living room in an old house or a high-turnover apartment. His left leg had been wrapped in a dark blue compression splint with metal bars running down each side, and a couple of red throw pillows had been tucked underneath his knee and ankle, elevating his foot—which had been covered up to the heel with one of Tallah's purple bobby socks.

Slowly, painstakingly, he shifted his body into a seated position, something he regretted almost instantly. He felt dazed and weak— highly medicated. His thigh was throbbing, but the pain was tolerable as long as he kept his movements to a minimum.

Isaac looked around. A pair of aluminum crutches and a collapsible wheelchair were leaning up against the wall by the front door, as if he needed another tangible reminder of the condition he was in. And if that weren't enough, there was a blue plastic bucket resting on the carpet next to the sofa, and judging by the stomach-turning smell it was exuding, he'd used it at least once, and probably more than that.

The room itself was modest: two bookshelves lined with paperbacks and college-level textbooks (psychology, organic chemistry), a wall-mounted television, a circular glass-topped coffee table, a brass floor lamp, a bright red beanbag chair, a sliding door that led outside to a small patio area. At the far-end of the room, the '70s-era carpet gave way to a patch of yellowish linoleum that he could only assume was the edge of the kitchen floor.

The voices he'd heard earlier had quieted. Every once in a while he could hear the sounds of flatware and ceramic dishes clinking against each other. Isaac cleared his throat. It felt as though he hadn't spoken a word in months.

"Hello?" he said.

A few seconds passed, and then it happened:

In walked Miss Leti Sanders from the kitchenette.

They talked for a long time—an hour at least. Leti sat curled up on the beanbag chair and looked at Isaac with those eyes of hers, and even in the state he was in, he could still appreciate the power that this woman wielded over him; in fact, she had such a profound impact that he wondered whether the painkillers he'd obviously been given had somehow amplified her magical effects. Either way, whether he'd been chemically enhanced or not, Isaac was picking up everything Leti Sanders was throwing down at the moment. Unfortunately, most of what she was throwing down was bad news.

As expected, the escape from the federal building a few days earlier (a few *days* had passed) was all over the news, much like the prior incidents had been—only this time, Isaac Williams wasn't the focus of the stories, which was also expected since he hadn't even been present at the time, or at least, his real face hadn't been. The focus of the current stories was a young, twenty-something, African-American, convicted drug dealer named Deron Coates, which would've been just fine if Deron had been the sole focus, or even the primary one. But he wasn't. Tallah was getting equal face-time in every single story, sometimes even more than Deron himself.

Yes, the video footage released to the public showed endless loops of Isaac's younger self rampaging through the thirteenth floor in the guise of Deron Coates, and yes, the news programs chewed up plenty of time (and the articles spilled gallons of ink, electronic and otherwise) debating the realism of what had been captured on camera, whether there were alternative explanations for the phenomena, and if not, what did it mean for modern society that random Black men were apparently developing the ability to defy the laws of physics for no obvious reason apart from natural, raw talent. But that wasn't all the stories focused on. Every reporter, every talking head, every host of every second-rate cable television show—all of them were enamored with the story of an eleven-year-old girl in police custody who'd been dramatically rescued by a felon twice her age. Who were they to each other? Were they related? Were they in a relationship? Tallah's face was being splashed all over the television, online, and in print. And it was all her father's fault.

"Where is she now?" Isaac asked quietly.

Leti gestured over her shoulder.

"She's watching Anthony for me. Last I saw, they were sorting my nylons into two piles: those with rips and those without. It's a real project, believe me."

"How is she doing?"

Leti hesitated.

"Tal is pretty angry, Isaac," she said.

"Of course she's angry. Look at everything that's happened to her."

"No," Leti said. "She's not focused on what happened. She's angry at *you*, Isaac."

"For real?" he said.

"I'm afraid so."

"Come on, Let, you've got to give me more than that. How bad are we talking? Is she really mad?"

"I don't know the girl well enough to say," Leti replied, shrugging. "All I know is that you're going to have to deal with her feelings while you still can, Ize."

Isaac stared in disbelief. He honestly wasn't sure if he'd heard her correctly.

"Did you just say while I still *can?*" he asked. "What's that supposed to mean?"

"Sorry. That came out wrong, okay? I'm sorry."

"So what are you trying to say, then?"

Leti shook her head. Judging by the expression on her face, it was obvious that she had more bad news to share.

"Listen," she said. "That doctor friend of yours, Dr. Stick Figure? She came here a few days ago to patch you up, and she's been to the house looking in on you, bringing supplies, checking on things. Do you remember her being here?"

Do I remember?

Isaac thought about it for a moment.

"Not even a little bit," he replied. "Her name is Dr. Thompson, by the way. But she's not my 'doctor friend,' Leti. I barely know her."

"That's fine—none of my business. My point is that Tal reached out to her and she came over here. Multiple times. Hence, the sling on your leg, the pills, and so on, and so forth. She even took a vial of your blood, Ize. She's obviously really worried about your health."

"Me?" he quipped, thumping himself on the chest. "I've never felt better in my life. What could she possibly be worried about?"

Leti didn't smile, and she didn't answer right away. It looked like she was stalling, which was a terrible sign, given the way she usually relished getting directly to the heart of the matter.

"The doctor thinks you've got something pretty bad going on, Isaac," Leti said. "Not the leg. Something inside you. That kind of bad."

Isaac was silent. Even though he desperately wanted to put up a fight, to argue that he was fine and that Dr. Thompson was a charlatan who didn't know what the hell she was talking about, the truth was that he'd suspected for a while that there was something seriously wrong with his overall constitution. This just served as a confirmation.

"Anyhow," Leti continued. "The doctor wants you to come over to Valley Med and do some 'next-level testing' to help figure out what's going on. And speaking of that, I really don't care for how she talks about you, Ize—it's like she's *fascinated* or something. Like she thinks of you as some kind of medical specimen, something to learn from. I get no sense that she actually gives a damn about your well-being. She just enjoys the challenge you represent."

"But she'll help me. That's what you're saying?"

Leti shrugged. "She told me she'd try."

"Even though I'm a fugitive?"

"That's what I'm trying to tell you," Leti said. "Anybody with any logic—which you'd expect a physician to have in surplus, by the way—wouldn't come near your Wanted self if you paid them a fortune to do it. But this chick? She's apparently ready to lose her job, her license, her *life* over trying to administer sweet, sweet care to Mr. Isaac Williams, man on the run. It's unreal. Unless you're sleeping with her and not saying so, it doesn't make a damn bit of sense whatsoever."

"It's not even about me," Isaac said. "I think it's all about Tallah."

Leti's eyebrows raised.

"What are you talking about?" she said.

"I'm just guessing, yeah? But I'm pretty sure Dr. Thompson is trying to help Tallah by helping me. Strong fathers make strong daughters: that kind of thing. Maybe the doctor sees a little bit of herself in Tallah—I have no idea, honestly. But either way, I'm not about to slap away an open hand, not at this point. If she wants to help me, I'm ready. Help me, baby. Please."

"Fair enough," Leti said. "And I want you to get help, Isaac, believe me. I'm just telling you to get the right kind of help, that's all."

Isaac snorted. "Well, how about we call all the doctors we know, put them in a big room, and interview them one by one. Ask for references and all that. Sound like a plan?"

Leti was silent. Isaac cursed himself.

"I'm sorry," he said. "Okay? I'm sorry."

"You should be. And because you're so tore up and *stank* right now, I'm going to forgive you," Leti said, climbing out the beanbag chair and getting on her feet. "But let me tell you something: If you really want to go out into the world and see this doctor, we need to get you ready first."

"Get me ready how?"

"A good, long shower, first of all," she said, pinching her nose. "But after that, you need to do something about that face."

My face. He'd completely forgotten about it.

Isaac reached up and touched his forehead, his cheeks, his jawline, the back of his head.

"It's you, Isaac," Leti said, watching him. "The real you, I mean. Looking gorgeous, as always, I might add. Though I have to admit: I kind of miss that fine young thing we brought in here a few days back. Where'd that little boy run off to?"

Isaac smiled; he couldn't help it. And his smile felt completely natural—effortless—now that he was himself again.

"Anyway," Leti said, "that lovely face you were wearing is officially off the list, whether I like it or not. Now that it's been associated with Deron Coates: Wanted Felon, you can't ever use it again, Ize. We're going to have to go in a different direction with your appearance this time. I'm thinking older. Something distinguished-looking and gentlemanly."

"Fine. Older it is," Isaac said, adjusting his position on the sofa.

He suddenly felt energized, motivated, and oddly hopeful, in spite of the enormous odds he knew were still stacked against him. *Always forward.* He pulled the throw pillows out from under his leg and set them on the carpet, then turned his body slightly so he could start the painstaking process of *getting off his behind* (which felt plastered to the sofa cushion), but before he could rotate more than a couple of inches to one side, he felt an electric pain shoot from his thigh all the way up to his left shoulder blade. It was all he could do to keep from crying out. He looked up at Leti pleadingly.

She was standing, hands on her hips, near the kitchen entryway.

"Can you help me, please?" he asked.

Leti managed to transfer him to the wheelchair and prop his leg on the fold-down metal footrest, after which he pushed himself slowly down a hallway toward the guest bathroom. This was Leti's momma's house, he learned, so everything from the countertops to the bathtubs had been conveniently set up for a seventy-three-year-old woman with advanced Parkinson's disease. All the important items were low to the ground, stainless-steel grab bars had been bolted to the walls, and every single section of the house was designed for a wheelchair user, with wide door frames and ramps instead of stairs. On his way down the hall, he passed by an open doorway and saw Tallah seated cross-legged on the carpet next to a small boy—toddler-aged, maybe two years old, with rich dark skin and tight little angel curls. Leti's son, Anthony. The boy was elbow-deep in a drawer that someone had pulled out of the nearby bureau.

Anthony and Tallah looked up at him with twin sets of wide, brown eyes, but Tallah quickly looked away.

"Hey, sweetheart," Isaac said. His own eyes were welling up again.

"Hey," she answered, staring toward the carpet.

It wasn't the most lackluster greeting he'd ever received in his life, but it was probably one of the most painful.

"I'm sorry, Tallah," he said quietly. "I know this has been hard, and you've gone through a lot, but I'm so proud of you—the way you've handled everything."

Tallah kept her eyes focused downward. She reached into the drawer on the carpet in front of her, pulled out a pair of white athletic socks, separated them, and tossed one to Anthony, who immediately shoved the elastic end into his mouth.

Eventually she shrugged by way of a response.

"Tallah, please look at me," he said.

Reluctantly, she did.

"What," she demanded, rolling her eyes.

"Can you talk to me? Please?"

"About what?"

"Come on. I'm trying here, Tallah," he said. "Just talk to me."

Tallah shrugged. "Okay. Fine," she said. "I'm talking."

"Can you tell me what's on your mind?"

She snorted. "Let's see. I want everything to go back to normal. I want to go home. I want my phone back. I want to see Cherie. I want you to leave me alone. How's that?"

"Wait," he said. "Where's your phone?"

"The police took it," Tallah replied, staring daggers. "It's probably still in that building somewhere."

"Oh, I'm sorry, sweetheart. I really am."

"Then why did you do it?" she asked angrily.

"Do what?"

"Everything," she spat. "If you would have just left me alone, everything would've been okay."

"Left you alone."

"Yes."

Isaac shook his head. "At which point should I have left you alone, Tallah?" he asked. "At the school? When the officer had his knee in your back? How about when he pulled your hair? Is that when I was supposed to leave you alone?"

"Yes."

"I was supposed to just watch—is that what you're saying?"

"Yes," Tallah shot back.

"Well, you don't know what you're talking about, Tallah. Maybe one day when you're a parent, you'll understand why I wasn't about to stand there and watch my only child get treated worse than a rabid dog."

"I didn't want your help," Tallah said.

"I think you did, actually. But, in any case, you needed it."

"You're wrong," she said. "You should've let it happen. It was supposed to happen the way it did, and you ruined it."

Lord, have mercy. What is this child talking about?

"You're telling me that I ruined something by keeping your head from getting stomped into the floor. That's what you're telling me?"

"Can we just stop? I don't even want to be talking about this."

"No, we can't stop. Tell me, Tallah. What did I ruin by stepping in when I did? Tell me."

Anthony suddenly broke down into tears. Wailing. His mouth wide open. Tallah scooped him up and held him in her arms, rocking, shushing gently.

"You need to keep your voice down," she said, shaking her head.

"I'm sorry," Isaac said quietly, "but you need to answer the question, Tallah. Please."

"It doesn't matter anymore," she said. "As soon as I get a chance, I'm going to the police."

"And why would you do that?"

"I'm going to apologize for what I did and take the consequences."

Isaac stared at her for a few seconds, speechless.

"The hell you are," he said.

"I am. You can't stop me, and you shouldn't be trying to. You're supposed to be telling me to do the right thing. You're the grownup."

"The right thing isn't throwing your life away, Tallah."

She gestured to the four walls of the bedroom. "I'm hiding in a stranger's house, Dad," she said. "I have no life."

Isaac felt his anger rising again. He had to take a moment to collect himself before continuing.

"Sweetheart," he said. "I can understand how you'd blame me for what happened, because it was my fault in a way, but look—you're not getting thrown into the system, Tallah. You're not going to become a number in a cage somewhere. Do you understand? We're going to find someplace safe, you and me, and we're going to start over again, just like we did a hundred times before. We're just going to need to be more careful this time, that's all."

By that point, Anthony had made a full recovery. He was squirming in Tallah's arms, arching his back, trying to get back to his business. She let him go.

"I'm not going with you," she said.

"I hear you, Tallah. I hear you loud and clear. And we can talk about it more later, but for now, you don't make any moves without me, you hear? I'm dead serious."

Tallah didn't respond. She reached into the sock drawer, pulled out a pair of black dress socks, and dropped them into Anthony's lap.

Isaac didn't have time for this. He could feel the pain medicine wearing off, and in any case, the sooner he could get Dr. Thompson's help, the sooner he could talk some sense into Tallah and get them both out of the Bay Area, out of California, and out of the country itself, more likely than not. He was considering Canada, but Brazil was another possibility. Maybe somewhere in Africa—Liberia? Or maybe Ghana. Ghana was a country he'd heard was open to people from the United States.

"One more thing," he said. "Please. Let me say thank you, sweetheart. Thank you so much for helping me." He pointed to his leg, propped up on the metal footrest. "I don't remember much of what happened after we hit the ground, but Miss Sanders told me that you got me out of there. So thank you."

Tallah looked uncomfortable—he wasn't sure why.

"Okay," she said, shrugging.

By the time Isaac had finished showering, shaving, and dressing in some of Leti's late father's old clothes—a brown tweed suit with a herringbone pattern, a matching porkpie hat, and a white button-down shirt—it was early afternoon. Sitting in the wheelchair, positioned in front of the bathroom vanity, Isaac took off the hat and set it on the counter next to the sink, stared at his face in the mirror for a little while (it was strange seeing the old version of himself again), and then went to work.

Just like he did in the motel room in San Jose, he used a subtle version of his influence (what he'd come to think of as his *gravitational scalpel*) to alter his appearance again, only this time he didn't fight against the effects of gravity. He assisted them. Lowering his brow, drawing down the skin around his eyes, his mouth, his jawline, creating creases and folds where none had existed before, Isaac aged himself by forty years, at a minimum. And he didn't stop there. Because he no longer needed his face to match any particular image on an identification card (at least, not for the time being), he took liberties with his features that he couldn't have taken otherwise. He pushed his nose inward, flared his ears slightly outward, and added volume to his cheeks. By the time he'd completed his makeover, not only did he look like an elderly gentleman with an impeccable fashion sense, but he also looked like a complete and utter stranger. There was nothing left of his true identity whatsoever.

He put on the porkpie hat, arranged it at a slight tilt, and wheeled his way out of the bathroom. In the process, he nearly plowed right into his daughter, who was holding Anthony on her hip. When she saw him, her eyes widened. She looked absolutely terrified.

"It's me, baby," Isaac said. "It's okay. It's just me."

Leti drove him to Valley Medical Center in her mother's white minivan. She pulled into the circular driveway leading to the Urgent Care entrance and dropped him off, helping him climb into the wheelchair before driving away without a goodbye or even a backward glance.

Isaac had arranged to meet Dr. Thompson via a text message sent from Leti's phone. Same cubicle as the last time he was there—the infamous kidney stone visit. He wheeled awkwardly through the automatic doors, pushed through the crowded waiting area, bypassing the front reception desk altogether, and made his way to the treatment wing. No one seemed to give him a second glance, which confirmed what he'd always heard about getting older: that it's the process of turning more and more invisible until, one day, you disappear entirely.

When Isaac rolled up to the now-familiar cubicle, the bluish-green privacy screen was open and Dr. Thompson was sitting on the swivel stool, staring at the phone in her hand, her wire-framed glasses perched on top of her head. She looked just as gaunt and exhausted as he remembered, almost like he would imagine a prisoner of war to look.

"Hello?" he said, knocking lightly on the edge of the cubicle wall.

Dr. Thompson glanced up at him, then returned her attention to the phone. "You can't be back here unaccompanied," she said, swiping the screen. "You need to check in at the front desk, sir. I'm sorry."

"Lorietta," he said. "It's me."

Dr. Thompson lowered the phone, plucked the glasses out of her hair, and put them on her nose. Her eyes widened.

"Sweet Jesus on the cross," she said. "I knew you'd look different, but Lord—you weren't joking around."

"I tried to tell you. It's the same me, just wrapped in a more *sage* package."

Dr. Thompson pocketed her phone and got on her feet.

"All right, Mr. Sage," she said. "Let's find somewhere we can really talk, shall we?"

Dr. Thompson wheeled Isaac to her private office on the sixth floor, nothing more than a desk, two chairs, a filing cabinet, and a window. The walls were completely barren—no photos, no artwork, not even the requisite framed diplomas showing off her alma maters. The place looked more like a repurposed closet than a proper physician's office.

They sat across the desk from each other while Isaac reported how he'd been feeling, the symptoms he'd been experiencing, and whether he'd noticed any changes for the better or worse. Dr. Thompson didn't ask a single question—not one—about his broken leg, focusing all of her attention on exploring the physiological effects of what she referred to as "manipulating the continuum." She was hungry to know as much as she could—it was obvious. Her eyes wide, her posture straight and tall, she dutifully recorded almost every word Isaac said with a ballpoint pen and a yellow legal notepad like a lawyer preparing for trial. From an outside perspective, the conversation probably would have appeared perfectly normal—a physician talking with her elderly patient about his myriad health issues—which made it all the more ridiculous to consider that his health issues were caused by what amounted to a *magic power*, and the only reason he was elderly in the first place was because of that power's effects. The fact that Dr. Thompson and he could sit across from each other blithely discussing his condition as if it were an everyday medical occurrence or natural consequence of the ageing process made him seriously question their shared grasp on reality.

Eventually, Dr. Thompson seemed to run out of either questions or time, he wasn't sure which.

"Okay," she said, pulling a manila file folder from a desk drawer. "Your blood work came back, and based on that, plus the physical exams I've performed, plus the scan results from your last visit, I'm as ready as I can be to draw a conclusion about your condition."

She paused, looking at him expectantly.

"Uh. Okay," he said. "Please proceed."

Her face immediately brightened to the point that her identity appeared almost as altered as his own, and all at once Isaac saw her excitement on full display—her *fascination*, as Leti described it—revealing exactly what he represented to Dr. Thompson: he was an object of interest, and nothing more. But he was all right with that, truth be told. He didn't need the doctor to care about him on a personal level; he just needed her to *provide* a certain level of professional care. If Dr. Thompson got something tangible out of treating Isaac like a glorified science project, then so be it—in fact, he would have said she'd earned the privilege after all she'd done for him so far, especially given the multiple risks involved.

Dr. Thompson opened the manila folder, pulled out a stapled packet of papers, and set them on the desk in front of her.

"When I look at the collection of signs and symptoms you're reporting—taking them individually or as a whole, either way—they could be anything. Vertigo? Nausea? Disorientation? Muscle weakness? These are common symptoms of literally hundreds of maladies, Isaac, both common and rare. Taken alone, your reported symptoms are more or less meaningless."

"I appreciate that. Thanks so much."

"I don't mean 'meaningless' as a value judgment," she said, shaking her head. "My point is that these symptoms, in and of themselves, don't have a lot of diagnostic significance. They're still useful when examined in the larger context, of course."

Isaac shrugged. "Of course."

"Right. So, when I look at your reported symptoms, *plus* your recent health history, *plus* your scan results, *plus* your blood work, things start to get interesting." Dr. Thompson suddenly looked alive—*awake*. "First of all, your blood work shows the presence of calcium in excess—hypercalcemia, it's called. That was the reason for your kidney stones, by the way. It also points to the reason why your leg was broken relatively easily, in a pretty unusual location for such a serious fracture. Okay? So, here's the bottom line: you have severe osteoporosis, Isaac. Loss of bone density. It's real, and it's dramatic."

Isaac couldn't believe what he was hearing.

"Osteoporosis?" he said. "Come on, Doc. I know I look old, but come on."

Dr. Thompson shrugged. "You are experiencing severe bone loss, which results in increased calcium excretion. I don't know how else to put it."

"Lord. Unbelievable."

"Just bear with me," Dr. Thompson said. "That's not even the extent of it. It gets better."

Isaac stared at her.

"Better?" he said. "This is my life, Lorietta. Please remember that I'm more than just your next research paper, okay?"

"Of course. I'm sorry. I didn't mean 'better,'" she said. "What I mean is that once we add bone loss to the overall equation, a reasonably logical—though surprising—conclusion presents itself."

"All right, then. What is it?"

Dr. Thompson put an elbow on the desk and held up her closed hand.

"Nausea," she said, raising her index finger.

"Vertigo." She raised the next finger.

"Disorientation." She raised another finger.

"Muscle weakness." She raised her pinky finger.

"And now, acute bone loss." She raised her thumb.

"As luck would have it," she continued, "there's only one, select group of people who experience the onset of these exact symptoms over relatively brief periods of time, just like you have."

She paused, clearly enjoying herself and making no obvious effort to conceal it from Isaac, the unfortunate subject of her long, drawn-out announcement.

"Just tell me," he said. "Please."

Dr. Thompson smiled. "Astronauts."

It took Isaac a moment to process what she'd just said.

"Astronauts?"

"Those who have experienced low-gravity environments over a matter of months. Yes," she replied.

"You've got to be kidding me."

"No, seriously," Dr. Thompson said, still grinning. She looked like a child on Christmas morning. "Think about it. Low gravity environments have significant effects on the human body—it's well established. So, by extension, if you take a person who can create low-gravity environments, it might make sense that he or she would experience similar physiological effects. Again, this is just speculation—how could I know for sure? It's unprecedented. But you have to admit, the argument is compelling."

"That's fine, Doc, but what does it mean?" he asked. "Assuming it's true. What am I supposed to do next?"

"Well, when an astronaut returns to Earth and experiences Earth's gravity again, typically the body returns to normal functioning over time. So, if the theory is correct, you should be able to regain what you've lost as well. You just need to stop the underlying behavior."

Isaac thought about what she'd just told him.

"So I need to stop using my abilities," he said.

"If you want to heal. Yes. You would need to stop completely."

"For how long?"

Dr. Thompson stared toward the ceiling for a few moments.

"Well, if we're continuing the analogy, it can take years for astronauts to readapt to normal gravity after spaceflight, depending on how long they've been gone," she said. "If I were you, I would plan on quitting cold-turkey and not even think about using your abilities until you've healed physically—and that assumes that the damage you've done is reversible, which it may not be, Isaac. There's no way we can know until we watch and see how your body responds to rest."

Isaac was silent. He didn't know how to react. The truth was that none of the information he'd just heard should have surprised him as much as it had. If the past six months had taught him anything, it was that using his sway with abandon had been killing him, slowly but surely. He may not have known whether the effects were cumulative, but he knew that the effects were *negative*, that he was damaging his body, which shouldn't have required a doctor's confirmation for him to accept. Clearly he'd been in absolute denial. He'd wanted so badly to continue down the same reckless path, exercising his influence at will without any regard for his own well-being, that he'd never allowed himself to consider—to truly entertain the idea—that he might someday need to stop entirely. The idea felt the same as contemplating never using his arm again. Or his voice. The sense of loss he felt at the thought of abandoning his abilities was that significant.

But it was what it was. What could he do other than move forward?

"Are you okay?" Dr. Thompson asked. It seemed genuine; some of her core humanity had somehow broken through the excitement she felt over the discovery.

"I'm all right," he said. "I appreciate your help."

Isaac spent the next two hours in treatment. His leg was x-rayed, revealing a transverse distal fracture of the femur. The break was relatively serious, but not so serious that it would require surgery to correct—no pins, no screws, no plates, no external metal frame, and therefore, no added recovery time—which was the best piece of news he'd received in a good while.

Afterward, he visited the Cast Room, where a couple of technicians applied a full-length plaster cast to the leg, starting at his ankle and ending near his groin. He'd have to wear that cumbersome apparatus on his leg for three months, he was told. And that was the best-case scenario. It could be as long as half-a-year before the break would heal.

Once the cast had been applied, Dr. Thompson wheeled Isaac to an unmarked supply room on the second floor, and after waiting in the room for around fifteen minutes, a woman he'd never seen before delivered two unlabeled bottles of prescription pills (without an accompanying prescription, of course) and tossed them into his lap before scurrying away without a word. One of the bottles contained oxycodone for the pain, and the other contained *alendronic acid* to help strengthen his prematurely brittle bones, according to Dr. Thompson.

In short, Isaac received a full course of treatment, which was nothing short of astonishing. The fact that Dr. Thompson was able to arrange such a wide range of services for a person with no name, no identification, and no evidence of financial coverage was a minor miracle in itself, and although he had no idea how she'd made it happen (other than illegally), he wasn't about to refuse a single kindness he was offered, in spite of how underserving he felt. The only question was how he would continue to receive medical treatment—how would he get more pills, have the cast removed, verify that the bone had healed as expected, for example—when he was living as a fugitive out on the run, secreting himself in an unfamiliar place without any real money, resources, family, or friends. Isaac had no idea what he would do when the time came. But he couldn't worry about it at the moment. For now, he needed to take whatever he could get and be grateful.

Once Isaac had the pills, it was time to go. He used Dr. Thompson's phone to text Leti that he was ready, pocketed the smoked-orange medicine bottles, and wheeled his way out of the supply room and down the second-floor hallway toward the elevators, the good doctor walking by his side like a genuinely concerned and committed physician might. They passed a sign for the Cardiac Catheter Lab, another sign for General Surgery, and as they rolled by a third sign for Ambulatory Recovery, Isaac caught sight of a white man in a wheelchair struggling to back his way through an open doorway that led into an inpatient room. What struck him about the man was his clothing: he was wearing the full dress blues of a San Jose police officer, with one major modification—he was wearing short pants instead of slacks. Both of the man's legs were encased in bulky metal braces with long screws embedded directly into his swollen flesh.

Isaac recognized the man right away. This was the police officer he'd injured in the portable building at Tallah's school. Even though he was folded into a wheelchair, the man still looked every bit as tall and athletic—just as imposing—as he had on the day of the incident. Gates had said that the officer's name was Chauncey.

Without thinking it through, Isaac stopped, pivoted the chair, and pushed it in the direction of the room.

"Isaac," Dr. Thompson hissed.

He ignored her.

"Dammit, Isaac."

He kept right on going. At this point, Chauncey had navigated through the doorway, and was no longer visible. Before long, his chair came to a hard stop, and Dr. Thompson leaned over his shoulder until her mouth was a few inches from his ear. He could feel the warmth of her breath against his cheek.

"What are you trying to do here?" she whispered.

Isaac didn't know the answer to that.

"Do you know who that is?" he asked quietly.

"Of course I do. Everybody in the hospital knows who that is."

"Then you know why I need to do this. I have to—"

"No," Dr. Thompson said. "Actually, I don't know why, and you don't have to do squat other than leave."

"I'm just going to talk to him," Isaac said.

Was that the truth?

In reality, Isaac wasn't sure what he was going to do—in his heart he wanted nothing more than to maim the officer even more than he already had.

"Why, Isaac? What good could possibly come of interacting with this man, after everything that's happened?"

"Let go."

"What?"

"Let go of the chair, Lorietta," he said quietly.

There was a long pause. Isaac couldn't see her face, but he could imagine her expression—mouth pinched into a pucker, the worry lines carved deep into her brow.

"This is my job you're playing with, Isaac," Dr. Thompson said. "If you do this, don't expect any more help from me. I'm serious. You can figure everything out on your own from here on out."

"I hear you," he said. "And I understand."

"Good."

"So let me thank you for what you've done for me and Tallah. Please let me go."

After a few seconds, he felt her hold break. The resistance gave way, and he pushed ahead.

When Isaac reached the entryway to the recovery room, he saw Officer Chauncey seated in his wheelchair next to the window, staring outside. The man seemed older than he'd remembered—maybe it was the fact that Chauncey appeared more vulnerable with his legs propped up, or maybe the man was simply exhausted, a side effect of his recovery from surgery, poor sleep on an uncomfortable hospital mattress, or the media circus that had no doubt surrounded him over the course of the past few days. Whatever the reason, Chauncey looked like he'd rather be almost anywhere else. In fact, judging by his expression, if the window had been open, Isaac might have concluded that the man had been considering making the leap.

Before long, Chauncey turned to look at him. His blue eyes were so pale that they were almost indistinguishable from the surrounding whites.

"Can I help you find something?" the man asked.

It didn't come off as a veiled threat—Chauncey was being genuine as far as he could tell. The fact that the man hadn't told him to leave made it clear that invisibility wasn't the only byproduct of looking older: when people stopped seeing you, they also stopped viewing you as suspicious, as potentially dangerous. As a possible physical threat.

"I came to speak with you, actually," Isaac said.

Chauncey smiled.

"Well come on in, then," he said.

Isaac wheeled his way further into the room. The space had

been nearly filled to capacity with a kaleidoscopic array of helium balloons, elaborate floral arrangements, and at least twenty oversized, handmade Get Well cards from Mrs. Simmons' third-grade class at Summer Hill Academy. In the far corner, next to an adjustable bed and a few unfamiliar medical devices, was a child—a little white girl with long brown curls, not much younger than Tallah by the looks of her—seated in a green visitor's chair and staring at a tablet computer on the table in front of her. She didn't look up.

"I'm Alan," the officer said. "Alan Chauncey. And this is my daughter, Julie. Say hi, sweetheart."

"Hi," the girl said, still looking down.

After a few seconds of awkward silence, Isaac realized that he needed to politely reciprocate.

"I'm Calvin," he said. "Nice to meet you both."

"All right then, Calvin. As you might be able to tell, I'm planning on checking out of here at some point today and going home." He gestured toward an open suitcase lying on the foot of the bed. "So I'm kind of busy at the moment. But is there something I can do for you?"

"I just wanted to ask you about what happened at the school," Isaac said. "When you got hurt. I guess I just want to hear about it."

Chauncey frowned.

"I should probably stop you right there," the man said. "I'm all the way done with talking about the individual who did this to me, so if that's what you want to hear about, I'm sorry. I can't help you."

"No. Not him," Isaac said.

"Then what?"

"I want to talk about the little girl. Tallah Williams," he said. "I want you to help me understand why you did what you did to her."

Chauncey stared at him for a few moments.

"Why?" he asked. "You're some relative of hers?"

"I am."

Chauncey nodded, then rubbed his face with both hands a few times, exhaling loudly.

"Look," he said. "Normally I wouldn't be talking to you at all, sir, but I'll do you the courtesy of telling you the same thing I've told everybody since this whole thing blew up. I regret what happened. Period. I sincerely do. I already told the father—who I assume is, what, your son or your son-in-law?—anyhow, I told the father on the day of the incident that I didn't want it to go down the way it did. The school called the station with a complaint, I responded per the normal protocol, the girl chose to put her hands on a police officer, and she was lawfully detained as a result. I don't know what else to tell you."

"Lawfully?"

"Hell yes, lawfully," Chauncey said. "Look here. I understand that this is your family we're talking about. Blood is blood, no matter what happens, so I can see how it would be upsetting to watch from the sidelines. I can sympathize with that. But what more do you want from me, sir? The girl broke the law by not complying."

"And if she'd been your daughter?"

"What does that mean, sir?"

"If it had been Julie in that situation," Isaac said, nodding toward the girl. "Would you have been okay with a cop handling her the way you did? Even if she was in the wrong?"

Chauncey snorted. "My daughter would never be in that situation."

"That's only because the police would never have been called," Isaac said.

chapter nine

Leti picked Isaac up from the hospital.

They didn't speak much during the drive home—Isaac told her about Dr. Thompson's spaceflight theories, and that was the end of it. He wasn't in the mood for a heart-to-heart, not even with Leti Sanders. His conversation with Chauncey had left him feeling demoralized and defeated, and he wasn't even sure why. What had he been expecting? An apology? Some form of acknowledgement of his daughter's suffering at the man's hands? A promise to do something differently the next time he was called into the field to police a child? Whatever Isaac had been hoping to hear, the officer hadn't said it, and the truth was that he'd been foolish to hope for anything more. In fact, he'd probably been lucky that Chauncey had taken the time to talk to him at all.

Leti pulled the minivan into the driveway in front of her mother's house, shifted into Park, and killed the engine. She opened the garage door using a remote clipped to the sun visor, got out of the vehicle, came around to the sliding side door, and pulled out the collapsible wheelchair from in between two rows of seats. She set it on the ground and unfolded it, locking down the tabs on either side.

"Hey," Isaac said, watching her. She was straightening out the chair, testing its stability. She looked up at him.

"Thank you again for everything you're doing for me," he said. "I know I've asked for too much, but you still delivered, every time— even when I know I didn't deserve it. I appreciate you to the fullest, Let. Serious. I hope you understand that."

She smiled. "All true, every word," she said. "And you're very welcome. Now get your behind into the chair and let's get inside."

With Leti's help, Isaac climbed out of the minivan and lowered himself carefully onto the padded seat. She propped his leg on the folding metal footrest, and then Isaac pushed himself into the garage through the open bay.

Inside the main room of the house, Isaac found Tallah seated on the sofa with her feet tucked underneath her body, her long thin braids falling loosely around her face. She was staring down at her lap, and her hands were empty—no paperback, no magazine, no writing notebook, no electronic device. The television was turned off, and the room was quiet, save the crisp ticking of a wooden wall clock. As far as Isaac could tell, Tallah was just sitting and thinking, which would have been fine, perhaps even admirable, had it not been so far out of his daughter's normal character.

"Hey," he said.

She didn't look up.

"Tallah?"

"Hey," she said, still focusing downward.

Isaac stared at her. The simplest explanation was this: She was still upset with him over the idea of leaving the Bay Area, leaving her school, leaving her friends—Isaac knew that it would be a long time, if ever, before he'd be forgiven for this catalogue of offenses. But something about her demeanor still bothered him. None of it was typical *Tallah is angry at Dad* behavior. He'd seen his daughter upset with him more times than he could count, and in his memory she'd never chosen to handle her anger by sitting in a quiet room and staring intently at what amounted to nothing. Listening to music? Yes. Watching TV? Yes. Typing on the phone? Yes. Scribbling in a journal? Yes. Yelling at him? Absolutely. But sitting in silence and *pondering*? Isaac had never witnessed such a thing. And even when he took into account the current circumstances—the pandemonium of the past few days, the fact that she didn't even have access to her phone or her journal—her conduct was far enough outside the norm to make him noticeably uncomfortable. Especially since he could only think of one other reasonable explanation. She was planning something.

"Is it all right if I talk to you?" he asked quietly.

Tallah shrugged. "Okay."

She still hadn't as much as glanced in his direction.

Isaac suddenly heard the door to the garage open behind him, and Leti entered the room carrying paper grocery bags from Safeway in both arms. When she caught sight of the two of them, she stopped in her tracks, cocked her head to one side, and put on her incomparable "What on earth are you thinking?" expression.

"You all cannot be doing this right now," she said. "God knows you have issues to fix between you, and I fully support a good reckoning whenever possible, but there's no time for you to be sitting around like you're in the middle of formal arbitration, Isaac. You need to move. Do something while you talk. Work it out while you're working."

"I hear you, Leti," Isaac replied, returning his attention to Tallah.

Leti didn't move.

"I said I hear you, Leti," he repeated, waving her away with the back of his hand.

After a few seconds, Isaac heard Leti sigh deeply and adjust the paper bags in her arms, after which she stalked past him in the direction of the kitchen. Once she'd left the room, he brought the wheelchair as close to the sofa as possible, pushed the coffee table to one side, and pivoted the wheels until he was facing Tallah.

She hadn't changed position or even moved a single muscle as far as he could see. The girl was a shell of herself, almost mannequin-like.

"I need you to talk to me, sweetheart," he said quietly. "Anything you have to say. It's fine—just say something."

Isaac waited for what felt like a long time. Finally, Tallah looked at him. Her hair fell away from her face like an unveiling, and he could see that her eyes were wet.

"I'm sorry," his daughter said.

"It's okay, baby. Shh. It's okay." Isaac leaned forward, reached out, and put a hand on her knee. "We're going to figure all of this out, I promise."

Tallah didn't respond. He wasn't even sure whether she'd heard him at all.

"Baby? Talk to me," he said. "Please."

"I'm sorry, Dad," she repeated, sobbing. "I'm sorry."

Isaac leaned back in the chair, shaking his head. He wasn't getting anywhere. More than anything, his daughter needed time—time to recover, time to process, time to forgive him for what he'd done—which was unfortunately one of the luxuries he was lacking most. Unsure of what else he could do, he decided to just sit quietly with his girl, to simply *be there*, leaning forward to rub her ankle as she sniffled and wiped her eyes from time to time. In the background, he could hear Leti working on dinner in the kitchen and humming a tune that seemed vaguely familiar from when Tallah was a baby, Anthony banging against the tray of his highchair and gurgling happily, and the steady sound of the ticking clock. Tallah and he stayed that way for a while—maybe twenty minutes or so—before he felt his eyelids getting heavy as he started to drift off.

Isaac heard the metal screen door open to his left, then the heavy front door, startling him awake. Light from the outside spilled into the living room. He turned around in the wheelchair and saw a towering man standing in the home's entryway. Black t-shirt, gray ballistic vest, and a badge looped around his neck. It was Detective Gates. He was holding his service weapon and pointing it toward Tallah, who was still seated on the sofa.

"Be calm," Gates said quietly. "Relax, Mr. Williams, because I will pull this trigger if you make me, I promise you I will." Keeping the weapon aimed at Tallah, the man took a few cautious paces into the living room, leaving the door open behind him. "If you try and—whatever the fuck—hex me or use any of your goddamn witchery for any purpose whatsoever, I will shoot. Do not make me shoot a child, please, Mr. Williams. That's not what I came here to do."

Isaac's heart was hammering.

He raised his hands. "I hear you," he said. "I hear you, okay?"

At that moment, Leti burst into the living room from the kitchen with a dish rag in her fist, stopping short at the sight of the stranger standing in her living room.

"What the hell is going on," she demanded.

"Shut the fuck up," Gates said. He shifted the gun from Tallah to Leti and waved her over to the couch. "Sit down."

Leti hesitated. She glanced over her shoulder.

"My son is in the other room," she said. "He's alone."

"Sit your ass down," Gates repeated, motioning with the pistol. "Go and sit. Now."

Without another word, Leti went to the sofa, slid her way past Isaac's chair, and sat down next to Tallah, immediately grasping the child's hand tightly in hers.

Gates stared at Isaac for what felt like a long time.

"Look at you," the man said, shaking his head. "No wonder we couldn't find your slippery ass. Going all secret agent on me with your little disguises and shit. Looking like a grandfather? I mean, what the hell. You're unbelievable."

"Detective," Isaac said. "Please. Can you please—"

"Don't you say a word," Gates said. "There's nothing to discuss here. This thing is over. I've got a fucking battalion of officers on the way to this address, believe that, but your ass belongs to me. This is my goddamn takedown, nobody else's."

The man was breathing hard. He looked almost ecstatic, as though he'd just won a footrace at a track meet.

"Dad?" Tallah said, almost whispering. It was jarring somehow, hearing such a quiet voice amid the chaos.

Isaac turned to look at her.

"I'm sorry," she said, shaking her head. He could tell that she was on the verge of tears again. "I'm sorry. I had to."

"Hey," Gates said. "Don't you be sorry for anything, sweetheart. You're the only one in the room who tried to do the right thing here. I know it doesn't feel like it now, but trust me—you did good. You're a brave kid."

Everything was happening so quickly that Isaac was barely able to process this new information—*his daughter had just handed both of them over to the authorities*—but he came to one conclusion immediately, within seconds, whether it was based on exhaustion, fear, or an acceptance of the inevitable: he wasn't going to fight anymore. He would surrender himself and, by extension, his only child. Right or wrong, this was clearly what Tallah wanted, and if she was willing to go this far to put this ordeal behind her, then he wouldn't stand in her way.

"Dad?" she said.

"It's okay, baby," Isaac said. "It's okay. I understand." He managed a smile. "I love you no matter what, sweetheart."

Isaac turned around to look at Gates, raising his hands higher above his head.

"I'm not resisting," he said. "I've got nothing on me."

Gates didn't say a word. Still holding the pistol, he barreled across the living room, ripped Isaac's limp body out of the wheelchair, and bulldozed him to the floor. Within seconds, Gates had flipped him over onto his stomach and planted a heavy hand on the base of his skull, pressing his face down into the carpet. He heard a voice screaming—it was Leti's, judging by the pitch—but he couldn't understand any of the words she'd said, if she'd said anything at all.

Soon he felt a knee drop onto the center of his back, followed by the full weight of Gates' body driving down against his spine.

"Stay down," Gates shouted.

"I'm not resisting."

"Stop fucking moving."

Isaac heard the metal rasp of handcuffs. The weight on his back seemed to increase—it was as though Gates was ballooning in size, transforming into something gargantuan and monstrous, in real time.

"I can't breathe," Isaac whispered.

He heard a loud *crack*.

It was gunfire—Isaac knew the sound right away, and he could smell the burnt powder in the air. A searing pain bloomed somewhere around his left shoulder blade, spread quickly through his chest, and curled around his heart, clamping down. There was an immediate surge of warmth beneath his body. He felt someone's hands ripping at his clothes, yanking his arm. Eventually he flopped over onto his back and saw Gates' face looming above him. The officer looked terrified—eyes wide, flecks of spittle flying from his thin lips. He was shouting something that Isaac couldn't understand.

Isaac felt himself drifting off. Without making a conscious decision, he let go of the influence he'd been exerting over his facial features. He allowed the skin to relax, the underlying musculature to release, the tissue to sink back into place, the natural characteristics of his face to emerge again. The tightness was suddenly gone. He felt almost like himself again.

Gates was down on his knees leaning over his body, pressing down hard against his chest with both palms, but he didn't notice the pressure anymore. Everything in his world had become wholly visual. There was no sound, no sensation, only pure uncorrupted vision. As his eyes moved listlessly back and forth, falling in and out of focus, Isaac caught a sudden flash of movement above Gates' shoulder. Something rising slowly into the air and hanging there, suspended, ghostlike, somewhere near the ceiling.

It was Tallah.

His vision quickly fading, Isaac watched with detached wonder as his daughter hovered like a storm overhead, looming above them all. Her black braids were whipping in every direction as though blown by a terrible wind of her own creation.

chapter ten

I stared at the police officer, up close. Face to face.

He was hovering a few inches in front of me, his body stiff, his arms pinned down to his sides. The officer couldn't breathe any more.

I had learned a lot about respiration at school over the past year. In mammals, two lungs are located near the backbone on either side of the ribcage, and the lung on the left is smaller to make room for the heart. Underneath your lungs is the diaphragm (*dye-a-fram*). It's a muscle that helps the lungs bring air in (inhale) and push it out (exhale).

The officer's diaphragm wasn't working anymore. I wasn't letting it move the way it should.

The man looked so afraid. I honestly didn't know that they ever got this afraid. Not the way I do.

Miss Sanders was screaming at me and clawing at my leg from below, but I didn't stop. I couldn't make myself let go of him.

* * *

Miss Sanders, Anthony, and I were sitting together on the sofa when more police officers came barging in through the front door—six of them—along with two paramedics. All of the officers wore dark blue uniforms (not like the first policeman, who wore normal clothes), and they all carried guns, which they pointed at Miss Sanders, then me, then Miss Sanders, and then they pointed them all around the room, both high and low. After that, half of the policemen quickly scattered through the house like they were searching for something important, while the other half stayed in the living room to guard us. One of them put metal cuffs on Miss Sanders, but he let her keep her hands in front of her, on her lap, instead of behind her back. The policeman didn't put any cuffs on me, but he reminded me not to move at all. Not even an inch.

The paramedics carried their medical bags over to where my dad and the first policeman were lying on the carpet and tried to help them, even though I heard one of paramedics say that it was too late, they were both already gone.

Miss Sanders had tried her hardest to save them, but she couldn't.

Her hands were covered with dried blood—my dad's. The blood went all the way up to the middle of her arms because she'd pressed against his bullet wound for so long. She'd also left red handprints on the policeman's chest where she'd tried to push him back to life. But nothing had worked, not for either one of them.

Soon, the officers started taking turns asking questions about what had happened, and Miss Sanders did all the talking while I listened.

She told the police a lot of things that weren't true.

The biggest lie she told was that my dad was the one who had killed the officer, instead of me.

I knew that Miss Sanders would say that. Before the police had come to the door, she'd warned me that no one could know what I'd done, and more important than that, how I'd done it. She'd told me that I would have to keep my power a secret forever—otherwise, I would have no chance at a normal life—and I'd believed her.

As I sat on the couch, I spent a lot of time thinking about how scared my dad looked before he died.

He was afraid of me.

Or maybe that wasn't right.

Maybe he was shocked at what I was capable of. That was probably a better way to say it.

I wished that I would have told him about my abilities sooner and shown him what I'd learned how to do—especially because I'd learned it all from watching him. But for some reason I hadn't been ready to talk about it. I wasn't sure why.

I was glad that he'd had a chance to see me, though, at least once.

* * *

Miss Sanders had to go directly to the Santa Clara County Jail, and I had to live in a large building with bars on the windows where nine other girls lived—a group home called Utley House. I could still talk to Miss Sanders on the phone, but only during certain times when we were both allowed. Around once every week, it turned out.

I had my own room at Utley House. It was smaller than where I used to sleep at our old apartment, but it was all right. It had a small bed, a desk, a metal wastepaper basket, and a wooden box for the clothes they let me use, my toothbrush, a bar of soap in a plastic container, and some hair products. I didn't have to go to school (we were *homeschooled*, something I'd never really heard about), but I did have to go to meetings with the nine other girls, and also meetings alone with the main counselor, a white lady named Babbitt Davies. But we got to call her Dr. Beedie, for short.

Dr. Beedie was like a grandma from the movies—short, round-bodied, gray-haired, and always smiling about something special. But she could be pretty tough sometimes, too. During our first meeting, I lost privileges for too much backtalk, and during our second meeting, I lost privileges again for making up stories that weren't true. Dr. Beedie had a little sign on her desk that said, "I may not be gruff. But I don't take no guff." Guff is, basically, shit. And Dr. Beedie didn't take much of either one.

During our third meeting, Dr. Beedie told me that she thought I was feeling numb.

I mean, she didn't exactly use those words, but she told me that, as a way of dealing with somebody dying, sometimes people "dissociate," which means they *walk away from themselves* for a little while, so that they don't have to feel the pain up close. And that this was normal. Even okay to do.

I wasn't sure. Sometimes, I felt like I was floating through a dream and that my dad hadn't really died—that it hadn't actually happened at all—and other times I felt guilty because I knew that it had, and that it was all my fault for getting in trouble at school in the first place, and then for calling the police in the end. Whenever I remembered that my dad was really gone, those were the times when I would try my hardest to go back to feeling nothing, to dreaming my life instead of being inside it, to not believing anything.

* * *

I would sometimes watch videos about my dad during my screen-time privileges.

The news was talking about him a lot since he died, even more than before. Most of the stories said bad things about him—that he'd hurt a lot of police officers, murdered a detective, and caused hundreds of thousands of dollars' worth of damage to public property—but other reports said the total opposite: they talked about my dad like he was a hero. But I didn't care about any of that. I was only watching the videos to see him, to remember what he looked and sounded like.

* * *

Sometimes at night, after Dr. Beedie had called lights-out, I would think about the policeman.

I thought about his face as he struggled to breathe—his red skin and his wide, watering eyes. I thought about his mom and dad, wondering if they'd been a part of his life, and I thought about his kids, even though I didn't know if he had any or not.

I thought a lot about how I would die one day—would it be in the same way as my dad? And after I was gone, what would happen to my soul?

What I'd done to the officer was wrong—the worst thing I'd ever done to anyone, by far—and I could never take it back, no matter how much I wanted to. I couldn't even admit it to anyone as a way of trying to help myself feel better. Miss Sanders had told me that my life would be over if I did (she was right), and that my dad would've wanted to take the blame for me if he were still around.

I started thinking a lot about Hell. Demons and ghosts and torture that could last forever without end.

The officer hadn't tried to do what he did to my dad. Even at the time, I knew that. I could tell by the way he'd acted right afterward, screaming out *Oh my God* over and over, and then trying to stop the blood from pouring out everywhere. What I didn't understand was *how* my dad could've gotten shot if the officer hadn't wanted to do it— maybe the gun in his hand had fired accidentally?—but I knew that the policeman was surprised by what he'd done.

I knew it, but it hadn't made a difference. I hadn't been able to hold myself back.

* * *

Not long after moving into Utley, I had to go to the courthouse for my trial.

Miss Sanders had to go for hers, too.

The judge told me that I was being charged with Resisting and Obstructing a Police Officer because of my actions at school that day. It was a misdemeanor, which I knew was bad, but it wasn't as bad as a felony. Right before my trial was about to start, the lawyers made a last-second deal with each other—the deal was that I would spend twelve months living at Utley House (including the time I'd already been there), and then be on probation for another twelve months after I got out. My lawyer said I got such a good deal because I'd cooperated.

Miss Sanders wasn't as lucky as I was.

She was charged with one count of Being an Accessory After the Fact. When she told me about it over the phone, I thought she was playing with me. An *accessory*? What kind of word is that to use to describe a person? But then I learned that it just meant she'd helped my dad do something against the law. It was a felony, which meant that Miss Sanders would go to prison for a year, at least, if they decided she was guilty.

Which they eventually did.

After she was convicted, Miss Sanders got eighteen months in FCI Dublin, a prison for women in the Bay Area, and Anthony had to go live with his dad full-time. Once she was moved there, it was strange—I got to talk to her more often than I did when she was in regular jail. She called me every other night, and as long as I hadn't lost my phone privileges, I was allowed to talk to her for thirty minutes or more each time.

* * *

Six months had gone by since the day my dad passed, and not once had I used my abilities. Not once.

It had been so long that I wasn't even sure I'd remember how if I tried.

But I couldn't let myself practice. For one, I was scared of being found out by the folks at Utley—even though I spent time with some of them (Rachel, Tao, and Alicia), I didn't trust anyone with knowing anything that deep about me. Miss Sanders was right: If anybody found out what I could do, I might end up just like my dad did.

Another reason why I couldn't use my abilities was that I was scared for my own body. I knew from talking to Miss Sanders that the power wasn't good for you—it actually damaged your insides—so I could only use it a little bit at a time, or only in emergencies, if at all.

But these weren't the main reasons why I'd stopped.

The main reason I'd stopped using my abilities was simple: it was the memory of what happened the last time I'd used them.

* * *

There were two particular females at Utley—Lala and Orion—who would try and take commissary money from some of the weaker girls in the house, usually by tossing threats at them when no grownups were around, but sometimes by actually putting hands on them in the halls or in the bathrooms. Lala and Orion didn't work as a team or anything like that. They were independent, which was both good and bad. It was good because you were never outnumbered two-to-one, but it was bad because you had twice as many chances of getting yourself jacked.

Neither one of them ever bothered me, though.

I think it was two things. First of all, I knew deep down in my heart that I could hurt both of them badly if I needed to—and because I knew it, somehow they seemed to know it too. I never actually had to *do* anything to prove it to them. I didn't even have to *look* at them; they just had to look at me whenever I walked in a room, and that was enough.

Second of all, they knew the reason I was at Utley in the first place—what I'd done to the police officer at my old school—and that was something that really mattered inside the house. I wasn't there because of something small like weed, or because I'd taken a pocketknife through security, or because I'd shoplifted from Valley Fair. I was there for something real: I'd gone up against an actual cop and lived. When females think you don't care, that you'll do anything, they don't play around with you. I'd known that since I was, like, eight or nine years old, and it hadn't changed.

I'd never told anyone this (and I wasn't ever going to), but I'd actually gotten in trouble that day at school on purpose. It's true. I knew that if I ignored the teacher for long enough, he would call one of the security guards, and if I ignored *him* for long enough, he would call the police eventually, and then—in front of everyone, especially the four girls who'd been threatening me all year for my money, my jacket, my phone, and my shoes—I would send out a message: *I'm not the one.* I'm not the one you ought to be playing with. Move along to somebody else. That was all I really wanted at the time—to be left alone.

* * *

I had my twelfth birthday while I was in Utley.

Dr. Beedie brought in a Neapolitan ice cream cake from Baskin-Robbins, and seven other girls ate it with me in the house kitchen. Paper plates and plastic spoons and juice pouches. I didn't have to do cleanup chores that night, or go to meeting. I got ten dollars added to my commissary account as a present from the staff, plus they gave me an extra hour of screen time to use whenever I wanted.

I really missed my dad, though.

So much.

The folks at Utley only knew it was my birthday because my file said so. They didn't know because they knew me. And the only grownup who did know me (at least sort of) was Miss Sanders, and she had no idea what day I was born on. Even though I was pretty sure these grownups cared about me—at least Dr. Beedie and Miss Sanders did—I also knew that caring was a different thing than love. My dad had loved me, I was sure of it. But now that he was gone, I couldn't think of anyone else on the planet who felt the same way he did.

* * *

One night, when Miss Sanders called me on the upstairs phone (in Phone Closet B, which was, literally, a closet), I could tell right away that she had something serious to talk about.

We went back and forth for a few minutes about the normal, everyday stuff, but then I got impatient—if you have something to say, just get it over with—so I interrupted during one of her stories about Anthony's dad bringing him in for a visit.

"What's going on," I demanded. "I know you're going to tell me something."

Miss Sanders went quiet.

I could hear voices arguing in the background—she called that kind of thing *prison stuff* whenever I asked what was going on.

"All right, Mouth," Miss Sanders said (sometimes she called me Mouth). "You're right. I do have something to tell you, so I'll get to the point."

"Good."

"Deron Coates," she said. "Do you remember that name? He was the prisoner your dad traded places with when he came to set you free. Anyway, long story short, Deron had been in jail for a while—"

"For what?" I asked.

"It doesn't matter what for, Tal. Just hear me out. So, Deron was in jail for something, but he escaped. He was running for a while, hiding in this place and that place, but the authorities caught up to him last week."

"So?"

"Well, if you'll let me finish, I'll tell you," Miss Sanders said.

At that moment, I heard a knock on the door of Phone Closet B.

I covered the receiver with my hand.

"What," I shouted.

"How much longer?" a voice asked through the door.

"As long as it takes," I answered. "That's how long."

"Well fuck you then."

"No," I said. "Fuck *you* then."

I uncovered the handset.

"Hello?" I said.

"Um. Hi. What was that all about?" Miss Sanders asked.

"Nothing. Just *house stuff.* You know how it goes."

"I see. All right, then. So where was I?"

"You were about to tell me why I should give a shit about Damon or whoever."

"Deron," Miss Sanders said. "And you need to start watching your mouth, Mouth."

I smiled.

I never would have admitted it out loud, but I liked it when Miss Sanders tried to get all *parental* with me. Sometimes I did things to push her buttons on purpose, just to get that type of reaction out of her.

"All right, then," she said. "So when they searched through all of Deron's stuff after they took him back to jail, they found something interesting. A piece of paper."

Miss Sanders paused.

For a moment, I thought maybe the phone had died.

"Hello?" I said.

"Just hold on. I want you to get serious for a second, Tallah. What I'm about to tell you is important."

"I am serious, all right? Just tell me."

Miss Sanders let out a long sigh. "The paper was written by your father," she said. "It was his will. Do you know what a will is?"

I felt something change inside my body.

It was like my heart switched off and my soul left to go somewhere better.

"Yeah," I answered.

"Listen. I'm sorry to be bringing him up like this. I know it's hard."

Miss Sanders waited for a while like she expected me to say something back to her. But I didn't.

"Anyhow," she continued. "His will was pretty simple, but it was clear. He wanted you to come and stay with me and Anthony."

I wasn't sure I understood.

"Like, *live* with you?" I asked.

"Live with me, eat with me, let me take you out clothes shopping, sleep in the room next to mine, argue with me about the rules—the whole nine yards. Which is what I want too, by the way. Once I get out of this place, I mean."

I couldn't believe it.

"You *want* me to stay with you?"

"I wouldn't have it any other way, baby girl," Miss Sanders said. "Ize and me had talked about where he wanted you to go if, God forbid, anything ever happened to him. He was on-board from the beginning."

The bridge of my nose started to hurt—it happened whenever I was close to crying, for some reason.

I hadn't realized it until that moment, but the whole time I'd been at Utley, I'd been worried about where I would go when I got out. Who would I live with? How would I get money? What city would they move me to? The questions had been crawling around in the back of my mind like rats—I always knew that they were there, and they were always bothering me, even though I couldn't see their hiding places. Now that I knew where I would go after Utley House, I felt completely different—like my mind was clearer, my shoulders were lighter, and my chest wasn't as tight.

I had a place to go.

And even better than that, someone wanted me to be there with them.

* * *

I spent a lot of my free time writing in a red spiral notebook Dr. Beedie gave me.

My whole life, I'd always written things—stories, poetry, stuff about myself, whatever I was thinking about. My dad used to say, "You can make anything by writing." It was a quote by someone famous, but I didn't ever find out who'd said it.

"Have you had your nose in the notebook this week?" Dr. Beedie asked one morning during Session.

We were sitting in the room she called the Main Office, but it really looked like somebody's bedroom without the bed. She'd hung up all these feel-good posters that said things like, "You have a choice—you can throw in the towel, or you can use it to wipe the sweat off your face" and "Believe you can, and you will." Some of them were okay, but a lot of them made no sense at all.

Like this one: "If you're tired of starting over, stop giving up."

I didn't get that one.

Almost every time I'd started over in my life—when I'd changed schools, repeated a grade, lost old friends and tried to make new ones, re-done a homework project—it was because I had to. Somebody had forced me. I hadn't started over because I felt like quitting something else.

I stared across the desk at Dr. Beedie.

For some reason she was really annoying me that day. Her pointless purple sweater, her frizzy gray curls, her boring background music with no words.

"Hello?" Dr. Beedie said. "Have you been writing at all, hon?"

"No," I lied.

She blinked a few times, took a sip from her coffee mug (it said "OCD: Obsessive Coffee Disorder" on the side), put her glasses on top of her head, and looked at me with her nonexistent lips pressed together. Whenever she did that, it made a thousand lines appear across her mouth, almost like it had been sewn shut with a thousand little threads.

Which I wished it had been.

"I have a question for you," she said, reaching over and turning up the volume of her bad music. "I'm wondering. When I ask you about your writing, does it feel like I'm *really* asking something else? Something totally different?"

I thought about it.

"I don't know," I said.

"Well, then, let me ask it another way. Sometimes a person might ask you a question about something, but they don't really want the answer to the question they asked. They're *actually* trying to lead you down a path to somewhere else. They're trying to get you to think about something, but they're not telling you what that *something* is. Does that make sense?"

I thought about it.

"Kind of," I answered.

"All right. So my question, again, is this: Does it ever feel like I'm asking you about your writing, but that I don't really want the answer? That I'm *actually* trying to make you talk about something you don't want to talk about?"

Dr. Beedie was right.

I did feel that way. I just hadn't known it until that moment.

"Maybe," I said. "I think so."

"Okay. So here is my follow-up question. When I ask you about your writing, what does it feel like I'm really asking about? Or really trying to *do*? Or really trying to get *you* to do?"

I thought about that for a little while.

Soon, the bridge of my nose started to hurt, and my eyes filled up with tears.

"I don't want to talk about this right now," I said.

"Why not?"

"Because then—I don't know. Then you win."

"I win?" Dr. Beedie asked. "How would I win?"

I shook my head. The tears were coming down my cheeks, but I wasn't crying—not really. It was more like having really watery eyes from allergies or something.

"I know what you're doing," I said. "You're doing it right now."

"Okay, Tallah. Tell me—what am I doing? It's okay to say whatever you think."

"You want me to write about him," I said. "You want me to think about him and talk about him. And if I don't, it means there's something wrong with me."

I started sobbing. I hated myself for it, but I couldn't stop.

Dr. Beedie reached across the desk and put her hand on my wrist. It felt rough almost like leather, but I didn't mind.

"There's nothing wrong with you, hon," she said. "You don't have to write or talk about anything you don't want to."

One morning I was leaving a stall in the first-floor bathroom when I saw Orion standing a few feet away by the sink. Just standing there, watching. I hadn't even heard her come into the room.

Orion was a big white girl with short pink hair and holes in her earlobes big enough to push a jawbreaker through—we weren't allowed to wear jewelry inside Utley, so her ear holes were empty, hanging down like loops of Silly Putty. During group meetings, she would spend her time pinching her lower lip between her fingernails over and over until it turned dark red and swollen (we weren't allowed to wear makeup in Utley, either, so maybe she was faking lipstick?). I'd heard somebody say once that Orion was fifteen years old, but I wasn't sure. All I knew was that I only came up to her shoulder.

We made eye contact for a second, but I didn't say anything to her. I didn't need to, and I knew it.

My head held high, I walked toward the exit, passing her by without a second glance.

When I reached out for the handle, something slammed into the back of my head, sending me stumbling forward face-first into the door. Before I could turn around all the way, Orion was on top of me, a handful of my hair in her fist, punching me in the side of the head with her free hand. As I clawed at her arm, trying to free myself from her steel grip, I took a bunch of hard shots to my ear, my cheek, my temple, and my jaw before I finally remembered what I could do.

I could stop her. Easily.

Without thinking about *how*, I let my power loose.

Orion screamed.

* * *

"Tell me about it," Dr. Beedie said.

We were sitting across the desk from one another in the Main Office, same as always. Same frizzy gray curls, same bad music with no words. The sweater was lime green this time.

It had been a couple of weeks since the fight with Orion, but I was still paying for it. No screen time for a month. My chores, plus hers. No commissary at all. Orion got some punishments too, but nowhere near what I got.

I leaned back in the chair and crossed my arms.

"How many times do I need to tell you? The girl put her hands on me first. For no reason."

"So you broke both of her arms. I know that. What I'm asking is how you feel about it."

"How do I feel?" I shrugged. "Like I've got too many chores all of a sudden. Like I want to watch TV. Like your music is horrible and your hair—I don't know—it needs some type of gel or conditioner or something. That's how I feel."

Dr. Beedie shook her head. She reached across the desk and turned off the music player.

"I'm sorry to hear it," she said. "Not because your comments are targeted toward me—I'm okay with that. I'm sorry to see you reverting right now."

"Reverting?"

"Going backwards," Dr. Beedie said. "Meaning, you're relying on your old ways of dealing with feelings, not the new ways we've been talking about. The things I've *seen* you do to process your feelings in a healthier way up until the incident with Orion—you're not using them now. Which I understand. It's difficult, and it takes constant practice. But I'm here to give you a gentle reminder, as someone who cares about you, that when you act 'too cool for school' and start mouthing-off like you don't care, you're not fooling anybody. At least not me. I know you're hurting, Tallah. And it's all right to let yourself feel hurt, and also, to let others see that you're feeling it. There's no shame in that."

Dr. Beedie paused, which meant that it was my turn; I was supposed to try and guess what she wanted me to say next, and then say it. But I didn't.

I uncrossed my arms and leaned forward in the chair.

"Do you know what would happen to me if I acted like you do?" I asked. "Wearing sweaters and talking about my feelings? Do you know what they would do to me?"

"Who, Tallah?" Dr. Beedie asked. "What *who* would do to you."

"I don't know—*everybody*. The world. People. Bitches inside Utley. Everybody."

"Tell me. What would they do to you, Tallah? It's okay. Tell me what would happen if you let people see you when you're hurting."

I thought about it.

"They wouldn't see hurt," I answered. "They would see weakness, like I was a sick animal. And then they would come and try to eat me alive."

* * *

Eventually, I apologized to Orion.

Not because I wanted to, and not because I meant it, but because I *needed to*; otherwise, Dr. Beedie was never going to move on, stop pushing me, and give me my privileges back.

Orion knew my apology was bullshit, just like I did, but she nodded and kept her eyes on the floor, which was fine with me. Even though both her arms were in casts, we shook hands (why do grownups always think this means something?) and went our separate ways. She joined a group of girls sitting in the kitchen eating chips and playing Truth or Dare, and I went back to my room to be alone.

That was one thing I'd noticed, ever since I'd hurt Orion—the females in the house had started keeping their distance, all of them, even the ones I used to be friends with. Maybe I'd been keeping my distance, too. I wasn't sure. But I could tell when I looked at them that something had changed. It used to feel like I was respected, but lately it felt more like I was feared.

* * *

It was getting close to my release date.

I was actually *happy*.

Even though my days were spent doing chores, being "homeschooled," going to meetings, getting cold-shouldered by a bunch of unbalanced females—and even though somewhere inside I still missed my dad, still felt guilty about the bad things I'd done, and still worried about what my future would be, if I had a future at all—I was still, somehow, happy.

The only problem was this—because Miss Sanders was still in prison, I didn't know where I would go after they let me out. Would they let me live in her house by myself? That sounded better than living with strangers, except for Anthony would probably be there, too, so I'd have to take care of him all the time, and even though I liked him, he was still a baby. Babies are a lot of work—a lot more work than they are fun.

Around a week before my freedom date, Dr. Beedie called me in for a special meeting at the Main Office. It was nighttime, a couple of hours after dinner, which wasn't a normal meeting time at Utley—after evening chores were finished, we usually had time to ourselves.

When I walked into the Main Office, Dr. Beedie wasn't sitting at the desk, like she normally did. She was sitting on the couch—the "love seat," she called it. Her face looked sad and serious; not like it usually looked whenever I walked through the door for one of our sessions.

"Come sit," she said, patting the cushion next to her.

Now I was sure that something was wrong.

Dr. Beedie was about to tell me something that I didn't want to hear.

I felt my heart shut down and my soul fly away to another place.

Like a robot, I walked over to the couch and sat down, faced forward, and stared straight ahead.

"Look at me, hon," Dr. Beedie said quietly.

I shook my head. She hadn't even told me anything yet, and already my eyes were filling up with tears.

"Just tell me," I said. "Whatever you need to—just say it. I already know it's bad. So just get it over with."

Dr. Beedie put a hand on top of mine.

I wanted to pull away, but I didn't.

"Leti Sanders passed away yesterday," she said. "I'm so sorry, Tallah."

* * *

A week later, I learned exactly what had happened to Miss Sanders: she'd been suffocated by her cellmate while she was asleep. Another example of a female hurting another female for no reason. Just like Orion. Matter of fact, Orion would probably grow up to be just like that murdering bitch one day, whoever she was.

I thought about Miss Sanders all the time.

I hadn't really gotten to know her well enough to miss her, exactly, but I did miss the idea of her—a lot. Until I found out she was gone, I hadn't realized how much I'd been looking forward to living with an actual mom—not *my* mom, but *a* mom, still—and I'd even been looking forward to more time with Anthony, as boring as he was. Without even being aware of it, I'd been imagining myself living in a real home again, eating real food, and even going back to real school. Making real friends. But now that I was alone again, I felt lost. I literally had nothing—no money, no parents, no home, no friends, no *life*, and no hope that I could ever get any of those good things back again. I sometimes felt like I wasn't even real—like there was an actual girl asleep in her bed somewhere, and I was just a character running around inside her worst nightmare. I would sometimes pray that the girl would wake up, open her eyes, and realize that it had all been nothing but a dream; everything would end, and I could just disappear into the light.

*　*　*

I spent as much time alone as I possibly could.

For some reason, when the room was quiet and I was lying completely still on my bed at night, I would think about Orion's bones. Not only the ones I'd broken. All of them. Her full skeleton, clean and white, underneath her skin.

Bones are scary but also beautiful somehow.

For my homeschool research project, I got to choose my own topic. So I decided to study the human skeletal system.

I learned that you have two hundred seventy bones when you're born, but that some of them fuse together. In the end, you have two hundred six.

The longest bone is the thigh bone, called the femur, which was the bone my dad broke before he was killed.

The smallest bone is inside the middle ear. It's only around a tenth of an inch long.

The area of your body with the most bones is the hand, fingers, and wrist—fifty-four bones in all.

Teeth are also technically part of the skeleton, but are not counted as bones for some reason.

The areas where bones meet are called joints. Muscles and ligaments hold bones together so that our bodies don't fall apart.

*　*　*

I started experimenting with my abilities again. I knew it was dangerous, but I couldn't stop myself.

It came down to a couple of things.

First of all, I was bored as hell. Something needed to be done about that.

Second, I just didn't give a damn what happened to me anymore.

Actually, that last part wasn't completely true.

It always felt good to say—*I just don't give a fuck*—but the truth was that I did care, at least a little bit: I didn't want to get hurt if I could help it, and I definitely didn't want to die. So yes, I was using my power, but I was being careful about it. I tried to keep things as balanced as I could.

My basic plan was this: I would only use my abilities on a small scale.

Micro, not macro, as Dr. Beedie would sometimes say.

That was one of the mistakes my dad had made—thinking way too big. He'd figured out how to pull off some of the smaller tricks—unlocking locks was the best one I'd seen—but nine times out of ten, he was trying to move the biggest thing on the map. People, cars, buildings—it was too much. I needed to do things different than he had. What I needed to do was to *get big things done* by pushing the smallest buttons, moving the smallest parts. Bottom line, I needed to think. To be smarter.

I needed to practice.

When I'd first learned how to use my abilities, I'd practiced (secretly) in the same way my dad did: I would try and move the objects he moved, complete the tasks he completed, make the changes he made, as soon as he wasn't around. I'd never been able to do all the things he'd done—some of them I couldn't, and others I hadn't even wanted to try—but I'd been successful at most of them, so successful that I started doing my own thing after a while. Experimenting in my own way.

For example, I'd used my abilities to build a small house out of some old Legos, to set up a line of fifty dominos in midair and make them topple over (the "floating domino effect"), to roll a set of dice and make my numbers turn up every single time, to write my name with a pen and also with a keyboard, to pull seagulls out of the sky and bring them down to the ground without hurting them, to make people (who I didn't like) trip over their own two feet. Things like that.

Most of the tasks I'd chosen on my own had been creative—I'd been building things, making things, changing things (mostly) for the better. But what I hadn't done was focus on the opposite. Breaking things down. Making them worse, in the best possible way.

I was about to change that.

I'd made the decision to practice causing pain.

I knew it was wrong, hurting other people on purpose. But if I was going to be alone in the world, which it looked more and more like I was, then I had to be able to (a.) protect myself at all times, (b.) force people to give me whatever I needed to survive, if necessary, and (c.) never let anybody know *how* I was doing (a.) or (b.). I'd decided that the best way to do all three was to become good—really good—at delivering pain. With subtlety and elegance.

Because I'd been studying the subject for my school project, I decided to start with causing pain by *moving bones*. Shifting them just enough to get a person's attention, at least to start with. The point would be to deliver the right amount of pain, using the smallest bone possible, using the least amount of power I could use to do the job.

* * *

Picking my first target for practice was easy.

Orion.

Believe it or not, Orion hadn't learned a damn thing from her arms getting broken—she left me alone, of course, but she was still spending quite a bit of her time bothering the weaker girls, even with casts going up to her elbows—so I didn't feel too sorry when I imagined her suffering a little bit more. It seemed all right, actually. Maybe even good.

I started during lunch.

In the kitchen at Utley, there was a round wooden table underneath a light fixture by the window where most of the girls ate, and then there was the center island. The island was basically a small countertop in the center of the room with cabinets underneath. That's where I sat, alone, on a padded stool during the lunch hour.

While the other girls ate their turkey sandwiches and carrots, I stared down at my paper plate, concentrating on a picture I'd memorized from a biology textbook showing the *ossicles*. That was the name for the *malleus*, *incus*, and *stapes*, the three bones of the middle ear.

Once I had the picture in my mind, I started trying to make the picture real by thinking about the ossicles inside a living person—inside Orion. And once everything felt real enough to me, I focused on the *stapes*, the smallest bone. *Stapes*, in Latin, means stirrup, but I wasn't sure what that meant, other than it had to do with riding horses.

Reaching out with my abilities, I took control of the stirrup, just like I'd done with a thousand other objects. I could tell when I had the bone locked down—I'm not sure how I always knew when I'd taken control over something, but the moment it was mine, I always knew. It felt almost like knowing when your fingers touched something, like a pencil on a desk, even with your eyes closed. You just knew. You could feel it resting between your fingers.

Orion suddenly screamed.

Her hand jumped up and clamped over her ear, and she fell off her chair onto the kitchen floor, twisting back and forth, sobbing uncontrollably.

* * *

I learned a few days later that Orion had gone completely deaf in her left ear.

I'd gone too far.

I felt terrible—I'd never wanted to take away her hearing; I'd just wanted to see if I could make her feel uncomfortable for a little while. It was never supposed to turn into a permanent change or anything.

Maybe I'd started off too small. I probably should have gone with finger bones in the beginning. The *phalanges*.

Next time, I would try and work with those.

* * *

I kept on practicing.

I decided to give Orion a pass and focus on Lala for a while—she'd been doing way too much, for way too long without anybody putting her ass in check. That needed to change.

One Friday night during Utley's monthly Film Fest (*Roots*, the miniseries, part one), we were sitting in what was known as the Lounge, which was basically a giant living room with a medium-sized TV, two sofas, plus five or six beanbag chairs. I took my usual spot—down on the carpet off to one side, away from the rest of the girls and the on-duty staff—while everyone else took the sofas or the beanbags.

Lala was lying on the couch furthest from the TV, chewing on her pinky fingernail.

I watched her as the show played. She was about as different from Orion as she could be, at least as far as what she looked like—she was as short as I was, with deep brown skin and long black hair—but their attitudes were almost exactly the same: straight hateful.

After around five minutes of *Roots*, I decided it was time.

Targeting Lala's left thumb, I reached out with my ability and took control of both the first bone (the distal phalange, which goes from the tip of the thumb to the knuckle) and the second bone (the proximal phalange, which goes from the knuckle to the base of the thumb, where the webbing is).

Once I'd taken control of both phalanges, I slowly—very slowly, and only by a millimeter at most—pulled the two bones away from each other.

Lala immediately jumped a little bit and yelped like she'd been bitten by a spider or something. She stared stupidly at her thumb, rubbing it with her other hand.

I didn't go any further; I let her go.

* * *

A week before Freedom Day (the name I'd given to my release date), I went to the Main Office for my session with Dr. Beedie, and I could tell right away that something else was wrong.

She had even more bad news to share. I was sure of it.

My heart shut down, and my soul slipped out of my body again. I sat down without a word.

"There's my girl," Dr. Beedie said. "The short-timer. How does it feel?" She smiled, but it wasn't real—she was forcing it. I could tell with a single glance.

I didn't answer. Instead, I focused on the desk between us. Her stacks of papers, her stapler, her gold-colored name plate (Babbitt Davies, PhD), her cup full of pens, one of every color I could think of.

"You've been talking about your big day for weeks now," Dr. Beedie said. "So I know it's on your mind. But what I don't know is how you feel about it. You know, whenever we have a life change like this one, it can bring on all sorts of emotions, all at once. People can feel relief, excitement, sadness, fear, anger, anxiety, confusion—just to name a few. I can only guess at what's going on inside your body."

I shrugged. "I don't know."

Dr. Beedie smiled. I could see her teeth out of the corner of my eye.

"It's okay not to know," she said. "And it's okay if that changes or even if it stays the same. Just pay attention, hon, to whatever is going on inside."

"Okay," I said.

"Good."

Dr. Beedie opened a file folder on her desk and started paging through the paper inside. After a few seconds, she stopped and looked at me.

"It's time to talk about where we go from here," she said. "That means a placement plan. We've been in touch with several families that are excited to have you stay with them, Tallah. I think we're going to find a great match for you."

Placement?

"Tell me what you know about foster care," Dr. Beedie said.

My stomach dropped.

I didn't know much about foster care. But I did know a girl who was in the system once, and judging by the way she'd described the experience—basically, she'd been a second-class citizen living in a third-class situation—I didn't want any part of it. No way in hell.

I felt the tears building, but I blinked them back.

"You're upset," Dr. Beedie said. "Tell me, Tallah. It's okay."

I didn't know what to say.

I'd been so focused on the idea of leaving this place that I hadn't really thought about where I'd be leaving to. Once I'd learned that Miss Sanders was gone and that I wouldn't be living with her anymore, I'd just stopped thinking about the details of life after Utley House. I hadn't replaced the picture in my mind with something new, a new home, a new family, a new situation; I'd replaced it with gray. With nothing at all.

Of course they'd try to send me into foster care.

I couldn't believe that I hadn't realized it until now.

"I'm not doing that," I said flatly. I shook my head. "I'm not."

I got on my feet.

Dr. Beedie looked up at me. Even now, she looked so kind—I couldn't hate her as much as I wanted to.

"Tallah—" she started.

I didn't listen to the rest.

I turned around, threw the chair aside, and ran out the door.

* * *

I didn't stop.

With tears streaming down my face, I burst outside through the front doors of the building and ran outside onto the crowded sidewalk. I had nothing with me—no money, no food, no clothes other than what I was wearing—but it didn't matter. I wasn't going back to Utley, not for anything.

I looked in both directions.

"Sweetheart?" a voice said.

A short white lady with a stroller was staring at me with wide green eyes—her boy looked like he was around the same age as Anthony.

"Are you all right?" she asked. "Are you hurt?"

I didn't answer.

I turned around and ran as fast as I could toward the skyscrapers downtown.

Tallah, the sequel to *Gravity Breaker*, is now available.

about the author

Jonathan R. Miller lives in the Bay Area of California with his wife and daughter.

www.JonathanRMiller.com

Made in the USA
Coppell, TX
02 September 2020

35438712R10118